The Pastor's Husband

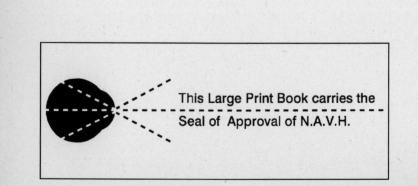

THE PASTOR'S HUSBAND

TIFFANY L. WARREN

THORNDIKE PRESS

A part of Gale, Cengage Learning

GALE
CENGAGE Learning·

Farmington Hills, Mich • San Francisco • New York • Waterville, Maine
Meriden, Conn • Mason, Ohio • Chicago

GALE
CENGAGE Learning®

ALL RIGHTS RESERVED
Thorndike Press® Large Print African-American.
The text of this Large Print edition is unabridged.
Other aspects of the book may vary from the original edition.
Set in 16 pt. Plantin.

LIBRARY OF CONGRESS CATALOGING-IN-PUBLICATION DATA

Names: Warren, Tiffany L., author.
Title: The pastor's husband / by Tiffany L. Warren.
Description: Large print edition. | Waterville, Maine : Thorndike Press, 2016. | ©
  2016 | Series: Thorndike press large print African-American
Identifiers: LCCN 2016003250| ISBN 9781410488503 (hardcover) | ISBN 1410488500
  (hardcover)
Subjects: LCSH: African Americans—Fiction. | Large type books.
Classification: LCC PS3623.A866 P37 2016 | DDC 813/.6—dc23
LC record available at http://lccn.loc.gov/2016003250

Published in 2016 by arrangement with Dafina Books, an imprint of Kensington Publishing Corp.

Printed in Mexico
1 2 3 4 5 6 7 20 19 18 17 16

ACKNOWLEDGMENTS

Another one in the can! I always have to thank God first, because He is the reason I am able to continue crafting these stories. I feel blessed every day that I have the opportunity to share my stories with readers.

I am nothing without my family. They are my backbone. My husband, Brent, is my best friend and travel partner. I am so glad to be on this journey with him. I have the best children in the world and I always thank them, because they take care of me. They cook, clean, iron, and make sure I don't forget stuff. Briana, Brittany, Brynn, Brooke, and Little Brent (Fatman) — I love you all!

My publishing team is the greatest too. Everyone at Kensington is dedicated to seeing their authors successful. My editor, Mercedes Fernandez, really is a champion for my quirky, faith-based stories. She really strives to *get* it, which is a rarity. My agent,

Sara Camilli, totally rocks. She is a bundle of energy and fire. I'm so glad to have her on my team.

I spent a great amount of time away from home during the writing of this book, so I have to list all of my friends and my support system who got me through the horrible time in D.C., living in my own fancy apartment . . . wait. So maybe it wasn't that horrible. But my bestie brigade is always on tap: Shawana, Afrika, Tiffany T, Rhonda, and Robin. Love y'all. My writer friends are better than yours! Victoria, ReShonda, Pat, Renee, Tyora, Angela, Vanessa, Sherri, Piper, Michelle Lindo-Rice, and Michelle Stimpson!

To the book clubs, readers, and Women's Ministries who continue to read my books and invite me to yummy outings, and show up at my events: God bless you, real good!

Last but not least, I'd like to thank my planner extraordinaire, LaSheera Lee. She gets me together with these blog radio shows and tour stops. Appreciate you!

Okay, enough mushy stuff. Let's read already!

PROLOGUE

Nightfall was near, and that was a good thing. Felicia needed the cover of darkness to execute her plan. She was cramped in her tiny, rented Ford Aspire as she impatiently waited for the sun to set. She couldn't possibly drive her own car. For this task, she needed to be anonymous.

The tools for the job, a crowbar and a gas can, sat on the passenger seat next to Felicia, and she glanced at them from time to time as if reminding herself of the reason she was there. Every time she thought about not following through, a little voice in the back of her head reminded her of everything Lance had done; of everything he'd stolen from her.

Felicia swept her long black hair into a ponytail and sighed. She wished it didn't have to be this way. It definitely wasn't what she had planned when she first saw Lance. He was supposed to be a blessing, but Felicia didn't feel blessed. She felt cursed.

Felicia touched one hand to her midsection, and shuddered as if she could feel the emptiness of her womb. It paralleled the desolation that she felt in her heart. All because Lance had chosen his family. He didn't love her, and worse, he'd lied about it.

Finally, the lavender dusky sky turned a deeper shade of violet. It was time to teach Lance a very expensive lesson.

And then . . . then it would be Nya's turn.

PART I

CHAPTER 1
NYA

Today could be my big break.

No, that's wrong. I should say this could be *our* big break, mine and Greg's. My speaking engagement today could take our ministry to the next level.

When First Lady Bowens invited me to her Women's Empowerment conference, I *knew* it was God. First Lady Bowens, or Lady Sandy as she likes to be called, is only the most popular pastor's wife in Dallas. She and her husband built their ministry, the Pathway Church, from a Bible study in a high school gym, and now they have ten thousand members. Speaking in the pulpit of their church could launch a minister into the very lucrative speaking circuit. This could mean invitations to conferences and churches all over the country. All over the world, even.

It's exactly what Greg and I had in mind when we started our little church, Love First

International. The international part was partially an inside joke between me and Greg. We weren't anything close to being international when we started. We still aren't. We're a local storefront church trying to impact the community with a little bit of money and a whole lot of love.

But the other reason for our church name is because God showed me in a vision that we would be known worldwide. It almost makes me cringe to tell people about that vision, because *everybody* is a prophet these days. A person can call an eight hundred number to get a prophetic word over their life. These days, saying that you have a prophetic gift is almost enough to get you laughed out of town.

Except that I really do have the gift.

It runs in my family. My cousin Zenovia is a minister right now, operating in her gift at a church in Maryland. She's low key with it, and doesn't want to be famous for it, or even known for it. Maybe because the gift killed her mother, Audrey. Well, that's wrong. It wasn't the gift that killed Audrey. It was the combination of her gift and the schizophrenia that led her to take her own life.

I married Greg because he didn't run from me when I told him about my prophecies. He was intrigued by it; in awe of it even. And he believed that we would do great work together. A vision of us speaking in front of a crowd of thousands confirmed it for me, because I know the visions are real and from God.

Even still, I have to admit that when I received the invitation from Lady Sandy, I was a little bit nervous. Okay, not just a little nervous. I was terrified.

Greg is always at my side when I preach. We're a tag team. We prepare our sermons together and flow so effortlessly that we finish one another's sentences. I can tell when he needs a break and step in without missing a beat, and he does the same for me. Our congregation loves it, and it is effective for us.

But for this occasion, this Women's Empowerment conference, I have to do this alone. Lady Sandy said she was inspired by Beyoncé's all-girl tour, and she only wants women musicians, worship leaders, and speakers. All-girl everything. She said that in order to empower women, women needed to be in power. So I was invited to do this engagement without Greg.

When I told Greg about the invitation he was supportive, if not a little hurt about not being invited himself. Ultimately, though, he gave me his approval. I wouldn't have done it without his blessing.

Greg knows I would've been a fool to turn it down, but I don't know if I'm ready to do this without my husband by my side. These women are expecting God to show up with a prophetic word. The only reason I got the invitation to speak is because I gave Lady Sandy a prophecy about a woman in her congregation who was pursuing her husband, and it was true. Lady Sandy believes in the gift and wants to show these women something miraculous.

So they're waiting to hear what God has to say about their lives. And I have to deliver. Talk about being under pressure.

The problem with the gift is that God cannot be scheduled. He does not move just because there's an arena full of women. He speaks on His timing and only when He has something to say. I hate to tell people that, though, because they think I'm a fraud if I can't give them what they want.

Believers don't understand that faith is trusting God without getting confirmation, and that God wants us to trust Him. Hearing a word from God for one person's situation is so rare for me. When it happens, it is truly a miracle, so I've tried not to build my ministry on the prophecies. I study and prepare to expound on a scripture and provide a word of wisdom straight from the Bible. And when God doesn't give me a prophetic word, I preach, pray, and speak blessings over the women.

Usually those prayers and blessings are enough. But today is different. My reputation is going to rest on me being able to deliver a fresh and anointed prophetic word from God.

My nerves are getting to me as I sit backstage at this church, waiting for it all to begin. The hustle and bustle seems more like a television production than a church conference. There are makeup artists, hair stylists, and assistants for all of the speakers — except me. I'm a newbie, and I only have my best friend, Tina, who is a beautician and has volunteered to stand in as a stylist.

Tina points her perfectly manicured nail toward a makeup chair. "Sit down and let me airbrush you," she says.

"Do you know how to use that?"

"I had one of the other girls at the salon show me how. It's pretty easy, actually." She gives a shrug, like this isn't all that important.

I know I can trust Tina with my hair, 'cause she's been doing it since we were teenagers, but I'm not sure about the makeup part. This is definitely an experiment.

"Do you think I would have you out here looking crazy?" Tina asks when I still hesitate to sit down in that makeup chair. She flips her long wig out of her face and gives me a lifted-eyebrow glare. I guess I should know better.

"No, but you know how important this is! It's going to be streaming live all over the world, and on Daystar."

Tina nods and pulls me down into the chair. "I do know how important this is to you, honey. I want you and Greg to blow up. Shoot, you can be Oprah and I'll be Gayle. You can get me designer handbags. And we can sit in the front rows together at New York Fashion Week. I won't be mad."

This makes me crack a smile. Tina is talented in her own right, and she's gorgeous. Her hair is always on point. She has a different weave or wig every week, but she makes sure they look flawless. She should be doing hair for celebrities, and I think one day she will. That's not a prophetic vision, that's just me knowing my home girl is the bomb.

"You sure you know how to use it?" I ask again.

"Yes. I made all the other girls at the shop

let me practice on them. The only one who didn't look good was Ramona, and you know she is facially challenged anyway."

I shake my head at Tina and laugh. "That was not right."

"Maybe not, but it's still true."

I take one last skeptical look at the airbrush machine in Tina's hand, and then I ease back into the chair. "Go ahead and make me camera ready."

"Girlfriend, you woke up camera ready. I'm just frosting the cake. You know you're gorgeous."

I don't *know* that I'm gorgeous. I know that I have a different look for an African American woman, with this bright red hair and green eyes, and it makes people ask me if I'm "mixed with something." I've been hearing that my entire life.

"Make sure my freckles are nonexistent," I say with a chuckle. "I woke up with a few new ones."

"I think you ought to let them show," Tina said. "They're unique. They add to your aura."

More than anything I can't stand my freckles. They usually are what starts the "are you mixed" conversation. I am part Irish, but I don't claim that side of my family, because the majority of them don't know

17

I exist. Only my father knew me, but he disappeared long ago. It's crazy that I look more like him than my grandmother who raised me.

I'm not proud of it, but I spent my entire childhood being jealous of my darker cousins. They don't carry the same badge of dishonor that I do. I am the product of rape, just like my mom and my Aunt Audrey. Every time someone remarks on my red hair or green eyes, it only reminds me that my mother, my grandmother, and my grandmother's baby sister were all victims of a dirty lowlife who liked to put his hands on women he had no right to touch. The fact that he was a white man in the backwoods of East Texas protected him from the law, but not from my grandfather's revenge.

Tina makes a few final brushes and then stands back to look at me, admiring her work. "Like I said, you're flawless."

I take the mirror from Tina's hand, and I am shocked at my reflection. "Tina, you are a miracle worker."

"I sure am, although a miracle wasn't needed this time," she says. "Do you need me to do anything else?"

My hair is popped, my makeup is on point, and my outfit cost less than a hundred dollars, but it looks like it was more expensive. I think I'm good — on the outside anyway.

"Nothing left to do except make myself a vessel and hope God shows up."

"God's got you! He's always on time," Tina says.

Penelope Bowens, Lady Sandy's daughter, waves at me as she walks up to me and Tina. We've met before, and she's very sweet. Gorgeous too. Like Tina, her hair is always different. This time it's a two-toned weave that's curled in big waves that tumble down her back. She's so tiny that she looks frail in her cream dress, but her smile is huge and warm.

"Hi, Pastor Hampstead," she says as she stops in front of me. "You look wonderful. Your stylist did an awesome job."

"Oh, this is my home girl Tina, she's not my —"

"I did, didn't I?" Tina interjects, not letting me reveal that I don't have an actual stylist yet.

"You did," Penelope says.

"Are you going to speak tonight?" I ask, unsure about Penelope's role in the service.

"I was going to speak, but I think I'm just going to sing. My mom doesn't think I'm ready to speak yet. I'm still learning."

"Oh, well, I'm sure you'll do great," I say.

"I will talk to you later," Penelope says. "I need to go and drink some tea for my voice."

"She seems sweet," Tina says after Penelope leaves.

I nod in agreement. "She is."

Lady Sandy struts over to me in her perfectly fitted and undoubtedly designer dress. It's perfect for the spring season with its yellow top and flowered flare skirt. Her bright yellow stiletto heels have a red bottom that lets me know the shoes alone cost more than my entire wardrobe. And even though I just looked in the mirror and was happy with my reflection, Lady Sandy's expertly coiffed swoop bang that covers one eye makes me want to tell Tina to start over from scratch.

"You look beautiful, dear," Lady Sandy says. "This is your time! Get ready to walk in your purpose."

Although I think I've already been walking in my purpose, I smile up at Lady Sandy. I can't help it. Her beaming smile makes me feel like I just have to beam right back.

"I feel the presence of God here!" Lady Sandy says in a loud, booming voice, making it sound like an announcement.

Everyone stops to look over at Lady Sandy, and she bows her head and im-

20

mediately starts to mumble a prayer. I can't understand the words, but I respectfully bow my head until the moment passes. When she is done, she claps her hands and the staff and members backstage all say "Amen." I don't say anything, because I didn't hear the prayer. "Amen" means agreement to me, and I can't agree if I don't know what was said.

"We're set to begin in five minutes," Lady Sandy says, again speaking directly to me. "Your life is never going to be the same after this."

I don't know why, but her statement sounds more like a warning than a positive omen.

Next, Lady Sandy is directed to the stage area to start the service, while the rest of us are left to watch the service on jumbo TV screens.

"What was that?" Tina whispers to me. "It was a little strange."

"Shhh!" I whisper back. I don't want anyone to hear Tina and have her skepticism mess up my opportunity to speak.

I agree that Lady Sandy's actions were a little strange, but I think she's just eccentric, and she doesn't mean anything by it.

After listening to several well-known gospel artists sing praise and worship songs,

I hear my biography being read and see my promotional picture flash across the big screen. I've been praying this entire time, and I don't feel the same presence Lady Sandy says she felt. There's a certain tickle that I feel on the inside when the gift is about to kick in, and I don't feel it. But it's not like I can back out, so I follow the conference volunteer to the stage entrance.

As I walk out, Lady Sandy extends her hand to me in a welcoming gesture. She smiles at me, and I try to smile back, but I'm so nervous that I know there's more of a grimace on my face.

"I can't wait for you all to hear *God* speak through this amazing woman. I knew she was anointed when she spoke a word over my life that could only have come from the throne of grace. I want everyone to point one hand toward this podium and say 'Rhema word'!"

My breath catches in my throat as I take the microphone from Lady Sandy's hand. She said rhema — a Greek word that means "revealed Word of God." The deepy-deep church people only think of it as some sort of prophetic utterance. And that is what they expect from me today.

I clear my throat, and launch into my message. "Do you ever . . . sometimes want to ask God . . . why He's taking His sweet time with *your* breakthrough?"

As soon as I ask the question, I get the response I knew would come. The loud roar of thousands of cries of agreement rocks the auditorium. For a moment, I am sad. So many hurting souls out there, with so many issues.

I continue my sermon and share the verses that spoke into my spirit, hoping that the women find comfort in what comforted me. I feel like I'm part preacher and part motivational speaker, with phrases like "don't give up" and "you can make it" sandwiched between scripture expositions.

As I near the thirty-minute mark, women start to leave their seats and make their way to the altar. They've had enough of the appetizer, now they want the main course — the prophecies that will tell them their husband is coming (or coming back), their son is going to get off drugs, their daughter is going to come down from the stripper pole, they will make thousands of dollars selling homemade jewelry or body shapers. They want the prophecy and the promise.

I feel my heart rate increase as sweat saturates my brow. My hand trembles on the microphone and I grip it harder.

Then it happens. I feel the tickle in my

midsection. God *is* going to give me a vision for this group of women, and I won't get laughed out of here.

"Wait a minute, y'all. Yes, Holy Spirit. I'm listening." I hold up one hand to hush the crowd while I try to concentrate on being a receiver.

I close my eyes and wait for God to flood me with images of the women in the auditorium — nuggets of what their lives have been, are now, and what they'll be in the future. Instead, I'm flooded with images of myself. They fly by so quickly that I can barely make them out. I see myself wearing expensive clothes. I see myself running down the street barefoot. I see myself crying in a room that I've never seen before.

None of this has anything to do with these women.

When I open my eyes, a woman in all black is walking up the stairs to the stage. Security rushes in from both sides to subdue her, but when they do, she simply falls to her knees and cries out. She stretches her hand toward me.

"Pleeeeease!" she says.

The young woman is overweight by maybe thirty or forty pounds, but it looks like the dress she's wearing is a holdover from when she was thinner. It pulls tightly over her rolls, and the buttons down the front strain to keep the dress closed. She's wearing a long wig, and her face is pretty and a little plump.

I motion for the security to back off, and I walk over to the young woman with the microphone still in my hand.

Everyone is waiting for me to say something profound. A spiritually deep utterance. They want me to speak life into her situation, but all I can see is that broken version of myself from my vision.

I know the visions are true and from God. Rarely do I get them about my own life, and when I have in the past, they've only been confirmation of promises. This feels like another warning.

Then, one of the ministers in front of the church walks up to the young woman and places her hand on the woman's back. The minister looks up at me and points to the sky.

"Speak, Lord!" she says loudly.

Then the rest of the ministers join her, almost chanting.

"Speak, Lord. Speak, Lord. Speak, Lord. Speak, LORD! SPEAK, LORD!"

I glance back at Lady Sandy, who has both of her hands raised to the heavens. Only moments have passed, but it seems like time has ground to a halt.

I take a few more steps toward the girl and she wails louder. I don't need God to show me that she's at her rock bottom.

I lean in close and take her hand. "You're going through the most difficult pain of your life, my sister," I say, stating the obvious.

I send up a silent prayer. *Lord, give me something for her! Just one thing!*

"Help, Holy Ghost!" I say into the microphone, echoing my internal prayer.

As the girl continues to cry out, I make a humming sound in the microphone, as though I'm waiting for an answer — on hold from the Lord, if you will.

A hush comes over the sanctuary. It's so quiet you could hear a fly land on a raindrop. It's quiet enough to hear God whisper.

But He is silent.

I look down at the girl, out at the audience, and back at Lady Sandy. Silently, I repent for what I'm about to do.

"I am seeing you beneath a waterfall," I say, "the blessings of God pouring over you like rain. You've been waiting for a long time. You've cried. You've been lonely — you're still lonely, but God has not forgotten you. He says this dry season has neared its end and your rainy season is coming.

Rain that causes everything in your life to spring forth and flourish. Purpose. Relationships. Vison and destiny! Get ready for it, honey. God says your blessing is coming, and it's going to be sudden! A suddenly blessing!"

The girl is on her feet now and the crowd is in an uproar. Many women are shouting and dancing, including Lady Sandy, who is cutting a rug right on the stage.

I feel the excitement too. Energy beyond belief surges through my body. I even feel powerful.

"Suddenly!" I shout into the microphone, almost shocking myself with the growl in my voice.

Every time I say the word "suddenly," more women fall out onto the floor. Nurses are throwing down sheets left and right.

Spent, I walk up to Lady Sandy and give her the microphone. I can't say another word, because I am completely and totally wiped out.

The young woman is being escorted out of the sanctuary, and she's praising God the entire way. Praising and crying. I hope that things turn around for her.

Because I've got a feeling things are about to turn around for me.

CHAPTER 2
NYA

"Honey, what do you think about this?"

I walk over to Greg's desk in his study and hand him my phone so that he can look at the e-mail I just received. As he reads, he slowly strokes his jet-black goatee. I love the way his facial hair looks against his smooth, dark chocolate skin, but when he strokes that goatee it usually means he's pondering. And not in a good way.

The e-mail says that Lady Sandy wants to sponsor a ten-city tour for me with "Suddenly Blessing" as the theme. She wants to send me to her sister churches all over the country, and I would get to keep half of all the love offerings raised at the churches.

Greg hands my phone back and exhales deeply. I know that sound. This is definitely not good.

"This doesn't really sound like the vision we have for our ministry. Suddenly blessing?" he says. "We've always focused on

repentance, reconciliation, and relationship."

"I know, I know. But you were watching
the streaming broadcast. You saw how the
women reacted."

"Church folk always get in a tizzy about a
blessing. We know that. We could've been a
five-thousand-member church by now if
we'd gone that route."

"So are you saying you don't want me to
do it?"

"I'm saying that you need to pray about
the message you're putting out there."

"There's nothing wrong with meeting
people where they are. If we hook them with
the suddenly blessing message, we then have
the opportunity to reach them with repentance, reconciliation, and relationship."

"The other thing is . . . we're a ministry
team. Is she sending us on this tour or is
she sending you?"

Really, Greg? I know he didn't sit up here
giving that spiel about our ministry's purpose just because he's hurt that he's not being invited along for this particular ride. It's
not like we're going to preach together every
single time.

"She's making it an extension of her
Women's Empowerment conference, but
I'm sure she wouldn't mind you traveling

with me. Do you want me to ask for plane tickets for you too?"

Greg scratches his goatee again. Not a good sign. Then he shakes his head.

"If you're going to do this, somebody has to stay behind and take care of our church. We can't both abandon our congregation."

"Abandoning our church? I am not abandoning our church. Don't you see how this is an opportunity for us to grow?"

"It definitely could be an opportunity, but it sounds like you already made up your mind."

"No. I really haven't. But my reasons are different from your reasons."

"How so?"

I haven't told Greg that my prophecy wasn't authentic and that I should be nominated for an Academy Award for my performance. I don't think I want to tell him either. He's sitting here acting really judgmental regarding this whole thing. I already asked God to forgive me, and maybe this opportunity proves that He has forgiven me. I won't ever have to fake a prophetic word again. I can just preach and prophesy if God tells me to. It's a perfect solution.

"I just don't know if I'm ready for this," I reply. "Lady Sandy and her friends are on another level. I don't even have the wardrobe for this."

"Well, that is a real concern. Maybe you can ask God to suddenly bless you with some designer clothes and fancy shoes." Greg lets out a guffaw like this is the funniest thing in the history of funny things.

"You got jokes, I see."

"I said SUDDENLY!" Greg imitates my message and the little growly tone that I used. I can't help but laugh. He sounds hilarious.

"I didn't sound like that."

Greg laughs harder. "Yes, you did! I thought you were about to wave your hand and slay everybody in the Spirit."

I take a peppermint candy from Greg's desk and throw it at him. "Shut up!"

"No, but seriously, if you want to do this, you know that I'm behind you. Just don't get caught up to the point that we miss what we know God called us to do. You're the one who had the vision, right? Both of us preaching to thousands."

"I did, and it's going to come to pass."

"I know. It sounds like Lady Sandy trying to start an all-girl crew."

The sparkle in Greg's eyes as he jokes with me makes me fall in love with him all over again. Every time he laughs, I remember the first time we met. It was in the chapel at our college. He had led the Bible study for the week, and he was so eloquent and passionate in his speaking. He was on fire for Jesus, and so was I.

When we started seeing each other, a different kind of fire was lit. So, in our senior year we decided to marry instead of burn (with lust . . . or in hell, as the church mothers liked to remind me). It was the best decision I ever made.

And yes, my man still gets me hot. I thank God for that too.

"She is not trying to start an all-girl crew, but I think she is very big on women in ministry. She comes from a denomination that never let women speak."

"But she doesn't preach though. I find that strange. She puts on these conferences for women preaching, but she doesn't say anything herself," Greg says. "Do you think Bishop Bowens doesn't let her?"

This has never occurred to me, but it could be true. "Maybe she's not called to preach. If she isn't I appreciate the fact that she doesn't do it just because people say she should."

"I guess I don't want to travel with you," Greg says, "although it seems like it'll be exciting. Our church needs at least one of us on Sunday and for Bible study. We're still in growing mode."

"This will only help us get more publicity. It's almost like an advertising campaign."

Greg frowns. "The commercialism of the modern black church. Hate it."

"Ministry isn't cheap, babe."

"That's because we have to have our conferences in auditoriums and arenas. We need to do like Jesus and find a good hilltop and just preach to whoever wants to listen."

"And then feed them from five loaves and two fish?"

"Nah, we gonna need more fish than that. Especially if we talking catfish."

I crack up. "And coleslaw too. Maybe some fries."

"See, this is where it all starts. This how stuff gets expensive. Why can't they just have the fish and the bread?"

"As long as they have sweet tea to wash it down with, it might be enough."

Greg chuckles. "I bet they're not gonna have catfish sandwiches on your Suddenly Blessing tour. That might take away from the bottom line."

"Greg . . ."

"No, let me stop, 'cause I got you, Nya. You want to do this and I'm not going to hold you back. Just be careful with this crew is all I'm saying."

"I will. Thank you for not standing in the way, because you know I'd stop if you asked me. I wouldn't do it without your support."

Greg smiles and places a soft kiss on my lips. "I will always support you, babe. I got you, and you got me. Right?"

I know Greg always has my back regardless, and that even though he's not too keen on this idea, he's not going to stand in my way. And I've got a feeling in my spirit that it's going to be good for us, even if it doesn't look that way to Greg right now.

The beauty of all this is that my man has got me. Like I said, I fall in love with him over and over again. I'd marry him a million times.

Chapter 3
Felicia

I want to shout right now.

I knew God would bless me if I pressed my way to the Women's Empowerment conference. When I saw it advertised online, it felt like Lady Sandy was reaching her hand out to me through the computer monitor, like it was a personal invitation. I just knew I couldn't miss it.

Even though I had to use my unemployment check to book my flight from Atlanta, it was imperative that I be in attendance. And although I had to stay in a trucker's motel with dingy sheets and probably bedbugs too, I just had to be there. Something told me God was going to show up and He did. He's not far from the ones searching for Him.

I almost didn't get up from my seat when that evangelist started preaching. Nya Hampstead. I didn't come to the conference for her. I came for a touch from Lady

Sandy, but I could tell Pastor Hampstead is anointed too. Just the fact that Lady Sandy invited her was enough for me.

Then she looked directly at me, so I knew it was time to move from my seat.

I knew it was time for me to get up, but I didn't want to, because of the most superficial thing. My clothes were too tight. I hadn't realized how much weight I'd gained while I was sitting at home on unemployment, until I tried to put on the clothes I brought with me to the conference. I didn't have time or money to buy anything else, so I wore the clothes. I could almost feel my back fat ripple as I made my way down to the altar. I couldn't miss out on God because I'd been eating crazy.

When Pastor Hampstead looked at me, there wasn't any judgment or pity on her face. She's a prophetess, so I know she could see all the stuff I've done in my life. I know she saw some things that I'm not proud about doing. Some men I'm not proud about claiming.

She didn't do or say anything to make me feel bad about the men I've been with. She was so much like Jesus.

She didn't prophesy for anyone except me, which makes it even more incredible. God chose to move the atmosphere for me and only me. And this e-mail I just received, offering me a job as a grant coordinator for the Atlanta Crows, is confirmation of it all.

I've been unemployed for a year, and then three weeks after the conference, out of the blue, a recruiter sets up an interview for me? Yeah, God!

When I went on the interview, I still wasn't convinced that this was the blessing Pastor Nya had prophesied for me. I've got to work on my faith walk so I can be ready to move when God says move.

God could've just blessed me with any job. I would've been grateful at this point to be a bank teller, or a call center operator. At this point, I just needed something to pay my bills and keep a roof over my head. But I just got a job offer from the NBA. When God wants to open a door, He just shows out with it. That's how you know to give Him all the glory, praise, and honor for it.

I have to get myself together and lose these thirty pounds so that I don't look like a stuffed sausage in my business suits. I haven't had to wear them in a while. Being unemployed only required me to wear sweat suits. But you better believe I'm walking into that building looking like I've got a lot of zeroes in my bank account.

I told them that I can start in three weeks.

So if I do protein shakes for all of my meals and drink lots of water every day, I should be able to lose fourteen pounds by the time I start work. I've got to look good on my first day. First impressions are everything with the professional athletes and millionaires that I'll be seeing every day.

Speaking of athletes and millionaires, Pastor Nya said my relationships were going to be blessed too! God knows I want a husband almost as much as I wanted a job. Okay, maybe I want a husband more, but I won't say that out loud. He hears me in the spirit realm anyway.

The men I've had in my life in the past have been nothing but users and abusers. I know God has more for me in that area too. I just haven't trusted in Him the way I've needed to when it comes to men.

My last boyfriend was one of the associate ministers at my old church. He wasn't married, but he was engaged to a woman in another state. I didn't find out about her until he brought her to the church and introduced her as his new bride. I wasn't the only woman in the church wounded behind that one either. There was much crying and groaning about that.

It's definitely not easy for an educated black woman to find her match, and that's why hearing a prophetic word about relationships was an on-time message for me.

Something in my spirit tells me I need to clean house of all the relationships I've had in the past. I pull out my cell phone, and one by one delete every ex-boyfriend's numbers. I chuckle at some of the entries in my address book. James, the associate minister, is in my phone as Big Fat Liar. Carl, my high school sweetheart, is saved as Demon. Graham, my college lover, is in the address book as Don't You Dare Answer.

I feel a little bit of freedom with each deletion. Every time I press that button, it takes me one step closer to my destiny. I'm ready for greatness. I'm ready for my suddenly blessing.

CHAPTER 4
NYA

"That woman pressed her way through the crowd because she knew Jesus was present."

Greg grips the sides of the podium as sweat pours from his forehead. He doesn't need a microphone. The acoustics in our small sanctuary are good enough for his voice to carry to the very last pew.

"She *knew* the solution to all her problems was right there, within her grasp. All she had to do was stretch herself. She had to push through the hordes of folk. Get them out of her way," Greg says. "Don't you know that sometimes the only thing standing between you and your blessing is people?"

I rock back and forth in my seat, because I feel that familiar tingle. Someone here needs a word from the Lord, and He's about to whisper that word into my spirit.

I really and truly believe that if everyone took time out to seek God and listen for His voice, there would be no need for

prophets and prophetesses. We'd be un-
necessary. I think God wants this. He wants
to speak to us one-on-one.

I bite my bottom lip and close my eyes.

A young teenage girl, maybe fifteen, sits
on the side of her bed, crying. She holds a
pregnancy test in her hands. The positive
marking is there. She looks down at the
damning piece of plastic and sobs into her
hands.

Time speeds forward. The girl sits in an
abortion clinic. She looks at the pamphlet
and at the posters on the walls. She's
scared. Her entire body trembles in her
seat.

A nurse in blue scrubs comes into the
waiting room and extends her hand to the
girl.

"Are you ready, Melody?"

She stands, and with tears streaming
down her cheeks, she takes the nurse's
hand and touches her belly with her other.

I snap out of the vision and immediately
scan the congregation. There are about two
hundred fifty people here. Packed, for us.
Then I spot the girl. She's sitting in the back
of the church. Her short hair is pulled into
a tiny ponytail on top of her head.

41

Greg watches me as I stand from my seat. I give him a slight nod to let him know that God wants to reach someone in the crowd.

He keeps preaching. "When the woman touched Jesus, He felt power leave his body. What do you think that power was? That was the Holy Spirit. And immediately she was healed."

I walk down the side of the church and as I make eye contact with the girl, she looks terrified. Maybe she thinks I'm going to embarrass her and put her business out for everyone to hear. I hold one finger up to my lips.

She seems to relax a little, but her hand feels clammy and it trembles when I reach out and pull her into the aisle.

"It's Melody, right?"

The girl's mouth forms a small circle. She nods.

I whisper to her. "I'm going to say some things. You just nod if it's correct, okay?"

She nods once.

"You're pregnant still?" I hope the answer is yes. I couldn't tell if the vision is future or if it already happened.

She nods again. I feel a flood of relief.

"The father. Does he know?"

She breathes deeply and stares into my eyes. No nod.

"We can help you. You don't have to take your child's life," I whisper in her ear.

She begins to cry.

"Are you safe at home?" I ask.

This time she shakes her head and more tears pour down her face. The woman sitting next to the girl stands.

"What are you saying to my daughter?" she asks.

I bite my lip as it suddenly becomes clear to me. The father is her mother's man. Not the husband, and not the teenager's father. *Oh Jesus, help me.*

"Your daughter is severely depressed. I'd like to help her get counseling, if that's okay."

Greg pauses in the message, I guess waiting to see if I have anything to say. I give him the signal to continue. Still holding the girl's hand, I walk her down to the altar and ask a few of our ministers to pray for her.

I take the microphone from Greg's extended hand. "I need everyone in this congregation to pray for this baby right now. She is going through some things some of y'all wouldn't be able to handle. She needs the prayers of the righteous."

Greg starts to sing a worship hymn. " 'Reign, Jesus reign. Reign, Jesus reign. You're the king of Zion, Judah's lion. Reign,

Jesus reign.' "

He repeats the song as members of the praise team sing from their seats.

"That's right on time, Pastor. Jesus, reign supreme in this baby's life. You are in control of her situation. Of every situation. Reign, Jesus!"

I am overwhelmed for a moment as Melody falls to her knees at the altar. The acoustics carry the sounds of her cries through the entire sanctuary. I wave my hand to signal Greg to continue singing.

The worship atmosphere is so high, and I am so glad the Holy Spirit is here. Because, so help me, Jesus, my flesh wants to walk to the back of the church and have me pull every strand of weave out of that woman's head, then beat her to a bloody pulp.

She knows. She knows her man is abusing her child. And she's letting it happen.

This is the kind of prophecy that no one wants. It drains me to see it, but at least I don't have to live it. But, praise God, we're getting that baby out of that situation.

This is what my gift is for. Redemption. Reconciliation. Relationship. Nobody wants to tour the country on that platform. It's not shiny enough. Not blessed enough. Not sexy enough.

I remind myself, as Greg continues to sing

with the praise team, that we're just meeting the people where they are. Start with the blessing, get them to the relationship piece. I know God can do it any way he wants, but I'm praying that He uses me.

CHAPTER 5
FELICIA

Seventeen pounds off in three weeks, and I must say I look good. My hair is laid with a beautiful honey-blond weave, my Chanel suit fits perfectly again, and my makeup is flawless. I am too ready for my first day at work.

As I drive to the office, I listen to some of my favorite gospel songs. I blast Fred Hammond singing " 'Blessed in the city, Blessed in the field.' " I am definitely blessed beyond measure today.

The Atlanta Crows logo sits atop a high-rise in downtown Atlanta. The blue and silver letters shine as the sunlight hits them. I get excited, happy that I chose my electric blue suit for the first day.

I walk into the office with a big smile on my face, and the receptionist smiles back.

"You must be Felicia Caldwell," she says.

"I am."

"I'm Sharon, the receptionist and office

administrator. I was told to expect you. I can get you anything you need. Mr. Bailey is out this morning at a meeting, so I have the keys to your office."

"My office?" I chuckle. "I was expecting a cubicle."

Sharon laughs out loud. "Girl, this is the NBA. The last person in this job administered grants for five of the top players' non-profits."

"Oh!"

"Yes, girl. You have to have somewhere nice to meet with the players and their grantees."

I like Sharon's look. She's got big, naturally curly hair that seems to go in any direction it pleases. Her jewelry is big, chunky, and wooden, like it came from an island or the motherland. Her clothes are definitely cheap knockoffs of designer brands, but she makes them work. I can kick it with her.

"All right, then. Show me to my office."

"My pleasure."

When Sharon opens the door to my new office I almost pass out. Yeah, God!

The first thing I notice is the huge picture window with a picturesque view of downtown Atlanta. Then, the office furniture is the expensive kind. They didn't buy this mahogany desk and burgundy leather sofa at Staples. It even smells like money in here.

"Girl, close your mouth before something flies in there," Sharon says. "This is nothing! You ought to see Mr. Bailey's office."

Tears form in my eyes, and I quickly wipe them away. Sharon hands me a tissue.

"I'm sorry. I just got overwhelmed for a moment," I say as I dab my eyes. "I don't know what I did for God to bless me like this."

"Girl, go ahead and give God glory. This job was a blessing to me too. I don't usually share this with people when I first meet them, but I like your spirit. I have a couple of felonies, and it seemed like nobody would give me a second chance, but God used Mr. Bailey to bless my life. He's gonna bless yours too."

I can't remember ever feeling this happy about a job. That evangelist Nya is definitely anointed, but she didn't do this. God did it.

"You can get settled in," Sharon says. "I will send for some coffee if you want."

"Do you have chai?"

Sharon laughs again. "They have whatever you want."

Sharon leaves and closes the door behind her. I spin around in circles and squeal. This is *my* office! My purpose!

I walk over to the desk and ease myself

48

down into the soft leather office chair. I close my eyes and inhale the heavy woodsy scent. I imagine myself making moves and connections, and being invited to red carpet events, hobnobbing with Atlanta's elite.

A soft tap on the door pulls me out of my fantasy. I sit up straight and smooth out my skirt.

"Come in," I say.

The door opens and Lance Jarvis, one of the starting players of the Atlanta Crows, walks in. Of course he's tall. He's in the NBA. But his skin is so dark that it glows, and his jet-black curls are slicked back into a long ponytail. Honestly, he looks like he should be on the cover of a romance novel.

"Are you the new grant coordinator?" he asks.

I nod and stand to my feet. "Yes, I'm Felicia Caldwell."

"I'm Lance Jarvis, and I need your help."

I give a little flirty giggle. "I know who you are. What can I do for you?"

"There's a Boys and Girls Club in my hometown that's about to close and they need a grant from my organization. I told them yes, but we need to go through the process. Can you hold their hand for the paperwork?"

"Of course."

"Good. You are a lifesaver." He genuinely looks relieved. "I hope I didn't disturb you."

"No. It's my first day, and I was thinking about how to approach everyone to let them know about my arrival. Then suddenly you appeared and you made it easy."

Lance laughs, and I love the sound of it. "Suddenly I appeared?"

"Mm-hmm. When things like that happen, I pay attention. It usually means something."

"Like I was destined to be the first player you met."

"Yes, exactly!" He gets it. He completely gets it.

Lance bites his bottom lip and takes in my ample cleavage, which is benefitting today from a very snug push-up bra. He gives an approving head nod. I feel my heart flutter.

"Suddenly I want to take you for a late breakfast."

I glance down at the jewel-encrusted band on his ring finger. He follows my eyes to his hand and twists the ring.

"Do you have a problem having breakfast with a married man?" he asks.

"Only if you're happily married."

"I wouldn't say that. I wouldn't say that at all."

I pause for a moment. I *do* have a problem having breakfast with a married man, but an unhappily married man might end up divorced. Maybe his wife doesn't appreciate him. I would.

Since he's here, I'm going to believe he's part of my blessing. There's just a process to this thing, and I'm going to trust it. He's ordained everything perfectly so far. I'm not going to question His methods.

"Why don't we order in?"

This comes out in a sexy purr. I can't help it. He's looking at me with hunger in his eyes. Shoot, I'm hungry too. For more than breakfast. It's been a long while since I've been fed.

"I like the way you think," Lance says.

I feel butterflies in my stomach, because this is all coming together. Career in order? Check. Body together? Double check. Meeting the man of my dreams? I think I'm about to check this off too. Shoot, for all I know he married a groupie or his high school sweetheart. If he's ready for an upgrade, then I am here for it.

We don't always get who we're destined to have on the first time around anyway. Maybe God is trying to do something in both our lives. I am definitely willing to submit myself to His will.

Yeah, God!

CHAPTER 6
NYA

The first church on our ten-city tour is Breakthrough Central, a nondenominational church in Houston, where the first lady, Cheyenne Jacoby, is Lady Sandy's best friend. It's a megachurch too. I wonder if being a megachurch wife is required in order to be in Lady Sandy's circle of friends.

I don't have to speak until tomorrow evening, at a special Sunday night service, but today I have to go to high tea at Lady Cheyenne's house.

"What do you even wear to a high tea?" I ask Tina as I pull out different outfits.

"It's spring, so pastel colors and a hat."

"A hat? I don't wear hats."

"Well, you're gonna have to start running with this crew. This is the big-money first lady crew."

I roll my eyes. She sounds like Greg.

"Do you have any pearls?" Tina asks.

"Pearls? Are you kidding me? You know I

don't have any real jewelry."

Tina laughs out loud. She goes into her bag and hands me a pretty pearl-and-lace necklace.

"Fake it till you make it, girlfriend."

"Help me find something to wear in this suitcase."

I know Tina is my "fake" stylist, but she ought to be the real deal. She reached into my pile of rags and put together a halfway decent ensemble. A white blouse, powder-blue skirt, and blue sandals.

"I still think you should get a hat," she says. "There's a Ross and a Marshalls five minutes from here."

I don't want to admit it, but I don't have money for a hat, not even the deeply discounted ones they might have at Ross. Greg and I aren't balling out of control like these ladies and their husbands.

"I'm not getting a hat, but maybe you can do something about my hair."

Tina's eyes brighten. "I know. I will give you a ballerina knot on top of your head and we can use the bracelet that goes with that necklace as head jewelry."

I sit and let Tina do her magic. With the hairstyle, outfit, and glittery makeup, she's got me looking like Tinkerbell or some other fairy.

"What do you think?" Tina asks as she stands next to me in front of the full-length mirror.

"I look fourteen years old on my way to my first piano recital."

"Ha!" Tina says. "Black don't crack, baby. You do look young though."

"I wish you were coming with me to this. What if I say something stupid?"

Tina slicks down a stray red curl. "What could you say that's stupid? Don't feel intimidated by those women. Shoot, you're out of their league. Not the other way around."

I cock my head to one side and give Tina a questioning grimace. "What do you mean by that? They're rich, and if you hadn't noticed, Greg and I are poor."

"I'm talking ministry. You are light-years ahead of them. I would go to church with you and Greg as the pastors before I'd ever set foot in one of their megas."

"I know you're just saying that 'cause you're my girl, and I appreciate you for it."

Tina shakes her head. "When do I ever say anything just because we're friends? I mean that."

My phone lights up with a text notification. I pick it up to read the message. It's from Lady Sandy.

"They're downstairs waiting on me."

"Okay, well it's time to show and prove, mama," Tina says. "Go impress the heck out of them. Maybe ten cities will turn into twenty."

"Over Greg's dead body," I scoff. "I thought he was gonna have a coronary over the ten."

Tina hands me a small purse out of her suitcase. "Put your stuff in here. You can't carry that tired-looking purse you have."

"There is nothing wrong with my Coach purse."

Tina stares at the ceiling. "There was nothing wrong with it ten years ago when it was actually for sale in a store."

"These bags are made to last."

"Honey, that purse has seen better days."

I snatch Tina's little purse and cram my stuff in there. Then I hurry downstairs to the hotel lobby. I don't want Lady Sandy to have to wait too long for me.

When I get outside, the car that's waiting is a big stretch limousine. A driver hops out and opens the back door for me to get in. Immediately I feel underdressed, but it's too late now.

"Well, don't you look cute," Lady Cheyenne says. "Like a pretty little teenager."

I give her a smile as I get into the limo.

"Thank you, Lady Cheyenne. I wish I still looked like a teenager, though. I woke up one day and saw a line on my face that wouldn't leave."

Everyone in the car laughs. Lady Sandy and Lady Cheyenne are on one side, and Penelope is on the other side of the backseat, sitting next to me. They're all wearing beautiful pastel-colored ensembles. Tina was right. Only Lady Sandy and Lady Cheyenne are wearing hats, though. Lady Sandy has her hair braided into a tight bun, but Lady Cheyenne's auburn curls tumble from under the hat and frame her face.

"You can just call me Cheyenne. Save all that lady stuff for church," Cheyenne says.

"She's not like my mama," Penelope says. "She's down-to-earth."

Lady Sandy gives Penelope a little pursed-lip grimace. Penelope lifts her eyebrows and her smile fades. She is sufficiently checked, I suppose.

"So, I've never been to high tea," I say. "What should I expect?"

"There will be many different kinds of tea, sandwiches, cupcakes, and cookies. And we're dressed up, but the environment is relaxed," Cheyenne says.

"I want you to meet the rest of the inner circle," Lady Sandy says. "Love International is a perfect addition as a sister church. We make sure that we're all successful in ministry."

"How do you define success?" I ask. This is a real question to me, because I think that Greg and I are already successful.

"Well, first of all, both of you being in full-time ministry with no side jobs," Cheyenne says. "And debt-free."

"For the most part, we're there," I reply. "But Greg does taxes for the members during tax season."

"He actually does them himself? Or does he have a staff?" Penelope asks.

"No staff. He sets up at the church and does them himself."

All three of the women exchange disapproving glances.

"That's going to change for you after this tour," Lady Sandy says. "These services will bring in a couple million easy. Especially since you're going to give some prophetic words."

"I can't promise that," I say. "I can only follow the leading of the Lord."

"What do you need to do to ensure the atmosphere is charged for the prophetic?" Penelope asks. "Do you need people to come into the sanctuary early? To pray? To consecrate things?"

The limo feels too hot all of a sudden. I don't know how to explain to them that all the mystical, symbolic stuff that church folk do has no impact at all on my gift.

"I don't need anything special, Penelope. God doesn't need anything special from us for Him to show up. We can just have hearts of worship and praise and see what unfolds."

Lady Sandy frowns. "What is the contingency plan if you don't have a prophetic word?"

"I will preach. I have studied and I have a great sermon prepared."

"Hmm . . . ," Lady Sandy says. "Let's just hope that the Lord moves, honey. That's what this is all about. You spoke a blessing over that girl and we have gotten so many requests for that DVD."

"Really? Like how many?" I ask in disbelief.

"We've sold over fifteen thousand copies so far."

A knot forms in the pit of my stomach. In addition to the thousands of women who were in attendance at the Women's Empowerment session, thousands more saw me operating in fraudulence. I still can't believe I crumbled under pressure and did that.

"That's incredible," I say.

"I'm not surprised," Cheyenne says. "The

people love a good prophetic word. And that girl was perfection. It was almost like she was planted in the audience . . . Was she?"

My jaw drops. "No! Of course not. I have no clue who she was. I would like to get her information if possible, though. I want to follow up with her."

Lady Sandy nods. "I'm not sure if anyone captured her information."

"I can find out," Penelope says. "The ushers would know."

"Listen, Nya, your ministry is about to explode," Lady Sandy says. "You and Greg are used to being those touchable pastors that greet every member after Sunday services. You're going to have to shift your focus, and trust the undershepherds to tend to the flock. Your words will reach and invigorate thousands, maybe even millions. You're not going to be able to connect with each one of them."

"I am hands-on, though. Most of the prophecies I receive are personal. I typically don't even share what I'm saying with the audience. Only with that person."

"Oh no. That's not going to do," Cheyenne says. "Honey, you better up the theatrics. You were good at the Women's Empowerment session, but you need a little extra oomph."

"Oomph?" I ask.

"Yes, girl. You need a bright-colored dress, some high heels. I say do red, since your hair is so red. It can look like Holy Ghost fire," Cheyenne says.

"Or the blood of Jesus," Penelope adds.

"She needs a catchphrase," Lady Sandy says.

"No, she doesn't. Her catchphrase is 'suddenly,' " Cheyenne says. "Suddenly anything. She can say someone's got a sudden salvation, or a suddenly breakthrough. That's it! Put it on a T-shirt."

"You think I haven't?" Lady Sandy says. "We've got 'I'm suddenly blessed' sparkly T-shirts on deck for each of the ten cities. We're going to give a few of them away during the service."

I clear my throat. Merchandise? Should I copyright my message? I don't know what to think.

"Since we brought you in to speak for the Women's Empowerment conference, it is a work-for-hire agreement. Anything that happens during the course of that employment becomes the property of Pathway Church."

It's as if Lady Sandy is reading my mind. I guess it's only right though, that they own a fake prophetic word. Greg would think it's funny.

"T-shirts. I just don't know about that, but whatever you think is best," I say.

"Exactly. Trust me, darling. You don't know the first thing about building a mega ministry. But if you stick with us, you'll be able to stop preaching in clothes you bought at the outlet mall."

"I will always love a bargain," I say.

"The only people who say that are the ones who need a bargain," Cheyenne says.

They all laugh while I sit in silence. I try to have a pleasant expression on my face, but this has got to be the most uncomfortable moment I've ever had in my life.

Lady Sandy reaches across and pats my hand. "Don't worry, baby. We're gonna get you together. I promise."

And this is exactly what worries me. Today, high tea. Tomorrow, what? Designer shoes and sparkly T-shirts with prophecies on them?

"Aren't you excited about what God is doing?" Penelope asks.

I expand my plastered-on smile and don't respond, because what can I say other than yes?

"God is incredible, isn't He?" I say.

The women all squeal, because this is something we can all definitely agree on. We may not agree on bargain shopping and prophecy tees, but the power of God is a universal truth. Plus, I can tell, I'm going to need all of His power to get through this tour.

CHAPTER 7
FELICIA
___

Mr. Bailey has requested that I attend a team networking mixer in his place, because he's going on vacation with his wife. This is my first time out in front of the entire team, and I will be representing all the services we provide for the players and their non-profit organizations.

I also know that this is my chance to really make a personal impact on people in the community who will be my partners in charity galas, auctions, and everything else. Being in nonprofits is more about schmoozing than anything else. And I can schmooze with the best of them.

I chose a fitted white pantsuit and paired it with a royal blue tube top and silver heels. My hair is in big barrel curls and my makeup is minimal. I want to be attractive without being viewed as a threat to the NBA players' wives who are sure to be in attendance.

Besides, I'm only interested in one player — Lance Jarvis. I smile at the bracelet sparkling on my wrist. It's a gift from Lance. He and I have been going on breakfast dates in the early morning, the only time that he can get away from home, for now. But he's promised to take me on vacation to the Caribbean, and I'm here for it.

Sharon steps into my office and does a little twirl, showing off her outfit. It's a little unprofessional, white jeans ripped right beneath her butt cheeks and a one-shoulder blouse covered in sequins.

"Look at you looking like a boss," she says.

"Isn't that how I should look? I'm representing Mr. Bailey."

She nods. "I'm representing me, myself, and I. Trying to capture a high roller."

"You're fly enough. I'm sure one of those players will want to kick it with you."

"Oh naw, girl," Sharon says. "I'm not fooling with any of those players. They are some of the biggest hoes on the planet."

"Meaning what?"

"Meaning they will sleep with any and every groupie that drops her panties. Plus, we aren't really allowed to talk to them anyway. It's against company policy."

"Is it enforced?"

"The no-sleeping-with-the-players policy?" Sharon asks.

"Yes."

Sharon's lips curl into a grin. "Why? You bumping and grinding with someone?"

"No, but if I was I wouldn't tell you."

"I think that's what everyone does. There's a lot of not asking and not telling going on around here."

"So you're not asking."

"And you're not telling. Hey!" Sharon does a little dance like we're in on something together. We're not.

"You want to ride over to the sports bar with me?" I ask.

"Of course I want to ride up with the boss chick," Sharon says. "You ready now?"

"Yes. Let's go."

We take the elevator downstairs, where the office driver is waiting to take us over to the sports bar that's hosting the event.

When we arrive, there is already a line wrapped around the corner. Obviously someone alerted the groupies that the players would be congregating here tonight. I have never seen so much spandex and so many lace-front wigs in one spot.

"The hood rats are out in full effect, I see," Sharon says. "Thank God we don't have to wait in line."

Sharon is right, because we're ushered

from the car straight into the VIP section of the club. I think the hood rats came out for no reason, because none of them are able to get to where the players are located.

I scan the room until I find Lance. He sees me and gives me a tight head nod. I don't nod back, because he's standing next to his wife.

"Let's find a booth," Sharon says. "My feet are hurting already."

"You can sit. I need to work the room. Lots of people here I need to connect with."

I flip my hair and stride across the room to where Lance is standing with his wife. I can feel the eyes on me as I move, but I don't care about their attention. I'm only trying to catch Lance's eye.

"Felicia," Lance says as I approach. "Meet my wife, Jasmine. She's starting up her own foundation, and since it's with my money, you might be dealing with her too."

Jasmine looks me up and down. Her eyes linger on my cleavage and then she takes the rest of me in.

"Hello. You work at the Atlanta Crows office?" Jasmine says.

"I do. I'm so pleased to meet you. Maybe we can sit down and have lunch sometime."

Jasmine sips her drink. "I'm sure Lance will put us in contact if it's necessary.

Lance, baby, I'll be right back. Erica and them are here."

She sashays away, leaving me and Lance standing face-to-face. His eyes meet mine, and he says more with them than he can say with his mouth, since we're out in public.

"She's warm and friendly," I say. "I totally felt the love."

"Jasmine is a tigress, not a house cat. She can purr, but she can also rip out a throat."

"She's a tigress. I'm a lioness. Big cats roam the jungle freely."

"I see. Do you want me to introduce you to the rest of the team?" Lance asks.

I shake my head. "This lioness can stalk her own prey."

"Prey?"

Lance licks his lips and chuckles. His eyes rest the same place his wife's did, right on my boobs. I spin on one heel and walk away wearing a winning smile on my face.

I might look jolly on the outside, but inside I'm fuming. Lance's groupie wife looks like she purchased every one of her body parts. If you put her next to an open flame, she'd probably start melting from the amount of silicone and plastic in her body. But I can tell she has no intention of going anywhere.

That's okay. I don't care what her intentions are, and neither does God. Once He decides to open a door, no man can shut it, nor a tigress.

CHAPTER 8
NYA

It's been three months since the Women's Empowerment conference, and now the ten-city tour is over. Finally, I'm getting alone time with Greg. I was going to take him out to dinner, but I decided that the news I'm about to share should be discussed behind closed doors.

"What's that I smell?"

Greg's voice echoes through the otherwise silent house. He sounds excited that there's dinner, and I completely understand. He's used to me cooking every day, and I've been on a two-month sabbatical from the kitchen.

"Fried catfish, shrimp and grits, collard greens, and garlic and cheese biscuits," I announce as I peek out from the kitchen into the dining room.

Greg's eyes light up as he sits down at the table. Usually when I cook his favorite dinner, he gets an extra special married-folk treat for dessert, but that's not the purpose of me cooking this time. I need him to be in a good mood for another reason.

"I'm glad you're back home," Greg says. "That tour was a lot, but you did your thang."

"God is good."

I step out of the kitchen and place two plates, heavy with food, onto the table.

"I notice you didn't do too much prophetic word, though."

I nod slowly. I didn't do any prophetic speaking, because I couldn't. I didn't even get an inkling of a vision during that entire tour. Honestly, that scares me. It feels like losing one of my senses. God has been showing me things since I was a little girl. Then, I didn't even know that it was something that few other people had. It was like hearing, tasting, or feeling to me.

"No. Maybe the Suddenly Blessing message was enough."

Greg prays for the food, thanks God for how He's blessed us. It's a good opening to my news, but that doesn't stop my feelings of apprehension. When Greg says amen, he looks up at my face and frowns.

"Are you okay, honey?" he asks.

Quickly, I nod. What I'm about to share really is great news. "Yes. Let me just get this over with so we can enjoy dinner."

I reach into my skirt pocket and take out the envelope I've been holding close to my body for two days — ever since Lady Sandy gave it to me.

"What's this?"

"Open it."

Greg opens the envelope and pulls out the check. His eyes widen exactly like I'm sure mine did when I saw the amount.

"Four hundred eighty-five thousand dollars?"

"Half of the love offerings from the ten cities. Lady Sandy wants us to sow it into our ministry."

Greg drops the check like it has acid on it.

"People gave this much money?" he asks. "Repentance, reconciliation, and relationship doesn't raise this much cash."

"Blessings do."

"But you can't buy a blessing."

I let out a long sigh. This has always been our issue. Mine and Greg's. The reason we went into ministry was to become a beacon of light. The antidote to "the money cometh" preaching. We were going to show people that the blood of Jesus is truly a greater blessing than a new house, a new car, or a new love.

"Our ministry purpose hasn't changed,

Greg. Don't you know how much this money can do for our church?"

"So why haven't you deposited it yet?" Greg asks. "Why do you look worried? If this is such a blessing for us, why are you so concerned?"

"Because of you. I know you aren't truly, in your heart of hearts, supportive of this, but I believe that it's going to get us to our vision."

He slides the check across the table, back to me.

"So deposit it."

"You act like you aren't happy about this."

Greg shakes his head. "You're wrong. I am. We accept donations from all sources. Last Sunday a drug dealer dropped a thousand dollars in the offering."

"This doesn't compare to that though."

"Okay."

"Really, Greg. This money was raised during the course of ministry."

"Okay. Deposit it."

Greg stands up from the table. He tosses his napkin onto his nearly full plate and pushes his chair in. He's done.

"Aren't you going to finish eating?"

"I am finished. It was good, and I'm full. Thank you."

"Greg, talk to me. Don't leave. We need

to get back on one accord. I don't like feeling like we're miles apart."

"I don't like feeling that either, Nya. Tell me the truth. You didn't have one prophetic word while you were on that tour, did you?"

I shake my head. "I don't know what it was."

"I don't trust their intentions. Especially Lady Sandy. They are trying to build something and bring us along for the ride, but they're going through you. Not us. I don't like it. It feels divisive."

"I will always be here for our purpose, Greg. You know that. This is just seed money for us."

Greg sighs and leaves me at the table not knowing how to feel. I am just glad that this tour is over, and we can get back to living our lives and walking our destiny.

CHAPTER 9
FELICIA

Something startles me and wakes me from my sleep. I open my eyes and for a moment I am disoriented and forget where I am. Then my eyes focus and I remember. Luxury villa. Puerto Rico. With Lance. It's our three month anniversary present.

I glance to my right and notice what woke me up. Lance has gotten out of the bed and is texting or something on his phone. There's a smile on his face, though, so it must be good to him, whatever he's doing.

"What are you smiling about over there? I'm over here." I purr softly, stretching my body sexily under the sheets.

Lance looks at me and his smile fades for a second. Then it returns. It's a different smile though — a lusty one.

"A video of my son playing with a remote-control car," he says.

"Aww, cute. I want to see."

Lance locks his phone. I watch him put

75

the code in. Then he walks over to the bed. He is completely naked and the sight of his sculpted body makes me lose all sense.

"Or . . . we could do something else," he says as he slides under the sheets and cozies up to me.

"Where does Jasmine think you are?"

There is a long pause before he says anything.

"We said we weren't going to talk about my wife, Felicia."

"This isn't really about her. I'm just curious."

"I told her I was at a business meeting in Miami."

"Miami?"

"Why do you care about what I said to her? You should just care about the fact that I'm here."

"I am happy that we're here together."

"Good. No more conversation about my family then. It's all about us right now."

But it's never all about us. His irritated tone when I bring up his *family* proves that much. Even when he's with me, he's always on his phone, chatting with his wife (I think) and his kid.

When we started this, he acted like we were going to be together for real. My suddenly blessing was going to unfold before

76

my eyes. Now he's backpedaling. He's becoming an average man with an above-average capacity for playing games.

"You aren't really leaving her, are you?"

"I never said that I was."

This is the truth. He's told me lots of things. *You're the best I've ever had. You make me forget all my problems. We sure would make some pretty babies.* But he's never said that he was leaving his wife. Not once.

I don't know how I let myself get here again — to a place where I am the side chick hidden in the shadows. I thought when Nya Hampstead prayed over me, I was going to have something different happen with my life.

"You know I have love for you, right? I wouldn't be here with you, putting my marriage on the line, if I didn't care. This isn't just sex for me."

"It isn't just sex for me either."

I know what it is for me, but someone saying they "have love" for you isn't the same as them saying "I love you." I don't even know what "I have love for you" means.

I flip the sheet back and slide out of the bed.

"Where are you going?"

"To the bathroom. I'll be back."

Once inside the bathroom, I sit on the side of the huge Jacuzzi tub. Big fat tears roll down my cheeks quicker than I can wipe them. My body shakes as I try to sob silently.

There's a soft knock on the door.

"Yes?"

"Are you crying?"

"N-no."

Long silence outside the door. I hope he just goes back to bed. I don't want to talk to him anymore.

"I mean it when I say this isn't just sex, Felicia. I wish we had met at a different time in my life. If I'd met you years ago, Jasmine wouldn't be my wife — you would. Can we just enjoy what we have?"

I don't reply. What we have is nothing. What we have is what I've always had. A man who wants to walk all over me, use me, and throw me away. This doesn't look like anybody's blessing at all. It looks like a curse.

"You coming out?" Lance asks.

"In a minute."

I turn the water on in the sink, just in time to muffle the sound of me vomiting.

CHAPTER 10
NYA

Lady Sandy has invited me over for coffee, and I'm sitting in my car outside their home deciding on whether or not I want to go in. Since the tour is over, I was thinking of just cutting ties altogether. I don't think I want to be a part of their inner circle. But I think I owe her this fellowship. She just cut our ministry a check for half a million dollars. How can I say no to coffee?

I walk up to the door and Lady Sandy answers it. She's dressed down, like I've never seen her before. Wearing a track suit and furry slippers. I feel myself relax. Maybe this will be a different kind of meeting.

"How are you feeling, Nya? Glad to be back home and not traveling for a while?"

"I am."

Lady Sandy leads me to her kitchen table where she has coffee set up along with some kind of cake. We sit.

"How did you really feel about the tour

now that it's all over?"

I wonder if I should be honest about this. Should I tell her how I really feel about the seed offerings, the bedazzled T-shirts, and everything else?

"Lady Sandy . . ."

"Call me Sandy. I know my daughter thinks I'm not down-to-earth, but I am. So many people call me Lady Sandy that I decided to stop correcting them."

"Well, I don't know what to think about the tour. Those women gave so much, and some of them looked like the money would be better spent elsewhere. I don't want people to think that if they sow into my ministry that somehow they're going to magically reap a blessing down the road. That's not what Greg and I are about."

"I didn't think you cared for what we do. I was actually excited that you accepted my invitation to the Women's Empowerment conference. I didn't think you'd come."

"Really?"

She nods as she pours each of us a cup of coffee. "Do you take cream and sugar?"

"Yes, I do. Why did you think I would say no?"

"Bishop Bowens and I follow your ministry. You all bring something different to the body of Christ . . . something needed."

"But . . ."

"Listen, some of us in ministry have done our congregations a disservice. They've heard the seed-sowing messages for so long that it's a habit for them. You preach a good word, they sow a seed. They want to see you rich and in fine things. It means their blessing is on the way."

"They only believe that because that's what they've been taught."

Sandy sighs and nods her head. "I don't want to lose what we've built . . . We're not going to lose what we've built, but we believe that it is our responsibility to slowly turn the hearts of the people back to the Creator and not the blessing."

"I'm confused. We do a Suddenly Blessing tour because you want people to not focus on blessings?"

"We did the tour so that they can meet you, Nya. Thousands of people will be tuning in to you and your husband's Internet broadcast."

"We don't have an Internet broadcast."

"You do now. Bishop Bowens and I have already started working with Streaming Jesus on your behalf. We will assist with the expense of it."

"It's just . . . I don't understand."

"We chose you two, Nya. I would never

say this in front of my husband, but supporting your church is something like penance for some of the things we've done."

"Wow."

"I feel confident that you and your husband are going to take that money and do kingdom business with it."

I don't even know how to respond to any of this. It is a good thing that Lady Sandy is acknowledging that some of the things she and Bishop Bowens have done were not good for their church, but will they ever admit it to anyone else?

"We're going to get a new building with the money. Thank you for the opportunity."

"Now you know this conversation doesn't leave the kitchen, right?"

I chuckle. "Of course."

"My husband would frown upon such talk, but you are a woman who sees things. I always want to be completely transparent with you."

"And I appreciate you saying this to me. It really helps."

Lady Sandy claps her hands and makes a little chirping noise. I suppose that means she's happy.

"I have one more thing to ask of you," she says.

"Okay. Ask away."

"My daughter practically adores you. If you could nudge her in the right direction, I would appreciate it."

"I think she already has a great example in you, Lady Sandy. I don't know what else I can teach her."

"It's sweet of you to say that, but I am a first lady. I'm not an evangelist. I was never called to that. But I think my daughter wants to preach . . . and prophesy. Her ministry may be the future of our church."

"I am here for her anytime, Lady Sandy."

She makes the chirping sound again. "You have such a heart of gratitude, Nya. I hope you never lose that."

"Why would I?"

"Honey," Lady Sandy says with a smirk, "you are about to be a star. Just make sure you remember how you got your start."

Lady Sandy starts humming as she places goodies on a plate and sets them in front of me. She says all the right words. Exactly what I want, and what Greg would want, to hear, but there's an undercurrent of something else. I'm not sure what the something else is, but it worries me. It makes my spirit sensors stand on high alert.

I think this is a situation that embodies what the old mothers have told the young people in church since the days of dirt floors and fans in the ceiling. Watch and pray. I will be doing a good deal of both.

Chapter 11
Felicia

I always thought I would be happy the first time I got pregnant. I thought I would be in love with the father and he would love me back. That's the perfect way. The God way. The blessed way.

But this is not that.

I was afraid of how Lance would react to the news, so I invited him to my office like it's a business meeting. He doesn't want anyone here to know about our affair, so he will hesitate before making a scene. At least I hope he will.

He sits in the chair in front of my desk, looking as fine as ever, making me wish that he was mine. I wonder if our baby will look like him. Will he have that same ebony skin and silky hair? If he's a boy, will he be tall and play basketball, or will he take after me?

"You know I think it's time for us to have another getaway," Lance says. "How does St. Thomas sound to you?"

St. Thomas would sound great if we were planning to get married on the beach, then have our honeymoon before anyone could know I'm carrying our child. I know that's a fantasy because Lance hasn't made any moves to leave his wife.

"Lance, I have something to tell you."

"Are you okay, Felicia? Your hands are shaking. What's the matter?"

I look down at my hands and they are trembling uncontrollably. I sit in my leather chair and place my hands on the desk in front of me to steady them.

"Yes, I'm fine. I . . . I'm pregnant, Lance. That's what I need to tell you. Are you happy about it?"

Lance frowns. The opposite reaction of what I wanted.

"I thought you said you were on birth control."

"I was . . . am . . . was. Obviously, it didn't work. I didn't mean for this to happen. You do know that, right?"

"I guess. But how do I know you didn't stop taking your pills?" Lance asks.

I feel my heart rate quicken and my breaths become shallow. "You know what, Lance. Just leave. I don't need you at all."

"You don't need a child support check from me?" Lance asks. "Cut the games. You know you want that."

"I don't want just a check from you, Lance."

"What is it that you want, then? Oh, right. You want me to leave my wife and son."

"Yes, I do."

"And if that doesn't happen?"

"You tell me what happens next," I say. "Because I don't have a clue how any of this works."

Lance rubs his hand over his face with frustration. He pulls out his phone, scrolls through his text messages, and sighs.

"My son is playing pee-wee basketball now. He's good. Probably got my talent."

I stare at Lance and carefully hold my tongue. I don't care at all about his son's extracurricular activities. I know it sounds bad and not really like Christ, but I don't care about his son at all. I only care about the baby I'm carrying.

Finally, Lance puts his phone in his pocket and looks up at me.

"Well, we have to come up with a strategy," he says.

He stands to his feet and paces back and forth in my office with his hands shoved in his pockets. He looks worried.

At least he said *we*. Because this is definitely not just my problem.

"What kind of strategy?"

"I've been thinking about us — how we were in Puerto Rico, and how perfect it was."

I swallow hard and try not to get my hopes up. God knows I'm teetering back and forth between insanity and hope right now.

"It was perfect to you?"

He stops pacing and walks over to my desk. He takes both my hands in his and pulls them to his face. He kisses my wrists and palms, and I feel myself overcome with emotion.

"I don't think I knew how deeply you felt about me, until we were together this last time. And it made me realize how deeply I feel about you."

"So you aren't upset about the baby?"

He shakes his head. "No, of course not. This is my seed!"

I feel the smile form on my lips. I doubted God and the prophecy. And maybe this isn't how God wanted us to get together, because adultery isn't in His will. But it must be His will for us to be together. Otherwise this pregnancy would be the end of us.

"So why do we need a strategy?"

"Well, I don't know if you've noticed, but lately wives have been suing the mistress."

Mistress. I don't like that word being used

in reference to me.

"Don't call me that."

"I'm sorry. Wives are suing girlfriends and winning. We don't want that."

"No, we don't. So you need to make it so that I'm not your girlfriend."

"And that's what we need to strategize about. But right now we just need to focus on the baby."

I allow him to embrace me in his strong arms. This is what I've been waiting for this whole time. I thought he would panic and feel trapped. But he is here. He's going to be here for me and this baby.

"I don't want your wife to be hurt."

This is true. She's not done anything to me. It's not her fault that she's in the way of God's plan. We're just two big cats in the jungle, hungering for the same meal.

"Neither do I. It's up to us to make sure that she isn't."

"But how?"

"Let me think about it. I don't want you stressing right now. It's not good for the baby."

"Okay. I have a doctor's appointment this week, but you probably can't come to that."

Lance's eyebrows dip as if he's considering every option. Of course I want him at every doctor's appointment. Every ultrasound, every blood test, all of it. I know this is pretty much out of the question, but I just don't want to be doing the pregnancy thing alone.

"You know, there is a doctor that some of the other players have used when their girls got in similar circumstances. His name is Doctor Tomlinson and he's very discreet. If you want to get your care from him, then I can go with you."

"You can? You'll go with me?"

Lance kisses me softly on the lips. "Every one until our son is born."

"You think it's a boy?"

"I only make boys," Lance says. "This is a future NBA player you're carrying."

In this moment, I feel so much love for Lance. This is all coming together in such a special way that it can't be from anybody but God. I pray that my future NBA star is born wrapped up in all this love we're feeling right now.

I don't want to ruin the moment by bringing up the one thing that has me filled with doubt, but the fact that Lance is still married is a threat to our happiness. It's a threat to our blessing. But Lance told me he had a strategy, he told me he'd handle it, and I have faith that he's going to fix it. Without faith it's impossible to please God, so I'm

going to put my faith in God and in the man
that he sent me.

Amen and amen.

CHAPTER 12
NYA

Today, I'm not the superstar evangelist on the rise. Not the prophetic wonder touring the nation, speaking a word over the masses. Today, I'm a regular pastor checking on one of her members.

I check the small piece of paper with the address scribbled down, to verify I'm at the right door. I sure don't want to be knocking at the wrong apartment in this neighborhood. The best word to describe the apartment complex is filthy. There's a layer of dirt everywhere and flies are buzzing furiously around little piles of trash and dog poop. Even the children playing with water guns in the small patch of grass in front look dirty, like they've been outside all day.

Since I do have the correct apartment, I knock on the door and wait. The new member-intake unit at our church told me that they hadn't heard from Melody since we prayed for her that day in church. They had tried to follow up, but were blocked by the girl's mother. They gave up after a few times, and then I went on tour and got extremely busy.

I don't care how many thousands Lady Sandy promises we'll reach over the Internet and television. Not today. Today, I want to reach one.

Just as I lift my hand to knock a second time, the door swings open. It's Melody's mother. She's got a different color hair weave from when they visited the church. This one is dark purple. It kind of matches her lips, which have been stained that color probably from the Newports she smokes. There's an unlit one dangling from her lips right now.

"Hi. I'm Evangelist Nya Hampstead . . ."

"I know you. We come to your church sometimes. I'm Erica. You prayed for my daughter."

"I did. How is she?"

Erica shrugs. "I don't know. Something happened that day we visited your church. She barely comes out of her room now."

"Can I see her?" I ask, now completely worried about her welfare. She would be in her second trimester now.

I don't mention the pregnancy to Erica, because maybe she doesn't know. If Melody hasn't shared it yet, I'm definitely not going to be the one to do it. The knowledge might put her in danger, or at the very least on the receiving end of anger from her mother.

"You can see her. Me and Tyrone 'bout to leave though, so you can't stay long."

"Oh. Is Tyrone her father?"

Erica chuckles. "Naw, but he could be her stepdaddy if he play his cards right. We been getting extra close these days."

I glance over at Tyrone, who is sitting at the kitchen table wearing a tank top under-shirt, also with a Newport hanging from his lips. His is lit, and there's a thin plume of smoke rising to the ceiling. He grins at me and it nearly makes me shudder. I'm glad God doesn't give me any visions about him. I don't think I could even handle what's going through his mind.

"Melody!" Erica yells. "You got company."

"Who is it?" says a voice from another room, presumably Melody's.

"The pastor lady."

Melody doesn't reply, but slowly a door in the back of the apartment opens. Melody pokes her head out the door. When she sees that I'm here, her eyes widen.

"Hi, Pastor Nya," she says in a whisper.

"Well, come on out here and talk to her, since she came all the way to the hood to see you."

I hold out a package. "I've got a gift."

Melody rushes over to take the gift from my hands. I notice that she's plumped up some. Her face is fuller, but her belly is still flat. She sits on the couch and rips the paper off the tin of gourmet popcorn I brought her back from Chicago, one of the last cities on the tour.

"Thank you, Pastor Nya," she says after greedily tearing in and eating a huge mouthful of caramel popcorn.

"Tyrone, will you look at this greedy heffa," Erica says. "That's why you getting fat now. Eating all that junk food."

I feel my flesh rise up again. I want to scream *She's getting fat because she's carrying your grandchild by your boyfriend!* But I say nothing. Not yet. I will deal with Erica, but not until I have Melody out of harm's way.

"Have you gotten a chance to talk to any of the ministers from the church, honey?" I ask. I already know the answer is no, but I've got to try to engage her somehow.

She shakes her head. "They called a few times, but I didn't have a ride to the church, so I didn't go back after that Sunday."

"Don't be lying on me," Erica says. "Her lazy butt ain't get up for church. Me or

Tyrone would've dropped her off if she wanted to go."

"I have had a hard time waking up on Sunday," Melody says with a tremble in her voice.

"It's fine. I will give you my phone number, and anytime you wake up late, I'll make sure you still have a ride to church."

I grab my stomach. "You know, I'm hungry. I really would like some Applebee's. Erica, do you think it would be okay if I take Melody to Applebee's for lunch?"

Erica looks nervous, like she doesn't know if she should say yes. "Well, I guess, but only if she can bring me some of that chicken and cheese pasta they have as a to-go plate."

I force a smile and a chuckle, 'cause I still want to slap her. "Sure, she can bring you back something to eat."

"What about me?" Tyrone asks.

Lord. I know I should've asked Greg to come with me. He would be able to keep me calm right now.

"My Bible tells me that grown men have to work for their food," I say.

Tyrone lets out a sly scoff. "What kinda work you need me to put in, Evangelist? I can definitely give you what you need."

Erica flies across the room like a bird of prey and slaps Tyrone upside his head.

"Fool, what you doing? She a prophet."

I wish she was that proactive in protecting her baby from this monster.

"She a woman too, ain't she? And fine at that," Tyrone says. "What you mixed with? You got that good hair."

I ignore him and focus on Melody. "Let's go, sweetie. You like Applebee's?"

She nods. "She eat everything," Erica says. "That's why her booty so big."

I take a deep breath and take Melody's hand. I wonder if she can feel my trembling. Never in my life have I been this angry and this close to displaying wrath.

"This yo' car?" Melody asks when we get to my used Infiniti. "It's fly."

"I got a really good deal on it. Go ahead and get in."

As soon as I pull off, Melody starts crying. "I'm scared, Pastor Nya. My mama gon' kill me when she find out I'm pregnant."

"No, she isn't. I'm getting you out of there. Is Tyrone still bothering you?"

"Not since we came to church that time. It's like he don't even look at me now."

I get a sick feeling in my stomach. Partially anger because our church staff failed her. We let her go back to that house with no help. I didn't even think about this baby while I was out touring. But at least God kept her from being touched again. Lord, forgive me.

"How about we don't go to Applebee's. We can go get some another day. Right now, we need to make some plans to get you safe. You okay with that?"

"Is my mama gonna be in trouble?"

A child's love is so unconditional. She's getting raped by her mother's boyfriend and all she cares about is what's going to happen to her mother.

"I don't know, honey. If she didn't know about Tyrone, then she probably won't get in trouble. We're not going to worry about that right now, though. I'm more concerned about you."

When we stop at a red light, I pull out my cell phone and dial Tina's number.

"Hey, girl," she says after one ring. "What's up?"

"Hey. Your sister still a social worker for Dallas Child Protective Services?"

"Mm-hmm."

"I have an emergency case for her. A pregnant minor who needs sheltering right away."

"Okay," Tina says. "I'll have her call you right back. Is the child safe right now?"

"Yes. She's with me, but her mama knows

she's with me, so let's make something happen quickly."

"You know you can go straight to the police, right?"

"I know that, but I don't want her to get stuck in the foster system. Can we try to control that? There are some foster parents in our congregation."

"Wait to hear from my cousin. She'll take care of it."

"Okay."

I disconnect the call and look over at Melody. "I'm sorry we didn't take care of you before. But we've got you now. He will never touch you again."

"Thank you, Pastor Nya."

"You're welcome, baby."

I don't let on to Melody, but I'm afraid that my words aren't true. I pray that God covers and protects this child. If anybody needs a suddenly blessing, it's Melody.

Chapter 13
Nya

Greg, Tina, Greg's assistant, Lena, Mother Olivia, the head of the church's Mothers' Board, and I are standing in a movie theater that is in foreclosure. I'm hoping that this will be the building Greg chooses for our new church. We've been to a dozen different buildings, and he's found some reason to reject them all. It's like he's still hesitant to accept that this money is truly from God. But I've been praying so hard about this. I need him to want it as much as I do. I want him to take the reins and run with them.

"What do y'all think of this building?" Greg asks.

"It has a lot of potential," I say. "The seats only need reupholstering and the carpet has to be replaced, but I love it."

"Yeah, but the entire stage needs fixing," Greg replies. "We'll have to install a pulpit. That will be a lot of work."

"I like the parking lot," Mother Olivia

says. "Plenty room so folk won't have to park all down the street like they been doing. And they have a kitchen and setup to sell snacks and things."

"We've been wanting to have breakfast and coffee like they have at the white churches," Lena says. "That will be awesome. It'll bring more people to our church."

"That isn't only at white churches," I say between laughs.

"Yes, it is. Lady Sandy and them only have coffee once a year," Lena says. "You know people are greedy."

"Well, they have twenty thousand members over there," Greg says. "That's a lot of coffee."

"And cheese Danish," Mother Olivia says. Lord knows Mother Olivia doesn't need any pastries.

Greg shakes his head and looks at me. "God saying anything to you about this spot?"

I chuckle. Greg knows how sporadic the prophetic gift is. I truly believe that God just wants us to have faith about most things.

"Well, not this place specifically, but we know God's going to elevate our ministry. Why not just launch out? Why shouldn't this be the place? It has everything we want and need."

Greg smiles. "God did make that promise a long time ago. You know, I didn't like the idea of that tour at first, but maybe it was a part of the plan."

I feel such a wave of relief come over me as he says this. I didn't think Greg would ever cross this bridge.

"Finally!" Tina says. "I was about to start calling you a hater, Greg. I'm glad God touched your little heart."

We all crack up laughing at Tina's joke. She and Greg have a sibling-like relationship. She's probably the only one who could get away with saying that to him.

"Yeah, you just want your girl to blow up so y'all can have shopping sprees," Greg says. "You aren't fooling me."

"Ooh! Let God have His way!" Tina shouts and does a little dance.

Greg shakes his head. "I'm gonna pray for you."

"So are you feeling it?" I ask. "I think this is the place."

"Let's do it," Greg says. "The price is right and I can see us preaching right here."

"I have a question," Mother Olivia says. "Are y'all going to get a new house with some of that money?"

Tina gives Mother Olivia a high five. "Mother, that is the first thing I asked."

I don't say any anything. I'm gonna let Greg handle this one because I guarantee he and I are not on one accord when it comes to this. How do I know? Because I already asked this man if he wants to buy a house and he already said no.

Just like I thought he would do, Greg shakes his head.

"Now isn't the time for that," he says. "We need to focus on ministry. There is nothing wrong with our house. Plus, I don't want to give people the wrong idea about what we're doing at Love First International. They might think that Nya's Suddenly Blessing message means we're on the prosperity bandwagon."

I swallow hard. Greg is right about our house. It's fine. It would be nice to have a new one, but we can definitely do without.

"What do you think, Co-pastor?" Tina asks, as if I'm going to give a different response than Greg.

I know my girl. She's thinking that the money I made preaching is *my* money. I don't feel that way. There's nothing I have that I don't share completely with Greg.

"Greg is right," I say to Tina. "A new house isn't necessary right now."

Tina narrows her eyes at me but remains silent, as if she can hear the telepathic thoughts I'm sending her way.

"Lena, reach out to our Realtor to place our offer on the building," Greg says. "We're going to give them the asking price unless she says otherwise."

Greg reaches for my hand and touches my fingertips. He pulls me next to him. "Are you ready?" he asks. "Ready to take our ministry to the next level?"

"I am. God is going to help us change some lives here. I can feel it."

Tina says, "Speaking of changing lives. That little girl from the church, Melody, got placed in a very small transitional home that has four other pregnant girls. It's really nice, and run by one of our sister churches."

"Good!" I say. "And what about her mother, Erica, and that boyfriend, Tyrone?"

"I don't have all the details because it's confidential, but my sister did tell me that the mother isn't facing any charges. She claims to have no knowledge of the abuse."

"And Tyrone?" I ask anxiously. I don't want him to be able to hurt Melody again.

"He's gone, girl. Locked up."

I jump up and down and do a little Holy Ghost praise dance shuffle. I'm so happy that Melody is safe now, and not only that,

I'm happy that God hasn't taken my gift. I was afraid that He would stop trusting me with the prophetic. But even though I stumbled a bit, He's still got me.

"All right!" Greg says. "That's how we roll at Love First."

Greg pulls my hand to his lips and kisses it. "I love you, babe. I thank God for putting us together, and for opening doors for us."

"I love you too, Greg."

"I'm sorry I wasn't one hundred percent on board with all of this. I know you probably felt like I was hating a little bit."

"A little?" I ask with a chuckle.

"Okay. Maybe a lot. But I was wrong. All things work together for the good. We're going to do great things here. I can feel it."

I allow myself to rest in Greg's embrace as I feel his love surround me. "I can feel it too, babe. God is all over this."

CHAPTER 14
FELICIA

There is a smile plastered on my face as I watch my man, the father of my child, Lance, prepare us breakfast. He skillfully chops up a pile of raw spinach and kiwi. I wonder if he did this for his wife when she was pregnant. He's not wearing a shirt and his muscular chest has as much of my attention as the breakfast.

"I'm not sure I'm going to like the spinach," I say. "I've never had a green smoothie."

He glances up from his work and grins. "Trust me. It's going to be delicious. You won't even taste the spinach when I get done with this. And raw veggies are the best way to get your nutrients."

It's very early, not even eight o'clock in the morning, but he's here with me. I wonder where his wife thinks he is. And then I wonder if I care.

"How did you get away this early, Lance?

You don't want Jasmine to start asking questions."

Lance's good mood seems to fade. "If you have to know, I told her that I have daily morning workouts."

"That's pretty clever. She doesn't ask you where you work out? I would."

"She trusts me. She's got no reason to ask me where I work out. I'm a grown man. I come and go as I please."

This is funny to me. "Actually she *does* have a reason. She just doesn't know it yet."

Lance lifts an eyebrow as he dumps powder into the blender. I can't read his facial expression, but he doesn't look amused.

"What is that? I thought this was a green smoothie. Why are you adding powder?"

"Protein powder. I want you healthy. You're an NBA mother now, so you only get the best of everything."

I like the sound of that. NBA mother. Even if I'm not an NBA wife yet . . . I am still a mother. No one can take that away from me. Not even Jasmine.

"I love the way you're taking care of me," I say. "I have to be honest. I thought you wouldn't be this attentive to me."

"Why wouldn't I? I may not be the best husband, and I dang sure ain't the best boyfriend, but I love my kids with everything in me."

"Well, you're being a pretty good boyfriend right now."

Lance pours my smoothie in a glass and walks over to the couch where I'm sitting. He hands it to me and sits down.

"Drink up," he says. "I need my son to get all his vitamins and protein."

"Yes sir!" I say as I drink down the slightly sweet, but mostly nasty beverage. "That was gross, Lance. You said I wouldn't taste the spinach."

"You could taste it? Maybe it needed more bananas," he says.

I set the glass down on the table in front of me. "It needs some eggs, bacon, and pancakes. That's what it needs."

"You don't need all that fatty food, Felicia. You'll gain too much weight while you're pregnant."

I give him a huge smile. "So you want to make sure I still have my figure when all this is over?"

"Of course. But I'm more worried about you developing diabetes late in the pregnancy. It causes the baby to sometimes be born too big and can lead to complications."

"Okay, wow. You're an expert at this pregnancy thing."

"I went through all of this with Jasmine."

"Am I the first woman you've gotten pregnant outside of your marriage?"

Lance jumps up from the couch. "No. What have you heard?"

"Nothing. I was just asking."

My question seems to bother Lance. He paces back and forth in front of my coffee table. I pick up the smoothie and try to get it down my throat. It's as horrible now as it was on the first sip. It tastes like dirt.

"So what are you going to tell people at work when you start to show?" Lance asks.

The question catches me off guard. I hate the casual tone he used to ask that question. He just slid that in there like he was asking me which brand of deodorant I use. Like the answer to that question might not change everything.

"What are *we* going to tell people at work?"

Lance's eyebrows shoot up. "We've definitely got to play this safe, Felicia. My wife is friends with the other players' wives. We don't want this to get back to her until I've made all the moves that I need to make. I don't want you getting sued."

"Oh, right. You're so concerned about how this may impact my wallet. I keep forgetting. How about I don't care if she sues me.

If we're going to raise our child together, her little lawsuit is the least of my worries."

"Felicia . . ."

"No. You said you were coming up with a strategy for how to make this work. You said you wanted to be with me. I haven't heard the strategy yet, and I'm starting to think that there isn't one."

"There is. It is just going to take time to execute. I didn't want to tell you about this, because I really don't think it's any of your business, but Jasmine is cheating on me. I had an investigator follow her around and she's been sleeping with a guy we went to high school with."

"Wow. Are you okay? I know you two have been together for a long time."

Lance nods slowly. "I'm okay. Why would I think that she wouldn't be stepping out there on me? I've stepped out on her. Karma, right?"

"I guess."

"Look, babe. I just want you to trust me. I got this. Jasmine is not going to threaten our happiness. I promise you that. Just let me deal with things in my own way."

"Okay, babe. I trust you."

I allow Lance to hug me, but his affection doesn't erase my concerns. I hope he knows what he's doing and really does plan to address the Jasmine situation, because he doesn't want me to address it. And I will if I have to. No one, not even a first wife and a child, are going to stand in the way of my blessing.

CHAPTER 15
NYA

Bishop and Lady Bowens have invited me
and Greg to dinner at their home to share
some "exciting news." They called it exciting, but I'm assuming that they will want
our church to join the family of churches
under their mentoring. I hope I'm wrong,
because Greg will decline and it will be of-
fensive to the Bowens. And embarrassing to
me. They don't bring just anyone into their
inner circle. The churches in that group are
hand selected.

"What is this about?" Greg asks as we're
driving over.

"I have no clue. Maybe they're doing
another conference or something. Maybe
this time they want us both to participate."

"We don't have time for any conferences
right now. We're about to do the grand
opening of our new church. We're extremely
busy."

It's been two months since we closed on

the building, and although all of the renovations are not complete, we have done the majority of them and are ready to open our doors.

"Just hear them out, Greg. Don't be so quick to say no until you have all the facts."

"As long as you aren't so quick to say yes because it's the Bowens."

"I can't believe you said that. They have been a blessing to us."

Greg stops at a red light and glares at me. "God has blessed us — not them."

"Well, God used their ministry to bless us. Why are you so against being connected to them?"

"Listen, I'm sure they are nice people. I just don't agree with their ministry methods."

I let out a huge sigh. "Not this again. Do we have to keep having the same conversation over and over?"

"Nope. We don't have to have it ever again. I think you know how I feel."

"Good!"

I'm still angry as Greg pulls up to the Bowens' estate. The long circular driveway has a beautiful and meticulously groomed rose garden in the center of it. The smell of the roses almost overpowers me.

Greg walks into his office and slams the door. He looks different. It's the beard. He has a full beard. There is a bouquet of roses sitting on the desk, but Greg angrily pushes a stack of papers on the floor. Then he picks up his phone from the desk. He sees something that makes him smile. He presses a button and makes a call. The smile is stuck on his face like it's glued there.

He speaks. "Thank you. You don't know how much I needed that right now."

He laughs now. "Yes . . . maybe later . . . I would like that . . . Thank you."

He places the phone back on his desk and takes one of the roses out of the vase. The rose has wilted. He smells the rose, then tosses it in the trash.

There is a smile on his face. He looks content.

I snap out of my vision as Greg opens my car door. That was strange. I don't know what to make of it. I'm not sure what God is trying to show me. There is something — that much I know. I don't have a prophetic vision without it having meaning.

"You okay? You look a little pale," Greg says as I step out of the car.

"Yes, I'm fine. A little carsick, maybe."

I decide not to tell him about the vision until I have more time to think about it, maybe even pray for God to reveal its meaning.

We are ushered into the mansion by Bishop and Lady Bowens' daughter Penelope. She's only thirty years old and already she is a force to be reckoned with. She and I connected on the tour. She opened up in song for me every time I spoke, and her voice is definitely anointed. I was glad she was there with me. I felt less alone with her there.

"Hey, Nya!" Penelope squeals as she hugs me. "I can't wait for you to hear this news!"

"Wait, you know about it?" I ask.

"Yes, it's about both of us, but my mom has sworn me to secrecy."

Okay, now Penelope's really got me wondering what's going on.

Penelope reaches out and grabs Greg's hands. "Nya has told me so much about you, man of God. I'm so pleased to finally meet you. One day God is gonna bless me with a covenant partner like He did Nya."

Greg gives her a bashful smile. "I'm sure you have them lined up around the block."

"I'd prefer quality to quantity," Penelope says with a laugh. "I call them the men of the most low, because they can't possibly be from the Most High!"

Penelope leads us to the dining room, where Bishop and Lady Bowens are waiting for us. Lady Sandy looks classy as always in a cream-colored wrap dress. Bishop is a very small man. He's small, brown, and shiny. Standing next to Lady Sandy they look like wedding-cake toppers.

Bishop claps his hands together. "Pastor Hampstead! Or I should say Pastors Hampstead. Welcome to my home. Please, please have a seat."

We wait for Bishop and Lady Sandy to choose their seats first. And then Penelope. Greg sits next to Bishop and across from Lady Sandy. I sit next to Greg and across from Penelope. It feels strange, just the five of us sitting at this long table that seats about fifteen.

As soon as we're all settled, Bishop Bowens says a prayer over the food that's coming. When we say amen, the caterer's staff starts bringing in salad and bread as if they were listening on the other side of the door for the signal.

"So, Bishop Bowens, please don't keep us in suspense any longer," Greg says. "Nya and I have been discussing what the news could possibly be."

"Greg, please call me Bill. The news is all

116

because of how anointed your wife is. She really impressed some powerful people on that tour."

"She is anointed. I've known that since our very first date," Greg says.

"What did she do on the first date?" Penelope asks. "Was your date at church?"

Greg and I share a glance and giggle. Our first date wasn't exactly at church. It was worse than that.

"Our first date was at a youth conference. I wouldn't go out with him without a chaperone, so we went to service together the whole week." My hands fly furiously as I describe the memory. "We ate hot dogs, bags of popcorn, and church punch."

"I got so tired of hot dogs," Greg says. "I didn't eat another hot dog for ten years."

"I hope you don't mind that we're having hot dogs for lunch," Lady Bowens says.

For a half second I think she's telling the truth, but she bursts into laughter and everybody else laughs with her.

"What let you know that the hand of God was on her, son?" Bishop Bowens asks.

"I saw her prophesize for the first time at that conference. There was a prayer service before the main service, and she just laid hands and prayed for a young woman who was prostrate at the altar. She told that girl everything she'd ever done, and she led her to repentance that day."

"I remember her," I say. "I wonder what happened to her."

"I knew then that I wanted to marry her. I wanted to go into ministry with her," Greg says as he squeezes my hand under the table. "To me the single most important ministry function is repentance. We can't get to any of the rest of it if there is no repentance."

Bishop Bowens nods slowly. "What about the redeemed who are downtrodden? What about them? They're crying out, looking for their purpose, and they want to experience the abundant life."

Greg squeezes my hand. I wish that Bishop Bowens would just go into the news before he starts preaching a prosperity message to us.

"Listen, I know you don't agree with our platform," Bishop says to Greg.

Greg's eyes widen. "Sir . . ."

"You don't have to say it. I can tell by how you look at me with disdain when I said abundant life."

"It's j-just that . . ."

Bishop holds up one hand. "No, don't explain. I've had experience with much bigger and much more important preachers than you. They don't like me either."

"I understand, but I don't have any disdain for what you do," Greg says. "I just disagree that should be the focus."

"That is fine. What I'm about to propose to you doesn't require that you agree with my theology. And it should line up with yours. The reconciliation and relationship part."

Penelope is smiling now. Lady Sandy too. I wish I could share their enthusiasm, but of course they already know what's being proposed.

"What is it?" I ask

"Well, there was a producer from the Faith Women's Network in the audience in Atlanta. They want you and Penelope to have a faith-based TV show where you help people with troubled lives start over and discover their purpose. It'll be called *Suddenly Blessed.*"

"A TV show?" Greg asks. "For Nya and Penelope?"

Bishop Bowens nods. "Yes. It's a women's network. Their whole objective is to empower women, and they believe that you can help them. And Penelope will have a segment for at-risk teens."

"Where would the show film? Here in

Dallas?" Greg asks with a tremble in his voice.

"No, it will be in Atlanta," Penelope says. "But we'll only have to be there for a couple of weeks. We'll film eight episodes to start and see how the audience receives it."

Greg looks at me with a blank expression. I don't know what it means.

"This is a tremendous opportunity to grow your brand, honey," Lady Sandy says. "It's not often that a minister can find their signature message so early in their career. But you've done that with one prophetic word. That is an awesome move of God."

"How soon do we have to make a decision?" Greg asks.

"Yes, I want to pray about this before we go forward," I say in concurrence. But from the look of Greg's scowl, I said something wrong.

"*We* need to pray and fast over this," Greg says. "A signature message is great, but I don't know that Nya wants this to be her signature message."

Bishop Bowens says, "I believe Nya is the one who should seek God about her anointing. As husbands, it is sometimes difficult to see our wives coming into their season, maybe before we've realized our own goals. But just know that God has put the two of you together. Her destiny is intertwined with yours. There is no need to feel anything but blessed by this opportunity. It will enrich you both — spiritually and financially."

Greg scoffs. "With all due respect, Bishop Bowens, I am not in any way bothered by Nya getting an opportunity. I will pray with and for her, because I am her covering. She has shared with me what God has called her to, and *we* will pray together to see if this is in alignment with that."

I've never been so relieved to see food being brought to a table. I know Greg, and I can tell that he is plenty hot under the collar right now. The only thing keeping him from making a complete donkey of himself is the fact that we're talking to the most powerful preacher in Dallas. Bishop Bowens can make and break careers. Greg knows to tread carefully.

"Greg, I apologize, I seem to have offended you," Bishop Bowens says. "That was not my intent. I've just been where you are. I just want you to know that it's all going to work together for the kingdom. I pray that you come back with a favorable response. This is an open door for my daughter as well."

Bishop Bowens's apology seems to soften

Greg. He relaxes his defensive posture and slackens his shoulders, which were squared as if he was ready for battle. Bishop's words must've hit home too, because I definitely think Greg is only in his feelings about this because he is jealous. This hurts me. If it was the other way around — if Greg was getting this shot — I would be nothing but supportive of him.

"I don't know about you," Penelope says to me, "but I'm excited."

Lady Sandy touches Penelope's arm and shakes her head. "They haven't decided yet, honey."

"They will say yes. I feel it in my spirit. I'm praying with you both!"

I give Penelope a look that I hope says *I'm excited too!* because there is no way I'm going to let this chance pass me by. I don't know how many prayers and fasts Greg needs to do to get on board with the plan. Maybe he needs to put on sackcloth and rub ashes on his body. Maybe he needs to lie face down in front of our spanking-new altar until he gets a revelation. Maybe God needs to part the heavens and send down an angel to personally hand him a scroll.

Who does he think he is, anyway — the Ike Turner of the Body of Christ? Shoot, when the windows of heaven open, you

don't slam them closed and put on shut-
ters.

All of these blessings in such rapid-fire
succession make me think that perhaps that
prophetic word wasn't fake at all. Maybe it
was a word from God, and maybe it was
for me.

CHAPTER 16
NYA

Today is the grand reopening of Love First International. After two months of hard labor, we are finally able to share this wonderful building with our congregation and our community. Greg and I have prepared a special message, and I can't wait to deliver it. Then, Mother Olivia has planned a huge friends-and-family dinner. Everyone who attends this service, and we're expecting close to one thousand, will be able to get a chicken, pasta, or fish dinner, prepared by the church mothers and friends.

Greg stands in the mirror of his office, creating an intricate knot in his necktie. "Do you think I was wrong for not accepting Bishop Bowens's offer to come and consecrate our new sanctuary? He seemed to want to be a part of today's service."

I've kept mum on this, and I wish Greg wouldn't have asked me, because now I'm gonna have to tell him the truth. When

Bishop Bowens called Greg and asked if we wanted him to have words at our grand reopening, it was a huge thing. It meant that he and Lady Bowens accept us into their circle. That they approve of our ministry and what we're doing in the city.

It's also an endorsement, just like Lady Bowens putting me in front of the women at her empowerment conference and on that tour. An endorsement from the Bowens was priceless, but Greg had turned it down. To me, it seemed like an insult, but Greg had shrugged it off.

"I mean, how could I not have Bishop Lipford do it? He's our father in the gospel."

We love Bishop Lipford, and of course there is no way we would not have included him in this service. He is the one who helped us get started. He helped me hone my prophetic gift with prayers and fasting.

"We absolutely had to have Bishop Lipford, honey. I agree. But we could've allowed Bishop Bowens to have words too. You basically snubbed him."

Greg turns around to face me and he's wearing a scowl on his face. Even when he's angry, he's still incredibly handsome. I just noticed that he has a few silver strands in his goatee. It becomes him. I hope it's not because of stress, though.

"Why should I give him words? Because he's going to put you on television?"

My jaw drops a little. "Greg, I thought we were done talking about the show. We decided that —"

"No. *You* decided that you were doing it, and I told you I wasn't going to stand in your way."

I bite my bottom lip. I keep hoping that Greg will come around on the talk show. No matter what he thinks of the Bowens, he's got to admit that this is the biggest opportunity either one of us has ever had.

"Having Bishop Bowens speak, well it means that he is putting the stamp of approval on us. People in the neighborhood will come, just because they think we're connected to the Bowens."

"Did it ever occur to you that I don't want his stamp of approval on this ministry?"

"It did. But Lady Bowens is the reason we have this new building, honey. Don't deny that they've opened doors for us."

"God has opened doors for us."

"And He used the Bowens for that purpose. Don't be like that, Greg."

Greg relaxes and smiles. "Okay, maybe I'll let Bishop Bowens stand in and preach with me one Sunday while you're out."

"Or you could just let him have words this

morning. He's on the program."

Greg looks confused until he picks up a copy of this morning's program from our dresser. He scans the pages slowly then looks up at me.

"You invited him without telling me?"

"I extended an invitation from both of us. I explained how Bishop Lipford is the one who set us out on our ministry path, but that we would love for both Bishop and Lady Bowens to bless our service this morning. They said yes."

Greg closes his eyes and strokes his goatee again, smoothing the hairs down with each rub. I can tell he's furious, from the vein throbbing on his right temple. I watch his chest rise and fall slowly, as if he's trying to decrease his heart rate before dealing with me.

"Woman, you have lost your ever loving mind," Greg says. "The only reason I'm not canceling the invite *you* made is because that would absolutely be a snub. You've put me in a tough spot."

"It will be fine. It's not about Bishop Bowens today. He knows that. I gave them the history of our ministry, and Lady Bowens promises me that his remarks will line up with our mission."

"I hope so."

Greg and I follow Lena's instructions and enter the pulpit area just as service is getting underway. Bishop and Lady Bowens have on matching blue ensembles. Bishop Bowens's tie makes me cover my mouth to stifle a giggle. It's got huge green, orange, blue, and red bubbles all over it. Next to his royal blue suit, it looks like he's about to be ringmaster at the circus. Lady Bowens is no less gaudy than her husband. She's got on bright red, jewel-encrusted shoes that put me in mind of Dorothy from *The Wiz*. Next to them, Bishop Lipford in his plain, cream-colored preaching robe looks understated and underwhelming.

We enjoy singing by several different local choirs and a few soloists as the celebration begins. I watch Greg beam with pride at how the service is progressing and the hundreds of people in our new sanctuary. We just knew that when we first opened the doors there would only be a few more than our regular congregation, but there is an explosion of people. I don't know if it's because of the Suddenly Blessing message, or if people were just excited to have a new church in the neighborhood.

Now it's the time in the service for the words, blessings, and consecration. I feel a little nervous as our assistant pastor reads

Bishop Bowens's biography. He takes to the podium and the congregation roars with applause. He truly is a well-known face in Dallas.

"How many of y'all are excited about what God is doing at Love First International?" Bishop Bowens roars into the microphone, and the congregation roars back.

"I have to tell you, I believe God has planted this phenomenal couple right here in Dallas to do some kingdom building. Their youthful and relatable spirit is refreshing. My wife and I just love them with the love of Jesus."

I feel myself relax. So far, so good. Greg was worried about Bishop Bowens saying something crazy, but he's doing a great job.

"How many of you, in the audience, have heard Pastor Nya's Suddenly Blessing message?"

The roar is even louder than the first time, but Greg beams at me and joins in the applause.

"Church, I am believing God with the Hampsteads, for a supernatural breakthrough in their ministry. We know that Pastor Nya flows in the prophetic, and she's the real thing, y'all. We got a lot of imposters out here. A lot of prophe-liars, but not Pastor Nya. She is truly acting as one of the mouthpieces of God in this end-times dispensation."

Now I feel myself getting nervous. Partially because I did indeed prophe-lie. But more because Bishop Bowens's brief remarks are leaving the realm of brevity and entering the realm of lengthy.

"If you are believing God with me for this wonderful couple, I want you to do something very special right now. I feel led, in this moment, to be a blessing to them and to sow a seed into them. And I want to be very specific about this, because some of y'all might not know this about your pastors. Pastor Nya went on a preaching tour and put every penny of her earnings into the purchase of this building."

The applause is deafening, and if Greg had a superpower like X-ray vision, I would feel a hole burning in the side of my face from his stare.

"The man and woman of God sitting before you are incredibly selfless. They didn't have to use the money for that. They could've raised money from the congregation and had a building fund. But they didn't. They took what God entrusted them with and sowed it back into their ministry."

Bishop Bowens looks back at us and smiles. Greg gives him the blankest stare possible and I'm not quite sure what my face does. I'm just afraid Greg is going to pull out the hook and yank Bishop Bowens off the stage.

"Very, very quickly, I want you all to get an offering in your hand," Bishop Bowens says.

Greg's head literally snaps over in my direction. I can almost see the smoke coming from his ears.

"Get at least a ten-dollar seed offering, and if you're writing a check, don't write it to the church. Write it directly to your pastors. I want you to let them know that the burden of this wonderful building will not fall on their shoulders alone. And when you get that offering in your hand, bring it down to the altar and lay it here. To all that come, we're gonna pray a special prayer over your life."

As the people pour from their seats waving their offerings in their hands, I want to burst into tears. This is why Greg didn't want Bishop Bowens to speak, and he was so very right.

"I'm going to turn it over to this other great man of God, Bishop Lipford, to provide the prayer over you faithful givers."

Bishop Lipford has a very serious expression on his face as he approaches the

131

podium. He nods at Bishop Bowens as he takes the microphone from him, and Bishop Bowens goes to his seat next to Lady Sandy. She kisses him and pats his arm like he just discovered a cure for cancer. I see she's definitely his biggest fan.

Bishop Lipford looks out over the people standing at the altar, holding offerings. He is silent for a very long moment, and if I know him, he's praying for direction. On how to correct Bishop Bowens's wrong without disrespecting the man.

"Saints and friends," he finally says into the microphone. "I do believe that God is in the midst here with us this afternoon. And because He's here, I want to honor His presence. Those of you in your seats who desire communion with God and not just a blessing, move forward to this altar. You don't need any money in your hands, you just need praise in your mouth."

A slow smile starts on Greg's face, and he does a slow clap in support of Bishop Lipford's words.

"It is a wonderful thing to sow into the man and woman of God, and you will surely be blessed for your joyful giving spirit. But know this. God doesn't need your pennies, nickels, fifties, or hundreds to commune with you. He needs your heart. He needs unadulterated worship. Can y'all do that with me?"

" 'I need thee. Oh, I need thee,' " Bishop Lipford sings. " 'Every hour, I need thee.' "

Greg stands to his feet and lifts his hands in worship as Bishop Lipford continues the song. The musicians join in and so do those at the altar. As I stand, I glance over at Bishop Bowens and Lady Sandy. They're both on their feet, but neither of them has entered into worship with the congregation. Bishop Bowens has a sour look on his face too, as if he's been openly rebuked.

I know Greg is enjoying every moment of this, and normally I would too. Under any other circumstances, I would love to see Bishop Lipford turn a congregation away from foolishness and back to God. But this time, I feel like we may have stepped on some toes.

One thing we don't ever want to do is make enemies of the other pastors in this city, but if the look on Bishop Bowens's face is an indication, I've got some real damage control to do. I wonder what my next conversation with the Bowens will be like.

CHAPTER 17
FELICIA

"I have the results of your preliminary blood work."

Lance smiles and squeezes my hand, but something about the doctor's tone makes me tremble. Or maybe it's his serious facial expression as he sits down at his desk.

"Is everything all right? Is the baby healthy? I've been taking vitamins and drinking the protein shakes."

The doctor sighs. Anytime a doctor sighs, it is not a good thing.

"What's wrong?" I ask.

"Well, let me first say that I want to run some more tests to be sure. But it looks like your child may have a very serious condition called anencephaly."

Lance's squeeze changes to a strong grip. "What is that?" he asks.

"It's a neural tube defect that causes the baby to be born without major sections of the brain used for thinking and reasoning."

My stomach turns. "Can he survive it?" I ask. I don't want to lose my baby. He is a part of my blessing.

"Most children with this condition are born without a skull, meaning the parts of the brain he will have will only be covered in skin. More than likely he wouldn't survive the birth."

"But you're not sure, right?" Lance asks.

"What causes it? Did I do something wrong? Is it because we had sex? Lance, I told you we shouldn't . . ." I can't finish. My sobs punctuate my sentence for me.

"Ms. Caldwell. Sometimes this condition is caused by a lack of folic acid."

"Oh, then I know your test is wrong. I've been taking my vitamins. I have plenty of folic acid."

The doctor nods. "I understand. Sometimes we're unable to determine what causes this condition. I just want you to know that you did everything you could possibly do to make sure your baby was born healthy."

"So what's next?" Lance asks. "If your follow-up tests reveal the same results."

"I suggest that you terminate the pregnancy. It's still early enough to do so with only a relatively small amount of trauma to the mother."

I shake my head. "Absolutely not. God can do anything but fail. I'm not murdering my child."

Dr. Tomlinson shakes his head. "It's not murder. This child will be nothing more than a vegetable. Not only will the child be in a great deal of pain for the short time it's alive, it won't know you, bond with you, or connect. Terminating the pregnancy is the merciful thing to do. Is your God not merciful?"

I close my eyes as tears pour down my face. This is not what I came to hear today.

"It's not like we can't have another baby," Lance says.

Another baby. He wants to have another baby with me. That speaks to a future. Our future. I feel my nerves begin to calm, even though the tears still pour down my face.

"Dr. Tomlinson, how much time do we have to make a decision on this?" Lance asks. "I think Felicia needs time."

"Well, she's eighteen weeks. It will be better to do it sooner than later. The further along she gets the more traumatic it will be. I would say no more than a week."

Lance pulls me to my feet. "Come on. We'll go away for the weekend. We'll relax and you'll feel better about all this when we get back."

I know what this is. This baby was not supposed to live anyway. It's like when David slept with Bathsheba. David got Bathsheba pregnant and had her husband killed. Their baby didn't survive. But later, once they were married, Bathsheba had Solomon, and he became a king.

Our next child will be someone great. Our children will be blessed and anointed. If God requires this one has to be sacrificed for our sins, then I will accept it.

"I'm ready now. Let's do this and get it over with so we can go on with our lives," I say.

"Are you sure?" Dr. Tomlinson says. "I can schedule your procedure for tomorrow."

I nod as Lance wipes away my tears with a tissue.

"Go ahead and schedule it."

"You okay, baby?" Lance asks.

"I am."

This is, of course, a lie. I'm not okay at all. I want to scream at the top of my lungs. I want to cry out to God to save my baby. But you can't just trust God on the parts of His plan that you understand. You have to trust Him in all of it. As long as Lance stays by my side in all this, I'll be able to come out on the other side.

CHAPTER 18
NYA

I haven't talked to any of the Bowens since that service at our church. Not a call or text from Lady Sandy indicating approval or displeasure, and not a peep to Greg from Bishop Bowens.

So I'm surprised when Penelope invites me for coffee. I assume she wants to talk about our TV show, and I would love to hear her thoughts about it, because frankly I'm scared. I don't even watch these kinds of shows, so I have no clue what the content should be, or how I should act.

"The dedication service for your church was so nice," Penelope says as she flips her brand-new blond hair out of her face.

I wonder . . . do I need new hair, too?

"Greg and I were so happy that you-all were there with us. Especially since your mother inviting me to do that tour really was the catalyst of it all. We wouldn't have been able to close a deal on that property without the income from the tour."

I'm so glad that Penelope doesn't have anything negative to say about the service. Maybe that means her parents were okay with what happened.

Penelope shakes her head. "It was you, Nya! Don't you see it? My mother is great at many things, but she is best at recognizing talent. She knew that you had something special from the very first time you prayed for her."

"I have the same something special that she has — the blood of Jesus and the Holy Spirit. I give God all the glory."

"Praise Him in the highest," Penelope says as she lifts one hand to heaven and places the other one on her heart.

"So, the TV show? Who saw that coming? Being on TV was definitely not on my vision board," I say.

"It wasn't? Girl, it was on mine. I had a dream once where I was in a VIP airport lounge sitting next to actors, actresses, and singers. All A-list people. That's how I knew I was destined for celebrity status."

I wait for her to tell me the punchline. She keeps smiling and doesn't elaborate, so I guess there isn't one.

"I've never thought about being famous. Don't you think celebrities have pretty stressful lives? They're always under the microscope."

"And pastors aren't? Growing up as a pastor's kid, the spotlight has been on me my entire life."

"I didn't grow up as a pastor's kid. My grandfather did pastor a Holiness church, but by the time I was born, he had already retired. I didn't even grow up going to church really. My grandmother would give us Sunday school lessons at home."

Penelope puts her hand over her mouth and stifles a giggle. "That's a little bit weird, Nya."

At-home Bible lessons were the least weird part of my childhood. I wonder what Penelope would think if she knew we didn't have running water or electricity, and that we barely ever left our little shack. Or that my first contact with the outside world was high school — and that I was lucky for that.

"Maybe it seems weird to you. It is funny that I didn't learn any gospel hymns or any music really until I was almost grown. Sometimes Greg will bust out with a hymn during service and I'll be like, um . . ."

Penelope roars with laughter. I'm so glad my background is entertaining to her. I hope the sarcastic thoughts I keep having don't show on my face, because I don't think she means to offend me with her amusement.

"And even still, you're the most anointed preacher I know," Penelope says after her giggles fade.

"I just try to follow the move of God."

"Can you teach me how to operate in the prophetic?"

Did she really just ask me this? I don't know how to teach her to have the prophetic gift. Shoot, I didn't even ask for this. I was born with it. Sometimes I wish I didn't have it.

"It's not really something you can teach."

Penelope moves our coffee cups to the side so she can lean in. "But you can. Just like someone can learn to speak in tongues. It just takes practice."

I swallow hard. I don't want to offend her, but she sounds completely ridiculous to me. I believe that people should only be speaking in tongues if the Holy Spirit literally takes command of their tongue and vocal cords. Not because they practice.

"I've had the prophetic gift before I knew what it was. Before I knew Jesus."

"So, how do you know it's of God? You could be like a gypsy or a psychic or something," Penelope says. Her tone is irritated and taunting, as if she is somehow questioning me. Good thing I don't care what she thinks.

"I know that my gift is of God, because I belong to God. He gave me the gift before I chose to serve Him, but He definitely is the one who gives all our gifts and talents. This is somewhat elementary, Penelope. I know in all those years of sitting in church, you had to have learned this."

See. If she wants to do snippy, I can do snippy. I'd much rather we be friends though, and not snip, because I might just take off her head. I don't think she's ready for me.

"Oh, I know it's of God, girl!" Penelope says. "I just want to be able to move the crowd like you. I want you to be my mentor. After everything my mother has done for you, you should want to take me under your wing."

"Everything she's done?"

"Yes, she's made you and your husband enough money to buy a new church for your congregation. All I'm asking is that you teach me your prophetic technique. Like what do you do to get in the flow? Do you fast? Do you pray without stopping for days? What do you do to get God to speak?"

I take a long sip of my coffee. "You know, in the Bible there is a story about a man named Simon the sorcerer. Do you know that story?"

Penelope shakes her head.

"It's in the book of Acts. He saw the apostles lay hands on people and cause them to be filled with the Holy Spirit. He wanted to pay for that gift, and the apostle Peter told him the power couldn't be bought."

"I'm not asking you to sell me anything. I'm asking you to teach me like Elijah taught Elisha."

"But Elisha was also called by God. You should seek God for what He wants you to do in the kingdom, Penelope. Maybe it's not to give prophecies, maybe it is. I don't know. But I do know your singing voice is very powerful."

"A lot of people can sing, but not a lot of people can give true prophecies."

I wince at *true* prophecies.

"But not everyone who can sing can move people to want to turn their lives over to Christ. Don't sleep on what God's given you, thinking something else, or another calling, is greater."

Penelope sips her coffee now. She looks like she's thinking about everything I've said. I hope she thinks long and hard. This *gift* that I have comes with such a price.

"I still want you to be my mentor. Would you?"

I nod. "And guess what? Now, every time I preach or speak at one of these conferences, I want you to sing. You can open it up or sing at the altar call, or both. I think you'll be incredible."

"Yes, I'm gonna sing every time you hand me the microphone. But I am seeking God for that prophetic gift. I truly believe He wants me to have it. My father says that there is a process to everything. I will just watch and learn your process. You'll teach me without even realizing you're doing it."

If the expression on her face wasn't as serious as a sinner praying on his deathbed, I'd think she was joking with me.

"Did you hear anything I said?"

She nods. "And I just think my faith is bigger than the box you're trying to put me in. While I'm praying for power, I'm going to pray for your unbelief. Because we are destined to do great things *together,* Nya."

Father God in heaven. I nod and smile at Penelope, although she needs no approval from me. She's decided the path that she is going to follow, and I don't think anyone, not even all the apostles and Michael the archangel can tell her she won't prophesy.

I don't need the prophetic gift to predict a disaster in the making.

Chapter 19
Felicia

I wake feeling groggy. I guess it's from the anesthesia. I touch my midsection, knowing there's no one growing there anymore. I feel an emptiness in my spirit and in my womb.

The nurse walks over and checks my IV.

"You're awake. Good. How do you feel?" she asks.

"I have some cramps. Is my boyfriend in the waiting room? He can come back now," I say.

"He told me to tell you that he had an emergency, but he said when you're ready to be released, he will send a car service to take you home."

"He's not here?"

The nurse shakes her head. "Do you want some pain medication?"

"How long before I can go home?"

"A couple of hours or so. The doctor will want to come in and make sure your uterus is fine. Then we'll administer some antibiotics to make sure you don't have any infections."

My head is reeling. I just had to terminate my pregnancy and Lance couldn't even stay until I woke up. What could the emergency be?

"Can you please bring me my cell phone out of my purse?" I ask the nurse.

I take my phone from the nurse and open up Facebook. I navigate to Lance's page, but there's no new posts since yesterday. Then I log into Instagram and check Lance's profile. Again, no new posts. I close my eyes and sigh. I hate to do this, but I need to know for sure.

I navigate to Jasmine's Instagram page, and I almost drop my phone when I see the first picture. It's a family photo. Her, Lance, and their son. The little boy is wearing a Happy Birthday hat, and they're all smiling. The caption on the photo says, "My favorite guys."

Now, of course, I have no clue if this picture was taken today or some other time, but Jasmine seems to post daily, like Instagram is her personal diary. If Lance left me to spend time with his wife and son, while I'm here still bleeding after taking the life of our son, I don't know what I'm going to do.

What could be a bigger emergency than this?

I log off Instagram and call his number. It doesn't even ring once before going straight to voice mail. He's ignoring my calls now?

I dial again, and again I go straight to voice mail. I throw down the phone and burst into tears.

The nurse rushes back over to me. "Are you okay?" she asks.

"No. I am not okay. Not at all. He's not answering his phone. Why won't he answer his phone?"

The nurse pulls a chair up next to my bed and sits down. She takes one of my trembling hands and squeezes.

"Listen, baby, I see a lot of women here with their guys, and sometimes the men are supportive. Sometimes they're not. But you have to take care of you. You have to heal in your heart, body, and spirit. God will forgive you for making this decision."

"My baby . . . he had a birth defect."

She rubs my hand and nods. "Okay, then you can feel better knowing that you saved your baby from having any pain."

"I do feel better."

"Your boyfriend is just a man. You can't worry about him, and we can't control what men do."

No, I can't control what he does, that much is true. But I don't even need to do that anyway. God is in control. He has the final say. So Jasmine can post all the Instagram family photos that she wants to post. If God means for me to have Lance, then, by God, I will have him.

The next time I talk to him though, we're going to have to discuss his lack of attention to my situation and my feelings. I may be his woman on the side for now, but he might as well get used to treating me as the number one.

CHAPTER 20
NYA

This might be horrible, but I don't know any wife who doesn't do this. I just got Greg in a really good mood. A *really* good mood. Because I've got a pillow-talk confession to make. He's propped up on the pillows playing a game on his tablet when I hit him with the news.

"So, Greg. I talked to Lady Sandy the other day. We've got a book deal on the table from a major publisher."

Greg sets his tablet down on the bed and stares at me. The way his lips are pressed together in a straight line makes me worry what his response is going to be.

"A book deal? Nya, are you serious? Do you even write?"

I had prepared myself for Greg's skepticism about this newest opportunity. He laughed about the television show, but now he's just looking at me crazy. And I totally understand. I made a million objections when Lady Sandy brought it to me. Honestly, I'm just happy Lady Sandy isn't mad at me about what happened at our church dedication.

"Listen, I'm not writing an entire book. I'm writing about my testimony. Lady Sandy was offered a book deal and she wants to have a compilation of testimonies."

"A compilation. So that means there will be a lot of other ministers telling their stories? Is this another all-girl project?"

I nod slowly. "Yes. It's going to be like a women's devotional. But don't you think my story . . . the things that happened to me growing up . . . can help someone?"

"Of course. But I thought you didn't feel comfortable talking about being the product of sexual molestation. How will your family feel about that?"

"My grandmother is gone, and my mom . . . well . . . she won't like it. But she won't try to stop me."

"What about your cousin Zenovia? I thought you said she didn't even know about it."

"She doesn't. She doesn't know anything about it."

"Well, don't you think you ought to talk to her before you put out a book about your family secrets?"

I let out a huge sigh. Greg is right. Zenovia is in ministry herself, and she is an incredibly private person.

"Maybe I'll go and see Zee. I haven't seen my cousin in about five years."

"Why don't *we* go and see her? You're so used to doing everything by yourself these days that you've forgotten you have a husband."

Greg looks so irritated right now, but I don't mean to make him feel that way. Everything has been happening so fast lately, and I know I need to make sure he's a part of all of it.

"I'm sorry, babe. We can make it a long weekend trip. Zee and Justin will be happy to see us."

"Okay."

"What should I tell Lady Sandy about the book deal, though?"

"Tell her you're not ready to make a commitment yet. It shouldn't be a big deal. And if it is, you can send her to talk to me."

Greg had his chest puffed out a little bit when he said that. I don't know who is supposed to be scared of him, but it surely isn't Lady Sandy. She knows exactly what kind of opportunity she's putting in my lap. And she knows that I would be crazy to turn down being a part of this project. It's a real book deal with a publisher.

"Greg, can you believe that Penelope Bowens asked me to teach her how to be a prophetess?"

He shakes his head. "I wish I didn't believe it. I wish it was the most outlandish thing that I've ever heard. What did you tell her?"

"When she basically made it seem like I owed it to her, because her mom put me on, I told her about Simon the sorcerer."

"Good! Did that set her straight?"

"Not at all. She's really desperate to have the gift, and for it to be authentic."

"That's dangerous."

I've been going back and forth in my mind on this one. Whether it's truly dangerous or not. Maybe it's not such a bad thing to want to be gifted.

"I don't think it's desperate," I say.

"It is, and so is she. This is why I don't really want you around them, Nya. That kind of desperation is catching."

He doesn't have to tell me this. I caught a serious case of desperation at that Women's Empowerment conference. Now there's not a day that goes by that I don't think about how I failed God and the gift he gave me.

"Just admit it, Nya," Greg says. "You're enjoying the attention. A television show, for Christ's sakes. It's okay to say that this is fun and exciting."

"It is, Greg. It is! I know what you say is true about the desperation and getting caught up, but I have you to help keep me rooted and grounded. I'm not worried about losing my focus."

"Well, I am praying for you and us. Our church is growing so quickly that I need a bigger staff. We're starting a new minister's class and I think I'm gonna need some associate pastors."

"Associate pastors. Really? Are we there yet?"

"On the day of our dedication after Bishop Lipford ushered in the Holy Spirit, six hundred people joined our church."

"Wow. On the first day."

"Yes, God is up to something with us. And I just want you to be careful about the Bowens. After what they did at our church dedication, I feel they're capable of anything."

I will keep Greg's warning in mind while I'm dealing with them. My husband might not have a prophetic gift, but he does know a good man when he sees one. If he's still not sold on the Bowens, then they still have to convince me too.

CHAPTER 21
FELICIA

I took only a few days off to recover from terminating my pregnancy. Since my excuse was the flu, it's not like I could stay home for weeks. I don't want to be here though. I'd rather be back in Puerto Rico with Lance. But in order for us to go on vacation somewhere, he'd have to call me. He's been missing in action since he sent the car service for me at the hospital four days ago.

My boss, Mr. Bailey, asked me to meet with him this morning, and although I'm not really in the mood, I print out my status report and make my way over to his office.

The door is open, so I step inside. Mr. Bailey is on the phone, so he motions for me to have a seat in the leather chair in front of his enormous desk. Sharon wasn't lying about how they spared no expense for these offices. Mr. Bailey's office furniture is all cherry wood and bamboo. The pieces are so unique that it looks like they imported them all the way from China.

Mr. Bailey ends his call and finally gives me his attention.

"Good morning, Felicia," he says. "I'm sorry we haven't had much time to chat since you've been here. I think these two major fundraisers are finally planned and ready to go, so I can focus on going over some housekeeping items with you that I had forgotten."

"Housekeeping items?"

"Yes. You're doing a great job so far, by the way. That Boys and Girls Club in South Carolina sent you a thank-you card."

"Thank you, Mr. Bailey. I've never enjoyed grant writing as much as I do here."

"So, yes, the housekeeping items. Of late, there have been many infractions in our non-fraternization clause."

"Why does that concern me?"

Mr. Bailey chuckles. "Listen, the clause is in place to protect our beautiful female employees from advances at work. These players have lots of testosterone, and most of them are looking for a soft place to land. So the cheerleaders, dance team, and all of our female staff are off-limits to them."

"Are the players aware of the clause?"

"Oh, absolutely. But it doesn't stop them from trying to break it at every opportunity."

Lance knows that it was against policy to pursue a relationship with me. Is he ever planning to make me his woman for real? Or am I just a soft place to land?

"What happens to them if they break the clause? Do they get cut from the team?"

"No. Unfortunately, the team has invested too much money into each of these guys to lose them over that type of infraction. The woman, however . . ."

"Is fired." I finish Mr. Bailey's sentence. "That is extremely unfair."

Mr. Bailey shrugs. "I know that it isn't fair, and I can't say that I agree with it, but that is the way things are here."

"Thank you for letting me know! I wouldn't have wanted to get caught up with one of these guys. You make it sound like they're all on the prowl."

"Mostly they are."

"I have a pretty full schedule this morning. Is that all you wanted to share with me?" I ask.

"Yes, that is all. Please continue doing great work. I am happy that I hired you."

I walk out of Mr. Bailey's office feeling like someone punched me. The timing of this is completely suspect. Does he know about my and Lance's baby? Lance paid cash for the procedure so I wouldn't have to use my insurance coverage.

When I get back to my office, Sharon is waiting at the door with a cup.

"I brought you some chai. Hope you're feeling better."

"Yes, I am feeling somewhat better. Thank you. Can you reschedule my morning meeting? I have an emergency that just came up. I need a couple of hours to handle it."

"Of course. Do you want it rescheduled for this afternoon or tomorrow?"

"This afternoon is fine."

I go back into my office to grab my purse, and I hurry out to my car, not exactly sure of my plan or even where I'm going. I know where Lance and Jasmine live, but that is too cliché for me to show up at their house. And then what would I do when I got there? Tell Jasmine I just had an abortion? She would laugh in my face.

I take out my cell phone and send Lance a text If you don't want me to show Jasmine the video I took of you pleasing me in Puerto Rico, meet me at Caribou Coffee in fifteen minutes.

I'm at the coffee shop in ten minutes, and I keep staring at my phone for a reply from Lance. When the fifteen minute mark passes, I don't think he's coming. I don't have any video footage anyway.

Then, finally, Lance speeds into the parking lot driving his white Lambo. He pulls up next to my car and gets out, a furious expression on his face. I almost grin as I unlock my doors. I may not have all the power, but I do have a little.

"What video, Felicia?" he says after sitting in my passenger seat and slamming the door shut.

I giggle. "There's no video. I had to do something. You've been ignoring my calls and texts."

"I haven't been ignoring them. I just haven't replied."

"That's the same thing, Lance."

"What is it that you want? I left my son's school program for this, so it better be important."

His words are harsh. They feel like jabs. "Why are you being so mean to me?"

"Because, Felicia, you know I have my home situation going on. I'm not trying to neglect you, but sometimes I have to be attentive at home."

I feel tears welling up, but I don't let them fall. "You said that we were still going to be together after we lost the baby."

"Well, I'm thinking maybe that abortion was for the best anyway. I'm not even supposed to be seeing you. You could lose your job."

I close my eyes and shake my head. "Why are you calling it that? We *had* to terminate the pregnancy. It was God's judgment on us that our baby was sick."

"What are you talking about? God's judgment? We had an abortion, but now we have to move on with life."

"You said we could have another baby. You said we would still be together. I don't care about my job if we're going to be together. I'll quit right now if you say the word."

"I know what I said. I'm just thinking that maybe that's not for the best anymore."

"Were you going to tell me that, or was I just supposed to figure it out?"

Lance tilts his head to one side and sighs, like my questions are getting on his nerves. How am I annoying him? He is the one who started this — became my blessing.

"I don't know why you're acting like this, Lance."

"Acting like what? Look, we enjoyed each other. Maybe in the future we will enjoy each other again. But for now, let's just let this affair die a natural death."

A natural death. I can't tell if he's just not choosing his words carefully or if he's intentionally being cruel. I want to cry, but I refuse to let him see it.

"All right, then. I guess you can get out of my car."

Lance tries to take my hand, but I snatch it away. "It doesn't have to be like this," he says. "I don't want us to stop getting together from time to time, I just don't need the relationship right now."

"I understand."

" 'Cause, girl, you got the good stuff, for real."

I am suppressing the urge to dig my acrylic nails into his throat and he's telling me I'm good in bed?

"Get. Out. Of. My. Car."

Lance shrugs and jumps out of the car. He has a pep in his step when he walks back to his car, as if a burden has been lifted from him.

I don't know what to do next. I need to pray. I need God to speak some confirmation into my spirit about the promises He made to me through his prophetess. This calls for a fast. Yes, I'll fast. And then God will give me the next action to take.

CHAPTER 22
NYA

My cousin Zenovia and I leave our husbands and their teenage daughter, Jael, at home preparing a November barbecue so that we can have a private talk. We're near Georgetown, by the water. Zenovia's hair has grown so much since the last time I saw her. It's huge and curly, going in whatever direction it pleases, barely restrained by the headband she's put around the edges. She's older, but still has that pretty smooth, brown skin.

"It's been too long since you've visited," Zenovia says.

"Well, you should come on home to Texas every now and then."

She laughs. "Texas isn't home to me."

"You still have a little bit of family left there."

"I am okay here with my little brood," Zenovia says. "It's crazy how much you look like my mom."

"Aunt Audrey. I've seen pictures of her when she was little. She and my mom look alike too."

"They do. I escaped the red hair and freckles, but my baby didn't."

I chuckle. "No, she didn't. She looks just like your mother."

"Yeah, well, she more than looks like her."

My mouth forms a straight line. Aunt Audrey's mental illness was all Zenovia had to deal with growing up.

"Is she . . . like Aunt Audrey?"

Zenovia clears her throat. "You didn't grow up knowing my mom, so I don't know if you realize how bad it was. We left when you were little."

"I do remember Aunt Audrey vividly though. She used to do this thing with nail polish. Write crosses on the walls with it. I remember once Grandma spanked me because I was helping her do it one time. I didn't understand."

"I can't get an accurate diagnosis because she's so young, but I have a feeling she is schizophrenic."

"I'm so sorry. I'll pray for her healing."

"Thank you. Anyway . . . enough doom, gloom, and depression. What brings you and Greg to D.C.?"

"I have an opportunity that I wanted to

talk to you about. Greg says I should talk to you before I say yes."

"Okay, now I'm curious. I've been following you on the Internet. You're preaching up a storm these days."

"Yeah."

"Don't sound so excited about it. You really brought it with that 'suddenly' thing. Even I was moved."

I close my eyes and breathe deeply. Zenovia knows. She knows. I can tell.

"I'm surprised you were moved by that."

"Why? Because you faked that prophetic word?"

She's always been blunt like that. I think that came from taking care of a schizophrenic mother. She never had time to mince words.

"How did you know?"

She shrugs. "I just do. You know how we know stuff. We can't explain it, but we know."

"So why were you moved by it, then? If you knew it was fake?"

"I knew it wasn't a prophecy, but it was still a very powerful word that you spoke over that woman's life. God does bless people suddenly sometimes. I hope it came to pass for that girl."

"Me too."

"So what's the opportunity?"

"Lady Sandy got a book deal and wants it to be a compilation of women's altar-call experiences. I wanted to talk about how my mom, Aunt Audrey, and I were all the product of rape, and how that shaped my walk with Christ."

"My mother was the product of rape? Why am I just now learning this? Was . . . was I? Is that why I don't know my father?"

I shake my head. "From what I gather, your mother had a boyfriend that she wanted to run away with, and our grandfather ran him off when she got pregnant."

"Who was the rapist?"

"A man Grandfather worked for."

Zenovia's face scrunches into a frown. "So you're saying he raped three women in our family? How did that happen? I mean, how did the same man keep raping our family?"

"Zee. He was white. Klan."

"What happened to him?"

"He disappeared. But they say that the prophetic gift is in his family."

"Wow," Zenovia says. "He just disappeared?"

"The rumor is that he was killed, by a woman. But I don't know. Grandmother kept me away from it all. You should be glad Aunt Audrey ran away with you."

"Sometimes I am. But I missed out on growing up with cousins, grandparents, and everyone else. My mother and I were alone. And it was very lonely living with her."

I can't imagine what it was like living with Aunt Audrey, and I wish that I had grown up with Zenovia too. It would've been nice having someone my age who understood what I am, because she has the same gift.

"It sounds like you have your own testimony," I tell her.

"I do. In the midst of all the crazy that was my life, I made it through."

"Isn't that the truth? So, you're cool with me being a part of the book project?" I ask.

"It's your story to tell, but if you want my blessing, you've got it."

"I'm so glad. I knew you would be okay with it, but Greg insisted that I talk to you."

"It's good that you listen to him. I share everything with Justin, even if I think he's going to say the complete opposite."

"Greg has definitely been opposites with me lately."

"Nya, you know I always keep it real . . ."

My laughter comes out before my words. "What?"

"No, I'm about to say something serious. I need you to listen."

Her tone is immediately sobering. "Did

you . . . did you have a vision about me?"

"No. This is just some advice for you. Be careful with the prophetic gift. People will start to want the gift and not God. If the gift doesn't glorify Him, then what is it for?"

"Is that why you don't do speaking engagements, and travel and all of that? I'm sure you've been invited."

"I have. I go where God tells me to go. Right now, He has me preaching in our local assembly, when our pastor calls on me. And I am fine with that."

"Do you think I'm wrong for accepting these opportunities? Be honest."

"I don't know. It's not my place to say. That's between you and God. I just want you to be mindful of how you treat the gift. Respect it."

"I do."

"Then don't give false prophecies, Nya."

I shake my head. "No no. I'm never doing that again. I pray God forgives me for the first time."

"Me too, Cousin. Me too."

It's almost as if she seems uncertain about God's forgiveness in this, but we both know that He forgives. It's just that even with forgiveness come consequences.

CHAPTER 23
FELICIA

Sharon bursts into my office without knocking, and I scramble to put a positive expression on my face. I've been crying or on the verge of tears for days. I can't seem to pray my way out of this mess.

I've sent Lance about a hundred texts, called him about five hundred times, but he won't respond to me.

His wife keeps posting things on Instagram — hints that they have big news to share. I hope that it's Lance being sold to another team, across the country. Europe even. I don't want to see his face or hear his name being said by someone else.

And as angry as I am, I can't help but feel broken. But I didn't want anyone to see this, least of all Sharon. She thinks I don't know it, but she's the main conduit for gossip in and out of this office. I've caught snatches of her telephone conversations, and she always has something to say about someone.

"Oh, I'm sorry, I should've knocked," Sharon says.

"You should've."

Sharon walks over and sets a cup of tea down on my desk. "Are you all right, Felicia?"

"I will be."

She clears her throat. "So, I noticed Lance hasn't visited you lately."

I glare at her. "Don't do that, Sharon. Lance is one of the players, I help him with his organization. That's all."

"I know, I know. I just thought I should tell you that one of the player's wives mentioned to Mr. Bailey's wife that she thought something was going on between you and Lance."

"What?"

"Yes, and I've seen you crying . . . I know I shouldn't pry . . ."

"You shouldn't."

"But the last girl Lance stepped out on his wife with, he had to give her a huge cash settlement to keep quiet. I know, because the deal went down right in this office."

Now she's got my attention.

"Why did he have to give her a settlement?"

Sharon places a hand on her chest. "Please, Felicia, if I tell you, you can't tell anybody. I could lose my job for telling you, and you know how hard it was for me to get this job. I have felonies."

I shake my head back and forth, and motion for her to sit. "I would never betray you."

Sharon sits and looks me dead in the face. "I wouldn't be telling you this if I didn't think Lance was trying to run game on you too."

"I am not confirming or denying that there is anything going on with me and Lance, but please do tell."

"That last girl, her name was Nyoka. She got pregnant by Lance."

My mouth forms a tiny circle. "Pregnant?"

"Mm-hmm. He told her he was going to leave his wife."

"But he didn't."

"Naw, he didn't."

"That's pretty despicable."

"That ain't the worst part though. She sued him because he had some shady doctor talk her into having an abortion, told her the baby had some kind of brain disease. Come to find out wasn't nothing wrong with the baby at all."

It takes every shred of control I have not to let Sharon see me fall apart. She cannot see me fall apart.

"How much did he have to pay her?"

"I'm not sure, but she had her own doctor that she was going to and had proof that her baby was healthy."

"Well, that's a pretty juicy story, Sharon. Thank you for looking out for me. Fortunately, I don't have a similar story."

"Okay, well, if you ever need to know anything about any of these players, let me know. I got you."

I pick up the cup of tea and take a sip. "We got each other."

"I'll leave you to your work now. Holla at me if you want to get some lunch or something," Sharon says.

Out of frustration, I call Lance. I don't expect him to answer the phone, but he does.

"Hello." His punctuation is a sigh, as if hearing from me immediately stresses him out.

"I was wondering if you want to get lunch today."

A long pause. Too long.

"I don't think that's a good idea, Felicia. Let's just pause for a while and see what happens."

Something in his voice makes me feel like this is a brush-off. It makes me feel like I have exactly the same story as the girl

171

Sharon just told me about. Same plays, different players.

"How'd you know about Dr. Tomlinson, Lance? How'd you know he would be discreet?"

"Come on, Felicia. Guys talk. He's kind of an urban legend. He's been there for a lot of the players who get themselves in a bind."

"Is there a reason that he has more abortion procedures clocked than any other doctor in Atlanta?"

Of course, I have no clue if this is fact or fiction. I just want to see what Lance will say to that.

"Who told you that?"

"Really, Lance? These things are a matter of public record."

"I thought doctors had to have confidentiality."

"That's true. The stats don't show who he performed abortions on, just that he did them."

"Oh, okay." Lance sounds incredibly relieved.

"Do you know why he's done so many pregnancy terminations?"

"Probably because most mistresses and side pieces don't really want to be baby mamas."

"They'd just rather have a check, right?" I ask.

Lance is eerily silent. I wonder if he's choosing his words carefully. I bet he's worried right now, and trying to guess what I know.

"No . . . I don't think they want a check. I think most of them want to continue being with the guy they care about without having a child to complicate things."

"That's an interesting assessment," I say.

"You disagree?"

Now I give him the long pause so he can wonder what I'm thinking.

Finally I say, "I would rather have a child with the man I love. I wouldn't want a check, and I wouldn't think that a baby would complicate things unless he didn't love me."

"Well, then you should think long and hard about pursuing a relationship with a man who's already married."

No. He. Didn't.

I disconnect the call and sit staring at the phone in disbelief. Did he just really act like I pursued a relationship all by myself? I wasn't flying him to Puerto Rico, it was the other way around.

Now I feel that maybe I am just like the woman Lance and Dr. Tomlinson duped before, but I won't be like her at all. I'm going to call them out and make them pay with more than money. Starting with the good doctor.

Chapter 24
Nya

Today is the first day of *Suddenly Blessed* — the talk show. Our first guest is a woman named Bonita, who left an abusive marriage and is afraid to start dating again. The first segment of the show is me ministering to her and encouraging her. The second half of the show is something like *The Dating Game*, but hosted by Penelope. Bonita is going to ask bachelors questions, and they will answer them, but from behind a screen.

We're both in hair and makeup, and even though Tina is here with me, I am incredibly nervous. This isn't preaching. This is TV. This is scripted. No waiting for the Holy Ghost to show up here.

"Do you think I'll be okay?" I ask Tina as she paints on my eyebrows with a pencil. "What if I'm not entertaining?"

"You are entertaining me right now with this foolishness. Of course you're going to be great," Tina says. "You're perfect for this."

"I'm the one who should worry," Penelope says. "I'm riding your coattails. You already brought the substance with your message. I'm not sure what I'm supposed to bring to this."

"You're bringing us, Gospel diva," Monet Barnes, the executive producer, says as she walks into the room. "That's why you're here, honey. Just be yourself."

"Since myself is all I have, that shouldn't be a problem," Penelope says.

Monet touches my dress, still hanging next to the makeup stand and nods her approval. She gives Penelope a big smile when she sees her designer shoes.

"You two look incredible," Monet says. "This is going to be an awesome debut."

I say a prayer to calm my nerves, and then sip my coffee to make sure I have the energy I need. My phone buzzes in my lap, and it's a text from Greg.

Praying for you, babe. You're gonna be awesome.

Thank you, Jesus, my husband has my back. I mean, I know that he does, but I also know that he could do without all of it.

I thank God that he's allowing me to spread my wings without holding me back.

This text message from Greg calms me just as much as my prayer, and gives me hope that we will survive this challenge and go to the next level in God and in our careers.

Penelope and I are led out onto the set by two production assistants. We take our places in the chairs for our first segment, which is a conversation between the two of us. It's scripted and there are cue cards, but I memorized my lines. I don't want to look crazy on TV.

The producer gives me the cue to start, so I put a huge smile on my face. I hope it looks genuine and not like a TV smile. "Hi! I'm Nya Hempstead, this is my cohost, Penelope Bowens, and you're tuned into *Suddenly Blessed*!"

"So today we're talking about landing the first date," Penelope says. "I know you've been married fifteen years, so you probably don't remember your first date with Greg."

"I do remember. We were in college, and it was a church conference."

"That's romantic," gushes Penelope.

"And cheap. Did I mention we were in college? My husband was broke."

The studio audience roars with laughter

177

and I feel myself relax. Maybe I'll actually be good at this.

Our guest is a thirty-something woman named Bonita. She's pretty but doesn't have enough flair. She's educated but shy. We've got our job cut out in landing her a date with anybody, much less Prince Charming.

"So, what have been your experiences with first dates?" I ask Bonita while Penelope sets things up with the glam squad.

"I don't know how much I should share. Like, I want to tell them everything. That I want three children, and a house and a dog. Is that too much?"

The studio audience laughs again as I shake my head. "Maybe for the first date. Why do you think you're in such a hurry to talk about this stuff?"

"I guess I feel like I'm in a race against time and the other women. There are so many options for men that I just don't think I will be anyone's choice."

Now, on cue, the audience makes a sad noise. I guess it is pretty pitiful that she doesn't think anyone will choose her.

"Well, Bonita, first of all, I need you to believe God is going to send your Boaz. Do you know who Boaz is?"

"Umm . . ."

"He was a man who married a widowed

woman in the Bible. She had lost everything and he became the provider that she needed."

"I don't need a provider. I have a great career," Bonita says.

"That's great, but you need something, and God knows. He's going to send the one you need."

"Okay, but how do I know who he is? And what is taking God so long? Doesn't He know I have a biological clock?"

"God's timing is perfect, but today we're going to help you do some things to get ready for your Boaz."

"What kinds of things?"

"Penelope, send in the glam squad!"

Tina, a makeup artist, and a clothes designer all storm the set and walk up to Bonita.

"Get ready for a makeover, girl," I say. "And then we're going to pick a lucky bachelor for your first date."

"And cut!" the show's producer says after the glam squad takes Bonita off set.

They usher Penelope and me backstage, because we're going to have a hair and makeup change in order to tape a segment for another episode. This is weird, how it's all done. They're changing out the audience members and everything.

Backstage Penelope sits next to me in a makeup chair. "This is fun, right?" she asks.

"Yes, I guess it is. It's hectic, though."

"I love it. I wish we could do it every day."

"Well, Greg wouldn't want me doing this every day. He wants me home right now."

"He just needs to get on the bandwagon, because we're about to blow up."

I let out a sigh. This is what everyone keeps saying about Greg, but he's not having it. He's not a bandwagon kind of dude. I just need God to reveal to him how important this is for my ministry and for the kingdom, and then maybe he'll be on board. If not, I'm going to find myself suddenly back at home.

CHAPTER 25
FELICIA

I wish I had done like Lance's previous conquest and gotten my own doctor, so that I would have proof that he and Dr. Tomlinson lied about my baby. Unfortunately, I'm going to have to get my proof the hard way.

It's taken me some time, but I think I've finally gotten Dr. Tomlinson alone. I've had to follow him for days. His office is too busy for what I need to do, and waiting for him at his home might involve other people — witnesses. I don't want to be seen or noticed at all.

Luckily, Dr. Tomlinson is a creature of habit. He works out every Monday, Wednesday, and Friday evening, from seven o'clock in the evening until nine. On Friday nights, the gym is a ghost town. All of the fit people are going out for the weekend on dates or to clubs.

I wait for him to come out of the building. And he's right on schedule. I step out of my car that is parked two spots down from his. My hair is in a bun and I am wearing workout clothing. I do some stretches near my car so I don't look out of place, and to warm up.

When Dr. Tomlinson gets to his car and clicks his keyless entry device, he doesn't even look up at me. Doesn't even notice me walking toward him.

"Hello, Dr. Tomlinson," I say when I am finally close enough to touch him.

He jumps. "Oh, Ms. Caldwell. You startled me. Is this where you work out? It's a great gym isn't it?"

I shake my head as I step in very close. Close enough to whisper.

"This isn't where I work out," I hiss. "I came here to see you."

"If you'll excuse me, I have someplace to be."

I quickly reach into the pocket of my hoodie and pull out my secret. A little .22 caliber pistol. I jab it into his midsection.

"If I shoot, you'll probably survive. You may have to use a colostomy bag for the rest of your life, but you'll have a life. Not like the life you stole from my son."

Dr. Tomlinson's bladder empties on his shoes and the ground. Good. He should be scared. He is an accessory to murdering my son.

"Listen, p-please don't hurt m-me. My wife . . ."

"Your wife? Your *wife*?"

"Lance . . . h-he has me by the short hairs. If I don't do what he says, he could have my license revoked. I helped him once, and now I can't be free of him."

"Was there truly anything wrong with my baby?"

"Look . . ."

I press the gun hard into his side. "Tell me!"

"Your baby was perfectly healthy, based on all the tests we had done up until that point."

My eyes close. I feel myself swoon.

"Did Lance pay you to do this? Did he pay you to lie to me and convince me to have an abortion?"

"Lady, I could lose my license for this."

I twist the gun. "You think I care about your license when you murdered my child?"

"Not with you. With the other girl he did, and not a day goes by where I don't regret that decision."

"He didn't pay you."

Although my resolve is wavering some, I press the gun harder into Dr. Tomlinson's gut. He should work out harder. His abdominals feel like gelatin.

"He threatened to reveal to the media what happened the last time. He told me you were crazy . . ."

I ram the gun harder. "He said I am *crazy*?"

Tears pour down Dr. Tomlinson's face. He nods. "Yes. He said you threatened to hurt his wife if he didn't leave her."

I drop my arm to my side, feeling defeated. I didn't want this to be true. I wanted to believe that there was some hope left. Dr. Tomlinson sees his moment, jumps into his car and slams the door.

As he pulls out of the parking lot, I drop the gun on the ground and burst into tears. This is almost too much for me to take. Then, I feel the rage again, this time toward Lance. I pick up the gun and scramble to my feet.

I climb into my car and drive. Tears pour down my face as I speed onto the highway. I want to see Lance's face and tell him I know what he's done. That I know he's a murderer. He and his doctor friend murdered my baby.

I stop on the street in front of Lance's Buckhead mansion. I almost don't go through with it, but I need to lay eyes on him and see his reaction when he knows that I know.

Before I give myself the chance to change my mind, I pull my car up in the drive and stop in front of the home. There is still time for me to go on home and lick my wounds, but if I let Dr. Tomlinson get to him first, I may never get my chance.

I slam my car door as I get out, and jump at how loud it is. My sneakers don't make a sound on the concrete as I storm up to the front door. I touch the bun on top of my head and realize that my workout disguise probably has me looking crazy, but oh, well. I feel a little crazy right now, so my look matches my mood.

I ring the doorbell and wait impatiently for someone to answer. And I don't know why I'm surprised that it isn't Lance who opens the door. It's some sort of household employee. I should've known he wouldn't answer the door himself.

"Is Lance here?" I ask.

"How can I help you?" the man standing in front of me asks. "Do you have an appointment with Mr. Jarvis?"

I fold my arms across my chest. "I have a standing appointment with him. Why don't you go and ask?"

"Mr. Jarvis isn't available right now. Would

you like to speak with Mrs. Jarvis?"

I toss my head backwards and chuckle. "Yes. I would love to talk to her."

The doorman walks away and a few moments later, Jasmine is standing in front of me. She doesn't look nearly as pitiful as I thought she might look.

"Let me guess. You're here because you're sleeping with my husband?" Jasmine says. "I keep telling him to keep his hoes away from my house."

I blink a few times; wasn't ready for this. Wasn't ready for her at all.

"Yes, Lance and I have been having an affair."

She steps aside and holds the door open. "Do you want to come inside or talk about it standing outdoors?"

Again, I'm shocked, but I follow her inside. For a moment, I think I should've maybe gotten my gun.

She shows me to a sitting room, and Lance is right there. On the couch with an ignorant grin on his face. Like he's been expecting me.

"Dr. Tomlinson called," he says.

"Have a seat," Jasmine says to me. "Do you want me to stay or leave, Lance?"

Lance motions for her to sit. And she does. Right next to him on the couch. I sit in an armchair facing them both.

"As you can see, you have no leverage here with Jasmine. So if you were trying to destroy my marriage, that's not going to happen," Lance says.

"I'm not trying to destroy anything," I say. "I am trying to understand why you and Dr. Tomlinson conspired to murder my baby."

Jasmine rolls her eyes and Lance pats her hand. "Look, I did that for you. I knew you wouldn't have an abortion without thinking something was wrong with the baby. You don't really want to have a baby with me. I was trying to save your conscience."

My hands shake with fury and anger. I feel like I can kill him with my bare hands. I can almost see my fingers digging into his throat and ripping out veins. But the overwhelming feeling I have is shock.

"I hope you didn't come over here to save your little fling," Jasmine says. "All of you chicks have an expiration date. He's already moved on to the next one. A cheerleader named Sienna."

"You know about his other women?" I ask. "You're okay with that?"

She nods. "He's okay with my others too. We have an open marriage, but I bet he didn't tell you that."

An open marriage? What does that even mean? How are you married if you both have others?

"She wouldn't have wanted me that way," Lance says to Jasmine. "None of them want that. They don't want to share. They just want me all to themselves."

I clear my throat and stand. "You should've told the truth."

"I didn't. I'm sorry," Lance says.

"Ain't no sorry. Too late."

I walk back out of the house the way I came in. I reach into the car for my handgun. I hold it in my hand. Feel the weight of it. The cold steel touching my fingers. I could end his life right now. His and his smug wife's. And Dr. Tomlinson would probably make sure everyone knows why. He'd want to cover himself.

Then I set the gun down on the floor of the passenger seat in my car. I'm not going to shoot or kill anyone. God wouldn't want me to do that. But I don't know what He wants me to do. I don't know at all.

"Just leave, Felicia," Lance says. He's standing outside next to my car now. I wonder if he sees the gun.

"Why did you do this to me?" I ask. "You were supposed to be a blessing."

"What are you talking about? I am a married guy you slept with. It was supposed to be fun, and you got pregnant."

"You had no feelings for me?" I feel desperate to hear that our relationship was something. Anything.

Lance nods. "I did. But you know I wasn't in love with you. It was all about the fantasy. I wanted you to enjoy our time together. I did."

I swallow hard. I have to leave before someone gets hurt, and before I do something stupid.

"You *were* a blessing," Lance says. "I enjoyed you. Just think about the fun times we had together. They can continue if you want. Now that you know the truth."

My eyes narrow to the size of slits. I can't believe him. He's still talking about being with me after he and the doctor murdered my child.

"I have to go."

And I mean that. I have to leave right now, before someone gets hurt tonight. But this is not the last time Lance will hear from me. I don't think he's ready for what's coming to him. It's all about karma. And sowing. And reaping.

CHAPTER 26
NYA

All ten of the women who are going to participate in Lady Sandy's book-writing project have gathered at the Bowens' home with a ghostwriter. A ghostwriter named James Knowles. As if we're not capable of writing down our own stories. I don't know how I feel about this man sitting in front of us at Lady Sandy's long dining room table.

"I've written the biographies of several megachurch pastors," James says.

"Which ones?" one of the ladies asks.

He chuckles. "I can't say. It's part of my contract that my help on these books remains a secret."

"Well, I've already written my part," Penelope says.

This makes me grin. First of all, why is Penelope even in the book? She didn't have an altar-call experience. She was practically saved in the womb. Born like a little baby apostle.

"I'm sure whatever you've written needs work," James replies.

Penelope's eyebrows shoot up. "I have a degree in English. I was just letting you know that you can put your energy into helping these other ladies. I'm sure you'll have plenty of work to do on their stories."

Lady Sandy cuts her eyes at Penelope. The last time I saw a look like that was when I was thirteen and my grandmother made me go get a switch off the tree when she saw me kissing a boy. That's a mama-don't-play look she's giving, and I don't want any part of it.

"Listen, I'm sure you are all capable of articulating your words. You're all evangelists. You're good with words," James says. "But you will find that preaching and writing are not the same thing. If you trust me with your stories, I promise to make them even better. I would like to speak to each of you alone for a few minutes to get a feel for what you're trying to do."

When James takes the first person into Lady Sandy's study, Penelope rushes to my side and grabs my hand.

"Can we chat for a little bit?" she whispers. "Outside of here."

I nod and follow Penelope out of the room. She takes me into a huge library with floor-to-ceiling shelves lining the walls.

"It's my father's library," Penelope says. "He writes some of his sermons in here."

"Wow. I know God has given him some good stuff in here."

"Yes, He has. My parents being so powerful puts a lot of pressure on me, though."

"How so? It would seem like it opens doors, if anything."

Penelope sits at her father's desk, picks up a Bible, and holds it to her chest. "It does open doors, of course. But I think because they didn't have a son, they want me to be the one to carry on the ministry torch."

"I thought that's what you wanted."

"Oh, I do want to be in ministry, no doubt, but I don't want to be stuck in a church. I don't want to do what they do. I want to travel all over the world, prophesying and praying over people. I think that's what I'm called to do."

"So do it."

Penelope sets the Bible down and shakes her head sadly. "You don't know what it's like to disobey my mother. She's . . . well, she's pretty tough. That's all I'll say."

"You can be and do whatever you want to do, Penelope."

"Not if I want my parents to finance it."

Now this is the part I really don't understand. I have never had parents who financed and bankrolled me, so I don't know what that looks like. As soon as I hit adulthood it was sink to the bottom of the ocean or bust my arms through the waves like I didn't have a choice. And I didn't. Swimming was my only option.

"Tell me what you wrote about," I say to Penelope.

"I talked about my real altar-call experience. Not when I first went down at the age of ten and asked to be baptized, but the one I had after my abortion when I was sixteen."

Now I feel bad. I totally judged Penelope before. I guess she really did have some adversity that she needed to take to God.

"That is going to be very powerful, Penelope. It will speak to the hearts of a lot of young women."

"I hope so, although I really wrote it for me. It's a secret I've been carrying around for a long time."

"A secret from your church family?"

"And my parents. They don't know."

My eyes widen with shock. "Are you going to tell them before the book comes out?"

"I'm thinking I will let my mom read it when she gets a draft of the book from the publisher. Do you think that's a good idea?"

"Only if you think it's best to blindside

her with the information."

"I think that if I tell her ahead of time she'll try to keep me from revealing it."

This is a lot. Then it occurs to me that Penelope must want my help, because why else would she be telling me about this?

"Do you want my advice on this?" I ask.

A look of relief washes over Penelope's face. "Yes, please! I don't know what to do. I've been carrying this guilt around for years. I just want it off me. I think that may be what's hindering my prophetic gift from blossoming through."

I feel a vein near my temple start throbbing. Not this mess again.

"Like when did you know you were a prophetess?" she asks. "I wonder if I'm just a late bloomer."

"We talked about this before, right? It was before I was saved, that part I do know."

"So was it when you were a little girl? Or were you grown? I'm just wondering if there are some signs that I may have missed."

Maybe, just maybe, if I tell her the truth of what it's like to have this gift, then she'll truly embrace what God has called her to do.

"The first vision I ever had was of my grandfather crying. I was little and it did scare me. I wasn't used to seeing my grandfather like that. He was strong."

"Were you able to give him a word, though? What did you say to him?"

"So I don't necessarily hear exact words from God every time. Sometimes I hear someone say something in the vision. Sometimes there is no vision, it's just a very strong sense that I should share a particular scripture with a particular person. I just trust it."

"Wow. I know God wants to use me that way. I have a feeling about that. I'm just going to trust that."

"God is already using you, Penelope. You've got to know that. You were great on the show episodes too."

"I was your sidekick on the show episodes. I was like Vanna White. I wasn't the main attraction."

"When we preach, God is supposed to be the main attraction. Let's not lose sight of what we're doing."

"Of course you're right. You are. This is why you're the prophetess and I'm the psalmist. I'll get there."

I don't tell her what I want to say — that some people never get where she's trying to go. And that even if she gets there, it probably won't be what she thinks it will be. I'm at what some people would call the top of my game, but my husband is acting funny, I had to fake a prophecy, and I don't know what else may fall apart.

Instead I say, "You're going to have exactly what God has for you, Penelope. I hope it's what you're dreaming about."

"It will be. God only gives good gifts."

Lady Sandy walks into the room and looks at the two of us as if we've been caught with a pilfered cookie.

"Penelope, it's your turn to talk to James," Lady Sandy says.

Penelope jumps up from the desk. "Okay," she says and rushes out of the library.

Lady Sandy turns her attention to me. "Do you realize how much of an opportunity it is for you to appear with some of these women? You'll be able to get your own book deal after this."

"I realize that. If I do write something else, it'll be a book with Greg about one-on-one encounters with Christ that happen in the New Testament."

Lady Sandy laughs out loud. "Nobody will publish that, because nobody wants to read that."

"Excuse me? People will want to read our testimonies, but not want to experience Jesus?"

"If you are ever going to be successful,

you need to learn about the people you are ministering to. Most of them don't really want Jesus, because they don't really want to change."

"Isn't it our job to give them Jesus anyway?"

Lady Sandy laughs again. "If they want Jesus, they'll get Him. He's not hiding."

I think she's wrong. I think the people are looking for Jesus. But when they do come looking for Him, we've been handing them blessings and prophecies. I wonder what will happen if I flip it. If I start giving them Jesus, will Lady Sandy notice? Will anyone notice the difference?

CHAPTER 27
FELICIA

When I get to my office the day after my failed attempt at terrorizing Dr. Tomlinson and my visit to Lance and Jasmine, Mr. Bailey is waiting outside my door. I smile. I knew this was coming. How could it not be? I don't think Lance would say anything, because he's as much in violation of the team policy as I am. But of course, Dr. Tomlinson's scared self snitched, and now I'm a danger to the team.

"Hello, Felicia. Can we step inside your office and chat for a minute?" Mr. Bailey asks.

"Why do we need to step inside? You can fire me from the hallway, can't you?"

Mr. Bailey clears his throat. "You might want to hear what I have to say. And I need to say it in private."

I glance over at Sharon. "Well then, maybe I could use a cup of chai."

Sharon looks at Mr. Bailey and he nods.

She jumps up from her desk and fixes the cup.

I walk into my soon-to-be former office and sit down at my desk for probably the last time. Mr. Bailey sits down in the chair in front of me. I wait for Sharon to come in with my chai, and I nod my thanks. She looks nervous as she rushes out of the office. I wonder if she played a part in this. If so, she's on my list too.

"So . . ."

"Yes, I'm sure you know part of the reason I'm here," Mr. Bailey says.

"I'm not quite sure. I think you should go ahead and tell me."

"I spoke with Dr. Tomlinson last night, Felicia."

I give him a fake confused look. "Why on earth would you be speaking with my ob-gyn? Did you have any questions about my health questionnaire?"

Mr. Bailey frowns. "I know you threatened him, and I also know why."

"Oh, so you know he murdered my baby."

"He stated that you chose to abort your child. If you're calling it murder, and that's your choice, you are the one who authorized it."

I feel my irritation turn into fury. "What is this about? Are you firing me or what?"

"I made you aware of our non-fraternization clause . . ."

"After it was too late."

"You were provided an employee handbook on your first day."

"Are you firing me or what?"

Mr. Bailey reaches into his suit jacket pocket and pulls out an envelope. "We're asking for a resignation, and this should sustain you while you find alternate employment."

I snatch the envelope, then toss my head back and laugh. "Will you also be giving me a recommendation letter to provide to my future employers?"

"I'm afraid not, but we will not make any negative statements regarding your time with us."

A security guard appears at the door.

"Oh, so this is how it's going to be?" I ask. "You're going to have me walked out by security?"

"After what happened with Dr. Tomlinson, don't you think that's a wise choice on my part?"

I laugh some more. This is all incredibly funny. Then I look down at the check. Twenty thousand dollars. That's how much my baby was worth?

"How much did y'all pay the other girl?"

"I don't know what you mean."

"The other woman that Lance impregnated and then had her child murdered. How much did you pay her?"

"If there were another such woman, I would assume that her settlement would've been private."

"Did you give her more than twenty thousand dollars for her baby's carcass?"

Mr. Bailey swallows. "Ms. Caldwell . . ."

"Pay me what you owe me or I'm going to the media and the police."

"Do you think they will believe a stalker?"

"I haven't stalked anyone."

"Hmm . . . I have heard otherwise. In fact, there are some police reports that have been filed by Lance and his wife, about a strange woman who has been lurking around their home. The woman hasn't been identified yet, but it's only a matter of time."

"Pay me what you owe me."

"I don't owe you anything, Ms. Caldwell. I was authorized to cut the twenty thousand dollar check in lieu of the unemployment you will not be able to seek because of your resignation."

"I'm not resigning for anything less than a million dollars. Your organization can afford it."

Mr. Bailey looks at the security guard.

Then he waves a hand to dismiss him. "I'll be out in a moment," he says.

I smile. "So am I going to become a millionaire today?"

"You'll be required to sign this confidentiality agreement, and you will not be able to pursue any recourse, media engagements, or publicity against the Atlanta Crows, Lance, or Dr. Tomlinson." He slides the papers across my desk and hands me a pen.

"I'm not signing this until I read it."

"I will have someone bring over the check in an hour or so. In the meantime, you can pack up your office."

"Wire transfer, please. A check can be cancelled."

"Wire transfer then."

"You can use the bank account on my direct deposit paperwork. I will vacate the office and sign your little agreement when the funds are transferred."

Mr. Bailey stands and leaves my office without even a good-bye. How rude.

I pull up my bank account information on my tablet and wait for those funds to hit the account. There's nothing here I want to pack up. Nothing I want to keep.

One million dollars may not be enough to compensate me for the life of my child, but it's enough for a new start. As crazy as this situation is, maybe it's the blessing. Maybe the money is what Pastor Nya's prophecy was about.

I've got to believe that. Because if I don't, then what do I have left?

CHAPTER 28
NYA

"Greg! Greg!"

I run through the house screaming my husband's name. Where is he? He's not in his office or the bedroom. Let me check the man cave.

When I open the door to the finished basement, Greg walks into the kitchen laughing.

"What is it, Nya?"

"Oh! Where were you?"

"I was in the bathroom. Am I allowed to use the bathroom today?"

I burst into laughter. "Yes, you are allowed to use the bathroom."

"I thought you changed some rules when you got back from filming your little fancy talk show."

My laughter continues. "It's fancy? My talk show is fancy?"

"Yes. You and Penelope Bowens trotting around wearing designer clothes and shoes and hair down to the middle of your back, fixing everybody's life. Real fancy."

I'm so glad to hear Greg being in good spirits about the show. Even though he's teasing me, when I showed him the recordings of the shows, he was proud of how Penelope and I ministered to those women.

"Well, guess what? It's about to get even more fancy! They love us. We got offered a full season by the network!"

Greg picks me up and spins me around. "You're gonna be a star, babe."

"I don't want to be a star."

"What if God wants you to be a star?" Greg asks as he places me back on the floor and strokes my hair.

"I think He wants us both to have an international ministry. He showed it to me — remember?"

Greg nods. "I remember. As long as you don't forget God's promise to *us,* I'm going to support you in this."

"This means so much, honey. I love you."

"I love you more."

"You know, they're offering me a nice check for this. A pretty nice check."

Greg laughs out loud. "How nice?"

"Nice enough for us to finally upgrade our house. Come on, Greg. We're not using funds collected by the church."

"You want an Arlington mansion?"

"I was thinking more like Southlake."

Greg's eyes widen. "Oh, that check is real nice!"

"Six figures nice . . ."

"I will think about it. Maybe if I can have my own personal ministry man cave."

"You can have whatever you want. This is our increase, not mine."

"Oh, I know what I forgot to tell you. You got a package today," Greg says. Then he steps out of the kitchen, presumably to bring the package.

When he walks back in, he is carrying a pretty sizable box. He sets it on the kitchen counter and uses a box cutter to open it.

"It's books," he says. "You're a real published author now."

I grab the book from Greg's hands and squeal. Here it is, in my hands, the first book I've ever participated in writing. *Take Us to the King: Women at the Altar* is the title, and our stories are accompanied by our pictures.

My cell phone buzzes on the counter, and when I pick it up I see Penelope's number on the caller ID.

"Hey, girl," I say when I answer. "Did you get your copies of the book yet? Is this the final version?"

"Hey. It's not the final. These are the review copies. My mom got hers first and read it already."

Her somber tone tells me that Lady Sandy must not have reacted well to the news about Penelope's abortion.

"What did she think of it all?" I ask.

"She accused me of trying to destroy her and my father's ministry."

I close my eyes and sigh. I knew that Lady Sandy was going to trip about Penelope's revelations, but I had no idea how hard she was going to take it.

"Do you want me to talk to her?" I ask. "I can if you think that will help."

"She won't listen to you. She doesn't listen to anyone, not even my father."

"Why don't you let me try?"

Penelope gasps for air like she's been crying for days. "O-okay."

"Calm down. I'm gonna call her right now."

I disconnect the call from Penelope and dial Lady Sandy's number.

"Is everything okay?" Greg asks.

"No, apparently not."

The phone rings four times before Lady Sandy answers it. "Hello, Nya," she says.

"Lady Sandy. I got the review copies of the books in the mail. Who should I share them with?"

This is me trying to break the ice before asking Lady Sandy about why she's persecuting her daughter.

"You shouldn't share them with anyone," she says. "I've just gotten off the phone with the publisher. These review copies are to be destroyed."

"But why?"

"Penelope's testimony needs to be removed. She, like an idiot, decided to share a family secret in her passage. We can't send these to anyone."

"I haven't had the opportunity to read it yet, but don't you think Penelope has the right to tell her own truth?" I ask.

"She can tell her own truth when she gets her own book deal and pays her own bills. She's not going to derail my project and make it be all about her."

"But Lady Sandy . . ."

"Did she ask you to call me? You don't think I notice how you two always have your heads together? I may not be young like Penelope, or look damn near white like you, so no one is asking me to be on anyone's television show. But don't think I can't make all of this disappear."

I want to tell her how much I don't care if

it all disappears, but I don't, for Penelope's sake.

"Are you going to let her write something else?"

"The ghostwriter will handle it. He will write what I tell him to write for Penelope."

"I guess that's that, then."

"It is. And don't get any ideas about telling anyone outside our circle about this."

"Don't worry, I won't. That's your family business."

"You got that right. I will see you at the book release party. It's going to be a grand affair. Ministers from all over Dallas are going to be there."

"I will see you then, Lady Sandy."

I guess the look of shock is still on my face as I set my phone down on the kitchen counter, because Greg tilts his head to one side and frowns.

"What was that about?"

"Lady Sandy. She's . . . she's not the woman I thought she was."

Greg shakes his head and sighs. "I could've told you that. But this is not about her, right? You're not doing it for her."

"No. I'm doing this for Jesus."

I wouldn't walk away from this book, television show, or the Suddenly Blessing movement now if someone paid me. Because I'm afraid. I'm frightened that she'll take my fake prophecy and spin it into something even worse and uglier. I have to stay the course until it runs out of steam and a new, hot, and fresh message catches on. It won't take long.

This is the monster I created. I have to be the one to put it in the cage . . . or worse, put it down for good.

CHAPTER 29
FELICIA

Finally, it's dark enough. I grab the tools from the seat of my car. Gloves, a can of gasoline, matches. And a crowbar. Time to do a little damage.

I thought about burning their house down, because I don't care if they live or die. But I decided not to damn my own soul to hell. Why would I do that?

I haven't done anything wrong. There's still time for me to get what God has for me. I never would've thought that Lance was the one if it hadn't been for that stupid prophecy. That lie from the pits of hell. That "suddenly" curse that Nya Hampstead put on me. She's to blame for this, but Lance played his part.

The gas can is too heavy to carry, so I drag it to its destination. The garage that houses Lance's car collection.

I use the crowbar to break the glass in one of the windows. Then I reach into the window to try and find a door handle or lock. Of course, it wouldn't be anything like on a TV show or movie, where the door handle is always right inside the window. Right inside this window is nothing but wall.

I can't get in this way.

I circle the garage, pulling the gas can next to me, and all I see is more glass windows exactly the same as the first. In frustration, I start breaking them all out. Then I stop. This is noisy, and I definitely want to do more damage than a little bit of broken glass. Is that an alarm I hear?

Then I have an idea. Since I can't seem to get into the garage, I'll just pour gasoline in through the windows. I can still start the fire without going inside. The only problem is that I can't hoist the gas can up to the window. It's too heavy.

I can, however, soak something with gasoline and toss it into the window. I look around for leaves or foliage. Anything that I can soak with gasoline. But there's nothing. Apparently, Lance's idea of landscaping is concrete, asphalt, and marble. I look down at my feet. My sneakers will do. I soak one of them in gasoline and toss it in the window.

Then I do the other shoe, and toss it in another window.

I light one of the matches and carefully drop it to the floor. I think it might not work for a second, and then I start to smell the smoke.

I know I need to do more before the fire alarms start to go off, so I step out of my leggings and tear them into pieces. I soak these along with pieces from my hoodie. After I soak them all, I push them through windows along with more lit matches, being careful not to get any gasoline on my body or cause an explosion.

The fire is taking off good now, but I want to give it just a little bit more fuel. I pull my human-hair lace-front wig off my head, and toss it to the ground. After soaking it in gasoline really well, I take it around to the front of the garage and light it. When I toss it in the window, I drop everything and run.

As I scurry back to my car in my Victoria's Secret undies, I'm glad I moved fast, because something explodes. The sound of it causes the lights in Lance's mansion to come on. I speed off in my rental car before anyone sees me, and the fire will take care of any evidence.

I know that Lance will be able to replace every one of those cars. He can bring those back and I can't bring my child back. But I want him to know that he's not forgiven.

It's not okay what he's done, and a million dollars won't do anything but give me more resources if I should ever choose to reach out and touch him.

But my work here is done. I don't have a bit more business with Lance, Dr. Tomlinson's weak, scared behind, or Jasmine's stupid, low-esteem-having self. They were low-hanging fruit.

Nya Hampstead is another story. No matter how long it takes, I'll figure out how to make her pay for what her lie has done to me.

I press hard on the gas pedal and increase my speed, because I don't have time to waste. I have a plane to catch in the morning.

I'm going to Texas, where they say everything's bigger. I'm planning to supersize my anointing, supersize my finances, and supersize my blessing. I'm sure they need grant writers in the big ole state of Texas. I can make a lot of money there to add to this stash I already have. Suddenly I'm feeling in my spirit that Nya Hampstead isn't ready for me. And that's exactly how I want her. Unprepared.

■ ■ ■ ■

PART II
FIVE YEARS LATER

■ ■ ■ ■

CHAPTER 30
NYA

After five years on the air, *Suddenly Blessed* is moving from its seven o'clock evening slot to a four in the afternoon spot. This is the time slot where Oprah, Ellen, and Dr. Phil became popular. The time when stay-at-home, middle-class moms have picked up their children from elementary school and have already fed them milk and cookies. It's the time for us to cross over and become mainstream. A sweet spot.

Because of this huge change, the network wanted to meet with me and Penelope about strategy, branding, marketing, and all that. We now have a *team.* We didn't have a team before; we had a few stylists and Monet Barnes calling the shots from the sidelines.

"The first thing we want is for Penelope to stop calling Nya 'evangelist' and 'pastor' during the show," Bill, the executive producer, says.

Penelope's eyes widen. "I didn't even realize I was doing that."

"We want you two to seem like girlfriends," Bill says.

"We are girlfriends," I reply. "We don't have to just *seem* like we are. We're not acting."

"And she is an evangelist," Penelope says.

Monet clears her throat and raises one hand to stop the conversation. "Everyone who follows you realizes that you both are in ministry. This isn't taking anything away from that. It's just that the show isn't a pulpit. It's a talk show. We're going to do makeovers and motivation. Penelope makes over their look, and Nya motivates them on what to do to get that blessing."

"Except that we're not going to call it a *blessing* anymore," Bill says.

Monet nods. "That's right. With the new time slot, the show is going to be called *Suddenly You.*"

I can't even fix my mouth to form words. Which is fine, because Penelope's mouth is already opening wide.

"So, it's not about Jesus anymore? Who exactly is Evangelist Nya . . . I mean just Nya . . . supposed to be motivating them with?"

"Listen, we're not saying it's not about

Jesus. We're just not going to say Jesus. We're going to say their faith, or belief system."

"But what if their belief system is devil worship or something like that? What if they're a witch?" Penelope asks. "I don't know what to do with that. I'm straight Jesus over here."

Bill looks at Monet with a confused expression. "I thought you talked this over with Bishop Bowens. Didn't he say this wasn't going to be an issue?"

"Bishop Bowens is making decisions on the show?" I ask.

"No, no he's not," Monet says. "He is simply acting as an adviser to us. He believes this approach will actually open the door to inviting more people to Jesus. You'll build a bigger following for your conferences, and that's where you can Jesus them to death if you want."

"Jesus them to life, maybe?" I ask. "I don't know about this."

"Think of it as advertisement for your churches that we pay you to do," Bill says.

"It's not like you aren't making money too," Penelope scoffs. "The advertisers must like us if we're switching time slots. Are we talking about a raise for us too?"

"Yes, that's the best part. You both will be

paid one-and-a-half million per season. We've already signed on for two seasons in this slot. That's unheard-of."

I blink at hearing the amount we'll be paid. We both got two hundred fifty thousand per season for *Suddenly Blessed.* That was a lot of money. More than I ever expected to make sitting down and ministering to people. This, and the insane amount of money we make from the conferences and speaking engagements, is almost scary. But our church is paid off, our house is paid off, we have a full-time staff at the church, who receive both salaries and benefits. We've adopted a ministry school in Cameroon and are building homes for twenty of the students' families. We are blessed beyond measure, and the rain continues to fall.

"Where do I need to sign?" Penelope asks. I guess she started calculating how many shoes and handbags she could buy with that check, and her misgivings disappeared.

Bill slides a new contract across the table to Penelope and one toward me. "I know you both have to let your legal teams look over these."

"Absolutely," I say. "And my husband."

"Do you think Greg will object to one-and-a-half million dollars?" Penelope asks.

Greg isn't motivated by money, nor is he

impressed by it. He wouldn't care if they were offering a billion dollars. If he didn't feel God was pleased with it, he wouldn't do it.

"He might. I don't think he will, but it's possible," I say.

"Well, you ladies better put your heads together and pray that he doesn't object. This is an opportunity that will only come around once. It's not often that network TV executives want to mainstream a pastor and a pastor's daughter."

"Not Jesus on the main line. Jesus on the mainstream," Penelope says with a chuckle. "Sounds like my daddy's dream come true."

I have no doubt that Bishop Bowens will press Penelope forward even if Greg doesn't want me to do the show. He'll want his daughter's name to be known in Hollywood, and by every soccer mom in Suburbia, USA.

"So, I hear you're something like a gypsy fortune teller," Bill says to me. "Do you think you could read my palm and tell me my future?"

The silence is so thick, one would think the air in here is made of corn syrup. Did this uninformed beast just call me a gypsy fortune teller?

"I don't do that."

Bill narrows his eyes and looks at Monet.

"I thought you said . . ."

"I said she's a prophetess," Monet says. "And it's not a joke. She told me something only God knew about."

"Well, what's the point of that? You already knew about what she told you?" Bill asks.

I stare at him, not blinking, trying to decide if I should educate him. Then, after a long awkward silence, I choose to explain.

"Sometimes when I prophesy to someone it's to give them confirmation about a decision they're about to make or to help them forgive themselves from a choice they already made. It's not always about learning the future, although many times it is. Sometimes it's about getting free from the past."

Bill looks skeptical. "So you're saying you can't see my future."

"I only see what God shows me. He's not saying anything about you."

"I feel like that was an insult," Bill says. "But maybe that's a good thing. If God isn't talking about me, maybe I'm not doing too badly at all. I might just make it through the pearly gates."

"You should probably visit Nya's and her husband's church," Monet says. "They'll introduce you to Jesus."

"I'm good. Seems like every time I visit a black church I get separated from my cash and hit on by a gay choir member," Bill says, his smirk almost looking like a sneer.

I gather the contract documents and slide them into my briefcase. I try not to let his negative view of the church take away from the fact that Penelope and I are about to reach a whole new audience.

"Well, you're always welcome," I say. "We don't turn anybody away."

"You're open to all the wretches, huh?"

I nod. "Absolutely. Who needs a hospital but the sick?"

"So you're saying I'm sick?"

"The Bible says it. We're available anytime for you to come get your healing."

"I'll remember that," Bill says. "Next Sunday, as soon as I kick the girl outta my bed, I may just come to church."

"Your choice."

I don't doubt that we won't see him anytime soon. People like Mr. Bill need something or someone to break them down before they go running back to Jesus.

Greg and I used to be able to touch these kinds of people with a message of redemption. Now something is missing, and it feels like we're just trying to make it from one day to the next.

CHAPTER 31
NYA

These days, Greg's laughter doesn't always come with the correct corresponding emotion. He's laughing right now, but it's not joyful. I've not said anything funny. I just showed him the new contract for my talk show. And his highly inappropriate response is laughter.

"What's funny, Greg?"

"You keep pushing. Harder and harder. This started with one little speaking engagement. Then one little tour. Then one little television show. You don't even know how to stop, do you?"

"Why should I stop walking through doors that God is opening?"

"I am still not convinced this is God's doing. Every opportunity you've got over the past five years has pulled you farther away from this ministry. And me."

"Everything I've done over these five years has given our ministry a voice. You're a household name all over the world now. We couldn't afford a website, let alone airtime on cable TV, but because of open doors, we've been able to truly become an international church. Our name isn't a joke anymore."

Greg shakes his head and tosses the contract on our bed. Our king-size bed with sheets so decadent I almost don't want to get out of bed in the morning. Sheets purchased because of my opportunities.

"When is the last time we preached together, Nya? Do you remember the tag team? You are a co-pastor, but in name only. Your congregation has to watch you on TV. It's like I'm a single parent."

A huge sigh escapes me. He's right. We haven't preached together in over a year. But it's not because I haven't wanted to. It just seems like we are never on the same page anymore when it comes to hearing from God. It's just easier to let Greg run everything at Love First. He's a great pastor. The congregation loves him.

"Do you want to preach together on Sunday?" I ask.

Greg laughs again. "What's the message going to be? Suddenly you?"

"No, Greg."

"Then please share. What do you want to

preach about?"

"I've been doing a study on the one-on-one conversations Christ had with people. I'm thinking of writing a devotional on these conversations."

Greg's not laughing anymore. He sits down next to me on the bed.

"Please continue," he says when I stop talking.

"Well, I'd like to start with the woman at the well. I know it's a much preached-about passage, but I just love how Christ dealt with her there."

"I know the passage. In John, chapter four. Jesus acknowledged her sin, told the woman who He was and . . ."

"How to worship. In spirit and in truth."

Greg smiles at me and takes my hand. "I guess you do still know how to tag team."

"How could I not, Greg? We are covenant partners. I love you."

"Let me run you some bathwater, then. What kind of bubble bath do you want to use?"

Now I'm laughing, but it's the joyful kind. "Who said I need a bath?"

"You just got home from Atlanta, and you are trying to prove your love to me. So get yourself smelling good and prove yourself, woman."

"I didn't say anything about proving my love."

"You didn't? Oh, then that must've been me."

Greg stands and goes into our huge master bath. I hear the water come on in the jetted bathtub that I insisted on having.

"Since you didn't reply, I'm putting that peaches-and-honey bubble bath in. It's my favorite," Greg calls from the bathroom.

I get up and follow him. The scent of peaches fills the air now, mixed with the steam from the hot water. A bath is actually pretty appealing right now.

"So, we can go over our sermon before I go do the conference this weekend. I leave on Friday."

"Oh right. Well, are you going to be back on Sunday?"

"My flight leaves Saturday evening. I'm on the last flight out of New York City."

"We can start on our sermon after you handle your wifely business."

I shake my head. "Ugh. We're gonna write a sermon after getting it on?"

"It's the perfect time. My head will be nice and clear."

I laugh out loud. "This is blasphemous."

"It is not! Sex is a gift from God. So we're about to get it on, and then give honor and

227

praise where it is due."

I slap Greg with a washcloth. "Okay. Get outta here so I can bathe."

"What if I want to watch? We can play David and Bathsheba."

"You are doing too much, Greg. They were adulterers."

"Yeah, well, they got married eventually. I bet he still watched her bathe."

"Out."

Greg chuckles as he heads for the door. "Okay. Well, I'll be out here waiting. Patiently. Well, not really patiently, so hurry up."

The nervousness I felt in my spirit regarding telling Greg about the new show disappears. I know that he isn't totally on board, but at least he's stopped standing in my way. He voices his objections and then keeps it moving. That much I do appreciate.

But out of everyone, I want him to be happy for me. Greg is truly my best friend. He's the one I know I can count on. He prays with and for me. I want him to rejoice with me too. I'm sure preaching with him on Sunday will be a good step toward getting our mojo back. Baby steps toward our destiny are fine. As long as we're moving in the right direction.

Chapter 32
Felicia

Today is my four-year anniversary being a member of Love First International, where my pastors are Greg and Nya Hampstead. They don't know me, though. No one here does. It's easy to hide in a congregation of thousands when you come in late, leave early, and don't participate in any church activities other than Sunday service.

But today is my coming-out party. It's time for me to meet the man and woman of God.

Actually, I'll just be meeting the *man* of God. Nya is out of town, again. This time, according to the church announcements, she is launching her Get Yo' Blessing conference in New York City. Every major gospel artist in the country is going to be there, and she'll be signing copies of her book, *Unlocking Your Blessings.*

I bought a copy. I am not impressed.

When I moved here with my hush money,

I bought a beautiful brownstone less than a mile from where my pastors built their home.

Making contact with Greg is not going to be all that easy. He's got a huge entourage. That happened after Nya got famous. But I'm patient. I've waited four years for this. Five years since Nya lied to me and told me I would be blessed.

For a while I was okay. Lance tried to come for me about those cars until I reminded him that he's a murderer. I paused on that move to Texas, because I was thinking maybe I was wrong. Maybe I wasn't supposed to go after Nya. I just waited for confirmation — a sign on what I should do. And then I started having pain in my pelvic area. I didn't think it was anything at first, maybe hormones. And then my abdomen started to swell. It was tender to the touch and warm.

When I went to the emergency room, I was told that I had a horrible infection from tissue left behind when I had the abortion. It had progressed so badly that I had to have a complete hysterectomy. It saved my life, they said. But now I can never give life again.

Even though the doctors tried to convince me that it wasn't my fault, I knew what it was. God wasn't through punishing me yet.

Atlanta is behind me now. It's in the rearview mirror. I'd thought about doing more to Lance and Jasmine; making them pay even more. But Lance has his own consequences coming from God, and who knows? Every now and then I may just reach out to make sure he knows I still have the power to get him, even if I don't act on it.

Anyway, the real person behind all of this is Nya Hampstead. Even though Lance was definitely on assignment from the devil, the only reason I fell for what he was selling is because I was looking around every corner for this blessing Nya had promised me. She said that I was lonely and God was going to send a relationship, vision, and purpose. None of what happened to me since she told that prophe-lie has been a gift from God. She is a false prophet and she must be exposed to the masses.

It's obvious to me that she shouldn't even be in ministry anyway. She doesn't honor her husband. She goes all over the country speaking and appearing on talk shows and whatnot. She has a Jezebel spirit. I can see it all over her when she struts across the pulpit with that fire-red hair. She looks like her name should be Babylon.

At the end of service, Pastor Greg stands

in front of the church greeting people, sur-
rounded by his entourage. He says hello,
prays for some, chats with others. And it's
only for a limited amount of time. When
the bodyguards say he has to go, he waves
to the rest of those waiting in line.

But I've been watching. I know the way
beyond the veil.

Right before service lets out, I walk up to
the front of the church and slide into a pew
next to the church's head mother-in-charge,
Mother Olivia. I have purposely dressed
very modestly for this occasion. My off-
white church suit has a skirt that falls to the
middle of my calf and while the jacket is
tailored and fitted it isn't snug. If I want to
cozy up to Mother Olivia, then I can't look
like a woman trying to get in bed with the
pastor.

Mother Olivia whips her head to the side
as I sit and gives me a scolding look.

"*This* is the mothers' row," she says in a
harsh whisper.

I nod and smile. "I know."

"Are you a mother of this church?" she
asks, when it's clear that I'm not an elderly
biddy like she is.

"No, but I wanted to talk to one," I
whisper. "The most important one. You."

Mother Olivia sits up straight and runs

her hand over her silver curls. "I am the most important one. You're absolutely right about that."

"I have been attending this church for a few years, and I am a professional grant writer. I heard Pastor Greg talking about needing volunteers to help apply for grants. I've done this for many years, and I would love to volunteer my time."

Mother Olivia pats my hand. "What's your name, baby?"

"I'm Felicia Caldwell."

"I will make sure to introduce you after service. You just sit right here."

I settle in next to Mother Olivia until the end of service. I knew she'd be easy. Like taking peppermints from a grandma.

When the congregation has been dismissed and the majority of them are heading over to the Love First café for the soul-food lunch buffet, I'm with Mother Olivia. We walk straight up to the front of the greeting line, arm in arm. No one tries to stop us — not even the church security. They smile at Mother Olivia and wave her on through.

Greg extends his arms to hug Mother Olivia as she approaches. I wait patiently while they say their hellos.

Then Mother Olivia reaches out to me.

"Pastor, I want you to meet this young lady. Her name is Felicia Caldwell and she's a professional grant writer. She can help you get that money we need for the youth center."

Pastor Greg shakes my hand. "It's a pleasure to meet you, Sister Caldwell. Are you a member?"

"I am. I've been here going on four years."

"Really? Wow. We've got all kinds of resources sitting right in the pews."

I nod. "There are several funding options that I've identified for your youth center. If there is after-school tutoring, a literacy initiative, and a gymnasium promoting healthy kids, I can get you close to a million dollars in grant money."

"Really?" I've got Greg's attention now. "And you've done this before?"

"Most recently I worked as a grant coordinator for the Atlanta Crows."

"The NBA team? We definitely need to sit down and talk then. Do you have a card where I can have my secretary reach out?"

I produce a card from my jacket pocket, and Mother Olivia takes it.

"Honey, if you give Pastor Greg this card it'll be lost and never found again. I will make sure to get you on his calendar for this week. What is your Wednesday looking like?"

I give Mother Olivia a huge smile. "My Wednesday is wide open."

"So Wednesday morning at ten a.m. it is," Mother Olivia says.

Greg smiles too. "Then it's set. See you then."

Step one was a breeze. Almost like God has His hand on this plan of mine. He clearly wants Nya humbled as well. I've got faith that our meeting will go as well as the introduction. Step two will be to show Greg exactly what he's missing, and how I'm the answer to his prayers.

CHAPTER 33
NYA

Greg isn't speaking to me this evening. It's not my fault that my flight got delayed and I didn't make it back for Sunday service today. I don't have any control over the weather. But it seems like lately Greg is blaming me for everything that goes wrong.

"Hey, babe," I say as I peek my head into his office. "I'm done unpacking. You want to go and get some hibachi or something? I'm starved, and way too tired to cook."

"No, thanks. I ate at the church café. I'm still full from smothered chicken and rice."

His dry tone bothers me, but I don't want to start an argument with him, so I keep my irritation to myself.

"So, I was thinking maybe we should sneak away for a few days. Let's just leave tomorrow and go to Miami."

Greg scoffs. "No can do. I've got meetings scheduled all week. While you're off touring all over the country, someone has to keep this ministry running."

"Can the meetings be rescheduled? I think we need to take some time for us."

"We'd have plenty of time for us if you weren't always gone."

"I don't want to argue, Greg."

"Well, then don't start an argument. I'll have Lena get me a date on your calendar."

"You're going to have your assistant pick dates for our getaway? That's not church business. That's something we should be doing together."

Why did I say this? Greg looks up at me and bursts into his inappropriate laughter again. There's sarcasm dripping from his tone.

"Together? That word isn't even in your vocabulary anymore. So let's not go there."

"Greg, I'm sorry that I didn't make it back in time to preach. It was the weather."

"If this was the first time, or the fifth time, or even the tenth time you did this to me, then maybe I would give you a pass. But this is every time you go to one of your conferences. Your phone magically goes to voice mail whenever I call, your flights end up rescheduled. If I didn't know you better, I'd think . . ."

"You'd think what, Greg?"

"I'd think you've got a lover traveling with you."

A lover? A lover! Oh no he didn't. I'm so furious that I can't even respond to this. How dare he accuse me of adultery when I'm out doing ministry assignments?

"My mother always told me that if a man starts accusing you out of the blue of cheating, he must have a woman on the side."

"Your mother said it? So that certainly makes it valid."

I feel my eyes roll before I even try to stop them. He's cracking on my mom now? This is extremely petty.

"So are we going away together, or what?"

"Nah. You're not going to sandwich me in between tour dates like I'm an obligation you forgot to keep. I'm good."

I step out of his office and storm to our bedroom with tears in my eyes. Sometimes I wish I never gave that suddenly blessing prophecy. Ever since, my life has been going full speed ahead. I want to put the brakes on, but now too many people are counting on me.

It's crazy how one little message could change so many lives. Did God know I would choose the wrong thing to do? Is this Him turning it all around and making it for everyone's good?

No. It can't be that, because God's blessings don't come with sorrow. And behind all of this, I feel only guilt and shame at the perversion of my gift.

God, I know that you are faithful and just, and forgive our sins when we repent. And I've repented for this sin over and over again. But please, Lord, I beg you to remove this shame from me. If you want for us to be blessed, please allow me to walk in victory. If I should walk away from this, Lord, create a path for me.

My silent prayer comes from my heart. I only hope God is listening. I will be looking, in faith, for the open door. And I pray, when it presents itself, that I have enough courage to walk through.

CHAPTER 34
FELICIA

This morning, for the first time since my baby was murdered, I woke up feeling well rested and refreshed. Maybe it's because today is my meeting with Pastor Greg. He has some of the kindest eyes I've ever seen. Those long eyelashes make him look almost angelic. I'm sure he has to fight off the women to maintain his marital vows.

That's why I have to take a different approach than I usually would. Pastor Greg is an extraordinary man, so the ordinary path to his heart won't work. Most men, you'd go straight to that little head that makes more decisions than the logical head.

Pastor Greg will be ready for that. And so will the staff that he has surrounding him — especially Mother Olivia.

I choose my outfit carefully. A simple green wrap dress. It is modestly sexy, but only because after five years of working out (and a few enhancements) my body looks sexy in just about anything I put on.

I've put together a portfolio of my previous grant work, and recommendation letters from some people that I've worked with in the past. Unfortunately, I don't have anything to show from my time with the Atlanta Crows, but I know that if Greg does his research, they wouldn't dare say anything negative about me. I think Mr. Bailey probably knows I had something to do with the fire at Lance's house. But who wants one of their star players to be charged with murdering my baby? They should be glad I didn't do more.

I drive over to the church in my white Range Rover. I have found that with black folk, it is always important to look like money. Because a woman with money can't be desperate for anything, especially not a man. A woman with money is viewed with awe and reverence, and church folk who always are looking for that financial blessing give more credibility to someone who has made it.

Coincidentally, I pull up to the church at the same time as Lena, Pastor Greg's assistant. We've not met, but I know exactly who she is. She's driving a little silver Hyundai, and her outfit, while cute, is clearly the inexpensive knockoff version of the designer original.

She waves as she gets out of her car. "Are you Pastor Greg's ten o'clock?" she asks.

"I am. You're his assistant, right?"

She walks over with a sunny smile on her face. I like her already, even though she could use a diet and a treadmill in her life.

"Yes. I'm Lena."

"I'm Felicia Caldwell. Girl, I gotta tell you, you are wearing that dress. Hot pink is your color."

Now she practically beams at me. "Thank you! People tell me I look good in cool colors. Truthfully, I wish I had your body. I'd wear bright colors every day."

"You can have it! All it takes is a little hard work and determination."

She shakes her head. "Uh-uh. God knew exactly what he was doing giving me these rolls. If I looked like you, I'd have a hard time staying celibate. I might just end up being a church hoe."

We both crack up laughing. Lena at her joke, and me at her saying God gave her those rolls. No, ma'am. Krispy Kreme, fried chicken, and biscuits gave her those rolls.

"Well, come on inside," Lena says. "Pastor Greg is already here. I usually beat him, but I was running late this morning. My little girl had a program at school."

"You have a daughter? How old is she?"

"She's five. She's in kindergarten."

"That's so precious."

"Do you have any children?" Lena asks.

"I did have a son once, and he died."

Lena immediately reaches out and touches my hand. "I'm so sorry."

"It's okay. He didn't live very long."

"Maybe God will bless you with another."

I shake my head. "Unfortunately, I can't have any children."

"Oh, Lord Jesus. Let me stop putting my foot in my mouth and get you inside the office for this meeting. I am so sorry."

"No worries, hun. You didn't know!"

"That doesn't stop me from feeling stupid."

"Now it's my turn to ask what might be a silly question. Are you married? I don't see a ring on your finger and I was wondering about the singles ministry."

"No, I am not married, but I do not participate in the singles ministry."

My mouth forms a little circle. "Why not?"

"Don't tell anybody I told you this, but it's a hot mess. All they do is sit around scheming on how to get married. I'm happily single. Right now, I'm raising my daughter, and I don't really want to bring a man into the mix. Her father is active, and pays child support on time. That's all I can hope for. I get tired of all the tips on how to get a husband, you know?"

"I do know! Honestly, Lena, I'm with you. I'm single, I am doing well financially, and I'm not out here dying to have a man. Maybe we can have our own little ministry."

"I would like that."

Lena shows me into the building that houses all of the church's administrative offices. It's not connected to the main sanctuary, like I've seen in many other churches.

"Let me see if Pastor Greg is ready to see you," Lena says. "You can have a seat on the couch for a few minutes. Would you like coffee?"

"Do you have chai?"

"We do. Let me get you settled with Pastor Greg and I'll get you some."

Lena is definitely in the bag. Five minutes at the church and I'm already on my way to being besties with Pastor Greg's assistant. It's almost as if God is opening these doors for me. I wouldn't be surprised. He wants false prophets exposed too. And if He's showing me favor, maybe that means my time of reaping consequences is over. I am redeemed.

Lena appears again. "Pastor Greg is ready for you. Right this way."

Pastor Greg's office is nice, not too flashy like a lot of pastors' offices. It's professional. Nice and clean with tasteful decorations. I wonder if the false prophetess decorated it for him.

Pastor Greg stands to his feet and motions for me to sit. "Please come in, Sister Felicia. I'm excited to get started on this."

"Me too!"

"I really thought about what you said last night when I got home. There is so much grant money out there that we really haven't tapped into. We actually had a grants professional before, and she left to go work for a corporation. We've been using the money we collect at church to fund all of our programs, but if there's money out there that we can use to expand, I definitely want to know about it."

"Of course you do. It takes a lot of money to run a ministry this size."

"It does. I can't tell you how many times my wife and I have had to go into our own pockets to make up the difference on an initiative or project."

I frown. "Oh no. You should never have to do that."

Lena walks in with a warm, steaming mug. "I didn't mean to eavesdrop, but I've been telling him the same thing," she says. "He and Pastor Nya do not have to always chip in. Some stuff can just be cancelled."

Pastor Greg lets out a deep laugh. The sound is so rich and full that it makes me shiver a little. I hope that neither one of them notices. I just can't resist a chocolate brother with a goatee and good humor. They are God's most perfect creations.

"We're not going to ever cancel anything we've promised our community, not if I can help it."

"You are a pastor for the people," I say. "That is what drew me to this ministry. You don't preach about seed offerings and the like. Well, your wife sometimes talks about blessings, but it's not always about money."

Greg's laugh fades and his lips form a straight line. I may have gone too far with that one. He doesn't look happy at all.

"Well, this ministry is founded on —"

"Repentance, reconciliation, and relationship," I say. "I know. I love that."

Greg's smile has returned. "Okay, good! The Suddenly Blessed movement can sometimes take the spotlight away from what we're really trying to accomplish here."

"It doesn't. I just look at it as Pastor Nya's personal crusade. What she's doing with these conference dates is amazing for the kingdom."

"That is a wonderful way to put it. Now tell me about this grant funding and how we can get some of it."

I show Pastor Greg my portfolio, and tell him about the grants that I would like to pursue. I tell him about the deadlines and time constraints and how we can aggressively go after funding even for programs that haven't been launched yet, based on the strength of the things the church has already accomplished in the community.

"Wow," Greg says when I'm done with my introduction. "I didn't expect you to be this prepared. Your level of detail and planning is refreshing. I hate to say it, but typically when I'm dealing with church members, I don't get this level of quality."

"Thank you, Pastor Greg. I went to graduate school for a degree in fundraising for nonprofit organizations. I didn't get this skill set sitting in the pews."

"Well, we're definitely glad to have you on board. Lena will be able to bring you up to speed on everything we've done so far. What kind of availability do you have?"

"I'm not working right now, so I have lots of availability. My last freelance assignment left me . . . well taken care of."

Greg claps his hands and blows a kiss toward heaven. "Look at God!"

"I can get to work immediately."

"As in today?"

"Yes. One of the grants I want to pursue has a deadline that is only a few weeks away. The sooner the better."

"Lena!" Greg calls, and she comes running, almost as if she was waiting on him to summon her.

"Yes, Pastor?"

"Please take Ms. Caldwell and have her fill out all of the paperwork needed for the volunteers. The code of conduct, background screening, and all that."

"Code of conduct? That's interesting," I say. Actually, it's more than interesting. It's strange. What kind of members do they have at this church if you have to sign a code of conduct? I wonder if it says anything about lying for personal gain, and I wonder if his crooked wife signed it.

"It's pretty standard. As long as you're living right, it shouldn't be a big deal, right?"

I chuckle softly. "It's not a big deal at all. I'm glad about your commitment to excellence."

"That's exactly what it's about."

"Lena, can you take a picture of me and Pastor Greg? My mom is worried silly that I haven't joined a church yet. I told her that I've been a member here for a few years and she doesn't believe me. She follows Pastor Nya online."

Greg stands next to me and smiles. I don't really care about having a picture taken with him. I just want to have an excuse to stand close enough to him for him to inhale my perfume. I notice he doesn't put his arm around me, not even in a friendly way. I know that we just met, really, but I did expect for him to put his arm around me at the very least.

"I hate to cut our meeting short, but I have a conference call," Greg says. "Lena will show you the rest of what you need today. Welcome to the ministry team."

"Thank you, Pastor Greg. We're going to do some great things together."

He gives me a huge smile. "I believe that."

Well, that's two of us. And when two or three touch and agree on a thing, heaven will unfold. It's called partnership. Something Greg's wife prophesied about, but clearly has no clue about. If she did, she wouldn't be in another state filming a talk show and doing conferences while her husband works like a dog building their ministry.

That's okay though. I'm here now, so Greg has a partner now. We're definitely about to do some great things. For the kingdom.

CHAPTER 35
FELICIA

My new friend Lena invited me on a shopping trip, which has been entirely fun and tiring. Now we're having lunch at an expensive steakhouse that I've been meaning to try since I got to Dallas — my treat. It's not like Lena can afford to eat where I eat, but I don't mind a little charity when she definitely has some things that I need.

I watch Lena flip through the pages on the menu, from front to back and from back to front again.

"You see anything you want to have for lunch?" I ask.

"Girl, the prices aren't even on the menu," Lena says. "You sure I can order anything I want?"

"Yep. We have worked up an appetite, don't you think?"

"I didn't do nearly as much shopping as you did."

I give Lena a smile that doesn't give away

anything that I'm thinking. First, I would like to take her wig shopping. In fact, I am going to take her wig shopping, I just have to figure out how to do it. If she's going to be going out in public with me, I need to help her step her game up.

And she is definitely going to be in public with me, because she's my in with Greg. I thought it was going to be Mother Olivia, but she's pretty sharp. Sometimes older people have an intuition about things. It's called mother wit, and she's got it. I'm not trying to have her reveal me before I get a foothold. Lena is much easier.

"I usually do much more damage than that," I say. "I think shopping with you today helped me pace myself."

"Can I ask you a question?" Lena asks. "How did you make your money? And can I be down?"

I give a little chuckle. There's no way I'm telling her what happened in Atlanta. I should've anticipated this question, especially around church folk who are always looking for their destiny come-up. I didn't really plan a good response to give people when they ask me this.

"Am I being too personal? I'm just asking because you don't seem to have a regular job." Lena glances down at the menu nervously, then back up at me.

"I have invested well, and although I don't have a regular job, I do freelance work. I write grant proposals for private companies, just like I did for the church."

"Oh, girl, I was gonna ask if you had a body shaper empire or something that I could get a piece of."

"Body shaper? Oh, those girdles?"

"Yes. This one sister at the church makes about five thousand dollars a month having those body shaper parties."

"I would never sell something that gives the illusion of proper diet and exercise. I think men get mad about those things."

Lena throws her head back and laughs. "Who cares about them? It's about how snatched we look in our dresses. They can be mad about it if they want."

"You have to care about how men think if you want to get one."

Lena laughs out loud. "I thought we were saved and single."

"Oh, right. We are."

"Well, are you dating someone right now?" Lena asks while she continues with her laughter. "And if you are, does he have a brother?"

I give her a tiny smile. "I am currently single, but when my Boaz finds me, I'm going to be ready to be his partner in every way."

"You mean like in business too?"

I nod. "Business, ministry, whatever he's called to do. I'm going to be ready to compliment him."

"Whoo, girl. I do not want a minister. I would never marry a minister."

Now she has truly shocked me. Most of the women I know who attend church dream of being a first lady.

"Really? Why not?"

Lena lifts her eyebrow. "Let me tell you, being a pastoral assistant, I have seen way too much. It's totally turned me away from wanting a man in ministry."

"Girl, get out of here," I laugh. "Pastor Greg is a saint."

"He may very well be, but the way these women scheme to get him is crazy. I would never want to be married to a man with that much access to available coochie. Excuse my French."

I drop my jaw and give her my surprised look. "Who would do that? I mean, I could see if he was single, then all bets are off. May the best woman win. But what can someone gain by chasing an unavailable man?"

"I don't know. But what I *do* know is that

if I was Pastor Nya, I would bring my behind home sometimes. She's away more than she's in town. If Pastor Greg wanted to, he'd have plenty of time to play."

This is information that I already know. Everyone knows that Nya travels a lot. That's not going to help me.

"Well, as long as Pastor Greg supports her in her ministry, I applaud Pastor Nya. She is making an impact in the kingdom."

"Operative words, as long as Pastor Greg supports her . . ."

"He doesn't? Girl, stop. I don't believe that."

She narrows her eyes and leans in. "I overheard him on the phone one time. He was practically begging her to come home."

"It's never a good thing when a man begs."

"Thank you!" Lena throws her arms in the air to emphasize her point. "Your husband shouldn't have to beg to see you."

"I wonder if Pastor Nya has anyone mentoring her, and telling her these things," I say, sounding way more concerned than I actually am.

"She's been groomed by Bishop and Lady Bowens. They've been her biggest teachers since she did that suddenly blessing prophecy all those years ago."

I feel my eye twitch. "Oh, I've heard about

that message. It's what put her on the map, right?"

"Mm-hmm. I was there. The girl she gave that prophecy to was a hot mess at the altar. God really moved that night."

I feel myself twitch again.

"I'm sure He did."

"Anyway, I'm definitely team Pastor Greg and Pastor Nya. I've been with them since the beginning. They definitely have a heart for the people, and Pastor Nya's speaking engagements have done so much for our church financially."

"I am in support of them too. I'm happy to be a part of this ministry."

"Just keep Pastor Greg in your prayers. Virtuous women like us have to hold him down."

"I will. I'll pray for Pastor Nya too."

And this is a true statement. I will pray for her. I'll pray that she is soon shown the error of her ways, and I'll pray that when she falls, that she finds the strength to get up again. Just like I did.

CHAPTER 36
NYA

"Tell me what you need God to do in your life, honey," I ask the young woman who has stepped out of the aisle and is approaching the front of the church.

I glance to the left and right cautiously, looking for the security staff. This is my first time in this church in New Orleans. Penelope and I flew in this morning from Atlanta to do this Suddenly Blessed conference. My spirit has felt heavy since we set foot in the city. I always feel that way here, or anywhere people make it a point to try and connect with the spirit realm. It is an unsettling feeling, because I can discern evil spirits as well as the Holy Spirit. I'm never afraid, but definitely uncomfortable.

I feel myself relax as the church security steps into place. Since the television show has gained more popularity, the number of people who show up just wanting face time with a celebrity has drastically increased.

"I need a healing in my body," she screams.

I can tell her cries are authentic. Now I start praying, because I have no clue what to do next. *Lord, please help me. Please empower me to help her. Show me something.*

I can feel God's Spirit quicken inside me. He's about to do something miraculous in here tonight. Jesus!

The woman sits in her doctor's office. He shows her scans of her breasts. They are full of tumors.

"It's stage four, and it has metastasized to your lungs and lymph nodes. We can try radiation and chemo, but there is no surgical option, because of where some of the tumors are situated. There is only time to shrink these tumors, but we can't get rid of them."

"How long do I have?"

"Could be weeks. I would say six months tops, and that is being optimistic."

The scene changes. The doctor's office is gone, and now there's a funeral home with a pretty white casket at the front. A little girl walks up to the casket and reaches in. She touches the woman's face. The woman from the doctor's office.

Oh no. Not this. My hands tremble as the vision fades. I can't tell her that I just saw her in a casket. I can't promise her a healing for her body. She's desperate, and there's nothing I can say that will give her solace.

"You have cancer," I say in the microphone. There's no growl or mysticism in my voice. I'm actually hoping that she tells me no, and makes me believe the vision is all in my imagination.

The woman nods as she approaches the front of the church. I take the microphone and hand it to Penelope, who has risen from her seat in the pulpit. I walk down the stairs, directly to the woman. I grab some tissues from one of the ministers and help wipe her face.

Then I whisper to her, "God wants you to find peace. Spend time with your little girl."

"You see my little girl?" the woman asks between sobs.

"I do. God showed her to me."

"W-was she okay? Is she gonna be okay?"

Although God didn't show me the fate of her child, I believe it's okay to comfort her. "She's going to be fine. She's going to be in God's loving arms."

The woman nods and wipes her tears with the tissues, and allows the ministers to walk

259

her back to her seat.

I am unable to continue, though. This has wiped me out. God has never done this to me before. Shown me a situation where I can't help. I look up at Penelope and shake my head.

Typically this is the cue for Penelope to start singing, but as the musicians start playing, Penelope holds her hand in the air and motions them to stop.

"Sister with cancer. Come back to the altar. God is not done speaking on your behalf tonight." Penelope's voice comes out like a husky, harsh whisper.

The ministers are confused. They know to take direction from me during the service, but Penelope is just the psalmist. No one takes direction from her except the musicians.

When I don't stop them, the ministers walk the woman back down to the altar area. I'm not sure what I should do, so I wait to see what Penelope has in mind.

Penelope starts to walk down to the woman. Then she kicks off her heels.

"Sometimes you've got to get rid of all your niceties and accoutrements when God is telling you to move," she says into the microphone.

The crowd is responding to this, and it

seems to give Penelope energy. I begin to pray internally that she's not about to do something crazy.

When Penelope gets to the woman, she places one hand on her belly.

"Ministers, I need y'all to be touching every one of her limbs. Not one of her extremities should go untouched."

There is a sense of urgency in her voice. She's getting everyone excited.

"One of y'all get the small of her back. Get your hands on her now!"

When everyone's hands are placed on the woman, Penelope leans her head back and starts to speak in tongues.

Every few syllables she says, "Yes, Holy Ghost!" or "Hallelujah." I wonder what she's doing, but I don't step in. What if it is a move of God? I don't want to be a hindrance.

After a few minutes of hearing Penelope speak and sing in tongues, she gets quiet. Silence falls over the congregation.

"God said you will be healed of your infirmity."

The woman gives her a confused look, and then she looks at me with questions in her eyes.

I want to snatch that microphone out of Penelope's hand, but Lady Sandy is stand-

261

ing with her hands lifted toward the heavens.

"Do you receive your healing, sister?"

The woman nods slowly, then more quickly, then she bursts into tears. She wants to be healed so badly.

But I know what I saw in my vision. And I know it was God. This is *not* God. This is worse than what I did with that girl in the Women's Empowerment session. She's giving this woman hope that she will live instead of allowing her to have peace with her situation. God wanted to give her peace and Penelope just gave her a lie.

I can't do anything except pray.

Even as I whisper the words to my prayer, I know that part of me is somewhat bothered by the fact that the woman chose to believe Penelope's prophecy over mine. When did Penelope have a proven prophetic word? What made her word more credible than mine? I know . . . it isn't about the prophetic word being credible, it is about it being incredible. And the woman's situation is beyond impossible.

Then Penelope starts to sing into the microphone. As the lyrics of "Break Every Chain" ring throughout the sanctuary, I feel more bound and trapped than I've ever felt before. I can't rebuke her or fix this, because who would believe me in here? We're leaving a woman more broken than she was when she got here. I remember my cousin's warning about respecting the gift.

Tears of repentance flow from my eyes. My false words started all of this. And now the gift has been perverted, again, in front of an entire crowd. And Penelope looks taller as she struts with her shoulders back, singing at the top of her lungs. People fall out in the aisles and it's a great spectacle.

A spectacle that has nothing to do with God.

As soon as service is over, Penelope and I retreat to the minister's room in back of the church. I sit at the vanity dabbing sweat from my brow. Penelope lounges on the velvet couch happily humming a worship song. I try to think of something to say to her that isn't wrathful. I can't.

"What was that you did in the service tonight?" I ask, my words sounding like rapid-fire gunshots.

Penelope looks up from her cell phone and smiles. "Don't you mean what did God do? He made me his mouthpiece tonight."

"Really? What did that feel like?"

"It was like I felt a rushing wind that no one else could feel. And when that wind hit me, the tongues came. As I began to speak, God gave me interpretation of the words. I have never experienced anything like that before."

"I had a vision about the woman too. It's funny. What you said to her was the complete opposite of what God showed me. I think . . . in fact, I know, you lied to her."

There. Blunt is best. I'm not about to play games with this girl tonight. I'm tired and I don't feel like verbally sparring. I just want her to know that I know what she did.

"I didn't lie."

"You did. My vision was of her in a casket with her little girl standing next to it. She is not going to be healed."

"Well, what did you say when you whispered in her ear?" Penelope asks with a scared tremble in her tone.

"I told her to spend time with her daughter and to find peace."

"Why would God want her to hear *that*? It's the most depressing thing I've ever heard."

I shake my head. "It is not up to me to decide what God wants to tell people. It is only my job to pass on the message."

"Did you tell her you saw her in a casket?"

"Not in those words, but what I told her pointed to the fact that her time left here is short."

Penelope shakes her head. "No. Your vision was wrong. I know what God wanted me to do and I did it."

"You're playing with the gift."

"I'm not!" Penelope whines. "I'm doing what you do. I fasted for three days straight. I asked God to speak through me, and He did. You're just mad that my prophecy was received and yours was not."

I feel a vein in my forehead begin to throb, because I know she's serious. As ridiculous and desperate as she sounds, I know she's dead serious.

I stand and leave the minister's room. I can't even share the air with Penelope right now. Tina is in the hallway waiting for me.

"You good, Nya? I could tell you were wiped out."

"This entire evening stole every last bit of my strength. I just want to go and lie down."

Tina looks uncomfortable. "Are you sure you want to go straight back to the hotel? You don't want to get something to eat first?"

"We can pick up some fast food. I just want my head to make contact with the pillow in as little time as possible."

"Um . . . the pastor wants us to have dinner with a few of his ministry staff. They want to take you and Prophetess Penelope to eat."

I tilt my head back and sigh. I'm not in the mood for this.

"Prophetess Penelope? Really?"

"Hey, they called her that. I was as surprised as you are right now."

"Okay to dinner, but I'm not staying all night," I say. "I can't be around Penelope without wrapping my hands around her neck and squeezing."

We ride over to the restaurant in separate cars at my request. I don't want to hear any more of Penelope's stupidity, and I don't want to say something that might hurt her feelings.

The gentleman driving us is one of the ministry staff, and he's friendly enough. He keeps pointing out things of interest in New Orleans, but I'm too distracted to pay any attention.

When we arrive at the restaurant we are shown to a table that has already been prepared for us. Immediately everyone starts talking and socializing. I'm quiet, though, still trying to recover from that service.

"You okay, boo?" Tina asks me.

"I'm good."

As we order our food one of the ministers keeps glancing at me and grinning, like he has something to say. We haven't met, and I don't even know his name, so his glances make me uncomfortable. I sure hope he's not going to try and hit on me, because after the night I've had, I just might cuss him out and then have to go to the altar to repent.

"So, Pastor Nya, do you think you've got a bit of competition here in Penelope?" the sly-looking minister asks. "She did her thing tonight. I've never seen such a display of Holy Ghost power."

I take a sip of water from the glass in front of me. I'm trying to stall, giving Penelope time to jump in and say something to contradict what this man has said, but she stays silent. Okay. She asked for it.

"I'm not in competition with anyone. What I'm doing is kingdom business. I say and do exactly what God tells me to say and do."

The minister cocks his head to one side. "Are you saying that Penelope doesn't?"

I open my mouth to speak, but Tina touches my arm. "Wait a minute. What's your name again, brother?" she asks.

"Gerard."

"Okay. Well, Gerard, my friend is tired, and what you're doing right now is on my nerves, so I know it's on hers."

Gerard laughs. "I apologize, sister. It was not meant to antagonize. I just wanted to give Penelope props for how she flowed tonight."

"Mission accomplished. Find a different topic," Tina says.

I love that Tina is here with me. I was afraid that when I asked her to leave her salon and come work for me full-time on the road and for the show that she would say no. I don't know what I would've done to convince her if she had, but I need her here.

Tina snickers and whispers, "Check out your girl."

"So, what did you say to that woman, Pastor Nya?" Gerard says. "We're all curious. We know what Penelope said, but not you."

"If she whispered it in her ear, then that means it was just for her. Isn't that right?" Penelope says.

I nod. "It was just for her. I don't feel at liberty to share."

"How does it work?" Gerard asks as he leans forward and stares intently at me. "I've always wondered what it feels like to operate in the prophetic. Did you ask God for that gift?"

"No, I didn't ask for it. Sometimes I don't want it. It's not easy."

"Can you see stuff about your own life?

Does God let you know what decisions to make like every day? Can you see what your husband is doing right now?"

These questions from Gerard are annoying. Not that I haven't heard them before. I have. Or similar to these.

"It doesn't work like that. It's not a crystal ball. I only see things for a specific purpose. And the purpose is up to God. I have no say in the matter."

"Do you want to be a prophet?" Penelope asks Gerard.

"If it'll take my ministry to the level it's taken Pastor Nya's here, then yes. I want everything God has for me. Maybe we'll end up together like Nya and her husband and start our own ministry."

Okay, that's it. I can't stay here. I have to go back to the hotel.

"I'm suddenly not feeling so well," I tell the pastor who hosted us for the conference and dinner. "Do you think someone can run me back to the hotel? Tina, you don't have to come if you don't want to."

Penelope gives me a strange look. Tina gives her one back.

"Don't worry, Penelope. You can stay here and still get your flirt on, but my girl is tired. We're going back," Tina says.

Penelope's mouth drops open, and Gerard laughs.

"You keep it all the way real, don't you?" Gerard asks Tina.

"Yes, I do."

"There's something to be said about a woman who speaks her mind," another one of the ministers says.

Tina gives the short, balding, and dang near drooling man an eye roll as she leads me out of the restaurant. We follow on the heels of the minister who is taking us back to the hotel.

"Was that little troll doll trying to holler at me?" Tina whispers in my ear as we get to the car.

"I think he was. He's better than that one sliding up to Penelope. He gave me the creeps."

We ride back to the hotel in silence, because we don't know the minister who's driving us. He could be the gossipy type.

When I finally get in my hotel room after the night's service, I check my phone and see that I have five missed calls from Greg. Why would he be calling me like that when I was in service?

I call him back and he answers on the first ring.

"Hey, honey," I say. "Is everything okay?

You called five times."

"Apparently I wanted something if I called that many times. You're just now calling me back?"

"I'm sorry. I'm just now checking my phone. Service ran late."

"I bet you went to dinner after."

"I did, but I didn't check my phone until just now."

"Who'd you go to dinner with?" Greg asks, an irritated tone in his voice.

"The other ministers on the roster. A couple of gospel artists."

"So there were men there?"

"And also women. Tina and Penelope were there too. Greg, what's wrong?"

He pauses for a long time before making another sound.

"Greg? Are you there?"

"Yes," he finally says. "There's nothing wrong. I just don't like not hearing from you all evening."

"I'm sorry, babe. I just didn't think to call after service let out."

"You never think to call. Do you realize we haven't spoken in days?"

"It hasn't been days."

"Check your call log. I'll wait."

Determined to prove him wrong, I press the call log list and scroll back. It takes me a couple of days before I see a call completed to Greg. On the contrary, I see plenty of missed calls from Greg.

"You're right. I'm sorry, babe. It has been extremely busy here. Something crazy happened tonight. I got a vision about this woman with cancer. She was in a casket. I don't know what God is trying to tell me. You should be here with me."

"I have the church . . ."

"Yes, but we have associate pastors. You don't have to be there every Sunday. Sometimes you can travel with me."

"And do what? Watch you from the VIP section while you're slaying everybody in the Spirit?"

"It's nothing like that."

"Have you seen the promotional videos for your conferences? They have captured every moment of you touching someone and them falling out. They even have you praying for Lady Sandy, and then she's on the floor. It's a mockery."

I shake my head and sigh. I haven't seen the video, but I'm sure that Greg is exaggerating about the content. Yes, there are times when women fall out at the altar. I wouldn't say that all of them are touched by the Holy Spirit. Some of them are just so overwhelmed with their situation that they can't see past it all. The prayers give them hope.

"When I have a night like tonight that taxes my spirit, I would sometimes like for you to be there. That's all I'm saying."

"Well, maybe it's time for you to retire from traveling. Maybe it's time for you to come home and stay home."

"I just don't believe that God would be opening all these doors if He didn't want me to walk through them. We just have to trust that this is for our good, and for the good of the kingdom."

Greg is silent on the other end except for his breathing, which is slow and even.

"What are you thinking about?" I ask.

"How much I want you here."

"Oh."

"Is this really that important to you? I'm telling you I need you home."

"You asking me to put our marriage before my ministry?"

A very long pause from Greg. "Yes. I am asking you to do exactly that."

The groan that escapes me is full of frustration. I know that if Greg could just come to one of these, and see what God is doing, he wouldn't feel the same way. Why is he trying to make me choose between him and God? Why would he try to make me choose anything over God?

When I get home, we're going to address this matter once and for all, because I don't believe God would want me to leave my marriage behind for the sake of ministry.

CHAPTER 37
FELICIA

The last time I met with Pastor Greg, I made sure to dress very modestly. I don't want him or anyone else to think I'm trying to seduce him. The only thing I do differently today is wear my hair loose, in big wavy curls, and put on a tiny dab of perfume. Still, no makeup other than a hint of lip gloss. My jeans skirt sweeps the ground, even though it's close to summertime in Dallas and hot as a concrete sidewalk at high noon.

The first person I see when I get to the church is Mother Olivia. She's standing in the parking lot next to her car, looking confused. I hurry to park my car and rush over to her.

"What's wrong, Mother? Are you okay?"

She looks up at me and squints. "Baby, do I know you?"

"Oh, my hair is different. I'm Felicia, the girl you met in church a couple weeks ago.

You introduced me to Pastor Greg so that I could help him with the grants for the youth center."

She gives me a sweeping look; takes in everything from my jeans skirt to my curled hair. She seems satisfied.

"Yes, I remember you. Is that what you're here for now?"

"I am. Lena and I wrote up some preliminary grant proposals and I just want Pastor Greg to approve them, because they'll be sent on his behalf."

"Mm-hmm. Well, I can't seem to find my keys. I thought I had them in my purse, but maybe I left them in Pastor's office."

"I'll walk back in there with you. If they're not in the office, I'll help you find them."

"Thank you, sweetheart."

Mother Olivia and I walk into Pastor Greg's office together and he grins at us.

"Mother, I was just about to come outside and bring you your keys. You left them right there on my desk."

She chuckles. "I guess I was just ready to go start planning this party."

"Party?" I ask.

"Yes, Pastor Greg and Co-pastor Nya have been married for fifteen years. That is something to celebrate."

"Fifteen years? Did you two get married

in middle school?" I ask.

"No. We were both twenty. In our senior year of college," Greg says. "It doesn't seem like it's been that long, though."

They have been married fifteen years. Five years ago Nya had already been with her man. They were already in ministry together, doing their thing. Living in pursuit of their purpose. Why would she have to lie to me?

"The entire congregation is going to be invited to this party," Mother Olivia says. "So put on your dancing shoes, baby."

"Dancing shoes?" I ask. "What kind of music are you going to have?"

Mother Olivia does a little line dance. "Honey, we gonna do the 'lectric slide, cupid shuffle, and that new line dance they made to that Beyoncé song."

"Oh well, I will definitely wear my flats then. I love line dances."

"We have a line dance class at the church on Tuesdays if you need to brush up on things," Mother Olivia says. "Lena teaches it."

"She does," Greg says. "And she's good at it."

Mother Olivia frowns. "Speaking of Lena, where is she? Didn't you say you worked on these grant proposals with her? Why isn't she here?"

Greg lifts his eyebrows like he has the same question. I should've known Mother Olivia's eagle eyes were going to catch the fact that Greg and I are meeting alone.

"She had to take her daughter somewhere this morning. Our deadline for the grant is tomorrow, so I had to come without her. Is that okay?" I ask in the most innocent tone I can muster.

Mother Olivia's frown doesn't budge. Then she sits in one of the chairs in front of Greg's desk.

"The party planning can wait. I'll just sit right here until you're done."

"Mother, that's not necessary," Greg says.

"She's right, Pastor. I don't mind it at all."

"But she doesn't have to . . ."

Mother Olivia dismisses Greg with a wave of her hand. "Go ahead and show him the proposals, baby."

Sufficiently chastised, I guess, Greg sits on his side of the desk. I pull out all three finished grant proposals and walk him through them one by one. I point out all of the goals, milestones, and performance indicators. Then I share some questions that I think the interviewers will ask.

"So someone will come in and interview me about this?" Greg asks.

"They will. These grants are for huge sums of money. They'll want to make sure you'll do what you say you're going to do. It's hard to recoup misappropriated grant monies once they've been disbursed."

"Thank you so much for leading this initiative and briefing me. You are an asset to this church. How long have you been a member again?"

"About four years."

"Well, it's about time you stood up and gave back," Mother Olivia says. "Too many folk sittin' on their gifts."

Mother Olivia approves of me, of this. Thank God, because she was going to be trouble if she didn't.

"I'm going to leave these with you, Pastor Greg. Lena will collect them from you when you sign in all the places that need signing. If you have any questions, my e-mail is in the documentation."

Mother Olivia nods her approval. I guess she likes the idea of him e-mailing me as opposed to calling. She obviously doesn't know what can transpire in e-mails.

"Come on and walk me out, baby," Mother Olivia says. "These old bones have trouble after sitting for this long."

"Mm-hmm," Greg says as he shakes his head. "I knew you'd be hurting."

"Hush."

Mother Olivia takes my hand and basically pulls me out of Greg's office. This wasn't how today's meeting was supposed to go, but I guess I do have time. I'm in no rush to make Nya atone for her sins. I've waited this long. A few more months won't hurt.

"Thanks again, Sister Felicia," Greg says. "I appreciate you."

I appreciate him too. Much more than that Jezebel wife of his. Pretty soon, I'm going to show him my appreciation in every way imaginable. But not too soon. It's got to be perfect, and I don't want anything to ruin what we're going to have.

CHAPTER 38
NYA

The knock on my hotel room door drew my attention away from my Bible study. We're leaving New Orleans this afternoon, and I want to look over the scripture text Greg sent me. He wants us to preach on it this coming Sunday.

I look through the peephole and am surprised to see that it is Lady Sandy. I swing the door open. She strides in with her nose slightly tilted in the air. She looks as if she's about to sit in the armchair, but then she stops and spins on one heel.

"Penelope tells me that you had a problem with her using her prophetic gift during service."

"Good morning to you too, Lady Sandy."

Lady Sandy presses her lips together and crosses her arms. "I save pleasantries for when I'm being pleasant. Right now, I want to know why you are so against my daughter's ministry."

"Oh, I see. This isn't a friendly visit, then."

I'm not sure I want this conversation to continue down this path. Clearly, Penelope's gotten to her mother first and filled her head with a bunch of mess.

"Do you have any idea how much my daughter looks up to you? She wants nothing more than to make the same kind of impression that you make with your prophecies."

"I know that."

"So imagine how devastating it was for her when you, her mentor, accused her of faking a prophetic word. She's literally heartbroken behind that."

I didn't see heartbroken at dinner after that service. I saw her grinning, cheesing, and flirting with ministers. But okay. I see she told her mother something different.

"Would you want me to not tell her the truth?" I ask. "I know that the prophetic word she spoke to that woman was as false as her eyelashes."

"You don't know that. You aren't God."

"I know what God showed me, and it was the opposite of what your daughter decreed and declared."

Finally, Lady Sandy sits on the couch in my room. She crosses her legs at the ankle, very ladylike, and stares me down.

"I have done a lot to make sure that you reach your destiny. The very least you can do is pull my daughter up to follow in your footsteps."

"I will help Penelope do and be exactly what she is called to do and become, but I won't let her make a mockery of the prophetic gift."

Lady Sandy leans forward, still staring. "Maybe I wasn't clear. We're now shifting the focus of these conference dates a bit. We want Penelope to be more in the spotlight. She's been relegated to your singing sidekick. That's not what we have planned for our daughter. She is poised to take over our church when my husband retires. We need her to learn to take the reins."

So all of this, all of it, was a setup for Penelope to get some exposure? What type of prophetic coattail-riding is this?

"Take the reins of what? Service? When I'm up there, God is always in control of what happens. I don't know that I ever take the reins away from Him."

"You know what I mean. We want Penelope to start operating in her anointing."

That's the thing. I don't know what she means. I only know that this feels very, very strange. It feels like Lady Sandy wants to tap into my gift only to elevate her daughter's platform.

"And you believe her anointing is being a prophetess?"

Lady Sandy nods. "Yes. Prophecies are what people want. I can market a conference with a proven prophet much easier than I can a singer. Black people aren't impressed by singers. We hear good singers all the time. But a prophet who speaks the truth, now that is a sell-out conference."

"What happened to turning the people's hearts back to the Creator?"

"Are we not doing that? Isn't yours and Greg's ministry exploding? You are preaching repentance until you're blue in the face, and these folk still want a prophetic word."

"You're right. We've failed the church."

"So what are you going to do about it now, Evangelist? If you want to leave this behind, quit the TV show and everything else, do you not know that someone will step right up to take your place?

"Seems like you want it to be Penelope."

"I can't say I'd be angry about it. She'll make more of it than you do. She'll be a sensation."

She'll be a hot lying mess, is what she'll be, but I feel my resolve slipping. I feel my retirement from this circus coming. I know that when I get home to Greg, he'll help me pray, and then God will help me choose.

CHAPTER 39
FELICIA

I have a mixture of feelings as I sit in Greg's office while we await the arrival of the interviewer from the funding board. They've reviewed our grant proposal, and as part of their selection process, the board sends out a representative to speak to the potential grantees.

I'm excited that we're getting the opportunity, but I can barely concentrate, being in the room with Greg. This man is so sexy, and I have to continue to pretend that I'm not attracted to him. Lord knows I didn't come here with seduction on my mind. I only want to make Nya pay for what she's done to my life. But every time Greg speaks, I feel shivers through my body.

Lena was supposed to be here too, but someone conveniently told her the meeting was at two o'clock in the afternoon instead of eleven. Of course that someone was me.

"Are you okay, Sister Felicia? You look a

little pale," Greg says.

"Now that you mention it, I am feeling a bit under the weather. I woke up with a headache."

"I hope you're not getting the flu. It's going around. A couple of the older ushers had to be hospitalized for really bad cases of it."

"I'll take some vitamin C when I leave. Thank you, Pastor Greg."

He laughs. "We need you around here, sis. Can't have you dropping off 'cause of a flu bug."

I laugh with him. "Did you reread the grant proposal? They will be asking very specific questions about our strategy, how we plan to implement the program, and how we're going to measure results."

"I did read it, but why would they expect me to know all the details? Obviously, I wouldn't be the one to administer the grant funds. That's what I have you for, right?"

I smile at Greg. He could have me for a lot more than administering grants, but I'm happy that he knows my worth and understands the value that I bring to this process.

Finally the members from the review board arrive. As soon as the two men walk through the door, Greg laughs out loud.

"Frat!" he says to one of the board members.

Then Greg turns to me. "Felicia, this is my fraternity brother Walter Meadows. We go way back."

"Like babies with pacifiers," Walter says. "This is my associate Scott Briggs. We're a part of the team that does all of the faith-based grants from First Dallas Bank. When I saw your church's name on that well-put-together proposal, I knew I wanted to be the one to come out here and interview."

"Feel free to have some of this lunch spread," Greg says. "Looks like Felicia ordered enough food for an army, so eat up."

"I love a woman who caters to a man's stomach," Walter says. "Are you married, Felicia? Seeing anyone?"

I blush and smooth down my snug navy-blue skirt. The man is incredibly fine, and any other time, I'd be using my best flirting ammunition on him. But I can't do that in front of Greg. I can't have him seeing that side of me.

"If you don't leave this woman alone, man," Greg says. "She is saved, sanctified, and on fire for the Lord."

"On fire, you say?" Walter asks and then winks at me. Um, um, um, that man is definitely fine. I'm going to have to make a point of keeping his information in case things don't go well with Greg. I never mind having someone to fall back on.

After everyone has their plates, we sit down at the conference table in Greg's office and begin the interview.

"Like I said before, you have put together an impressive grant proposal," Walter says. "What made you want to build this youth center?"

"Walter, man, you know how we grew up. If it wasn't for the Boys and Girls Club we would've been out in the streets doing who knows what. I want to take it a step further and provide a place that doesn't just get kids off the streets but gives them a venue and opportunity to explore their talents. We're going to have a science lab where our kids with a high aptitude for science, technology, engineering, and math can be developed even further. We'll have an arts wing that will provide free instrumental music, singing, dance, and art classes. All of this is an investment in *our* youth. Our kids are in school districts that can't spend extra dollars on these kinds of programs. The faith-based community needs to step up to the plate and close the gap."

I listen to Greg speak and hang on his

every word as if I haven't heard him express these sentiments before. He's so eloquent and passionate that if he were running for president, I'd vote today. And it's not just because he's a fine man, because Walter and Scott are just as mesmerized as I am. They almost forget to go on to the next question after Greg responds, because his speaking is so powerful. He is an amazing man.

Walter looks at his notebook and nods. "I think we have enough information here to make a decision. I will say at this point, it's pretty much a formality. You have a good track record of already making an impact in the community, which is really a huge factor in who gets these funds and who doesn't."

Yes, we've got this! Greg and I make a great team. I would add Lena in there too, but she really didn't do anything except make us coffee and order lunch. Greg and I did all the heavy lifting. I translated his vision into the grant proposal, and now it is going to come to pass. Yeah, God!

Greg walks Walter and Scott out of the building, and I sit patiently waiting in his office. I know I want to congratulate him, but I'm not sure how, or how far I want to go.

"Woo-hoo!" Greg shouts as he walks back

into his office and closes the door. "We did it! The youth center is going to be built."

I'm surprised when Greg hugs me and spins me around. When he sets me back down on the ground there is a moment where our lips brush. Greg quickly steps back.

"I'm sorry, Sister Felicia. I got a little carried away. I'm just excited about what God is doing here."

"Me too. This is the first of many. I'm looking forward to when this ministry won't need anyone's money, though. You'll be making grants to your members to start businesses, and providing scholarships. That's what I see in the future," I say.

Greg's eyes shine with excitement. "That is absolutely in our future. We will be the head and not the tail. We will not be the borrowers, but we will be the lenders. In the name of Jesus. I thank God for you, Sister Felicia."

"You can just call me Felicia, Pastor Greg. I hope that we're friends now."

He smiles at me, and it's genuine. "We are friends. Have you met Pastor Nya? It seems like most of the work we do happens when she's out of town."

My spirits drop a little bit at the mention of Nya. Why did he have to bring her up? I guess that might be a good thing though. Maybe Greg is so taken by me that he had to remind himself that he even has a wife.

"I haven't had the pleasure yet," I reply.

"Well, when she gets back in town, you have to sit down with her. She's got some initiatives that she wants to work on too. And I know you can help her out, just like you helped me."

I clear my throat and start to gather my things. Greg clearly does not understand the nature of our relationship. I don't want anything to do with that lying wife of his, but of course he doesn't know that. I'll just avoid meeting her at all costs.

She doesn't need to meet me until it's time for me to remove the mask, and by then it'll be too late for her to do anything. It's funny: If she's such a prophetess, why doesn't she know I'm here right now, about to snatch her man right away? A fraud. And the Bible says that liars will not enter the kingdom.

CHAPTER 40
NYA

I am tired. I mean truly tired. Traveling and doing speaking engagements and shooting promo spots for the show have made me weary. I just got an e-mail today from Melody, the young lady we rescued from her mother's abusive boyfriend. Her baby is about to start kindergarten. And it made me think about how many years I've dedicated to this.

It's like it never stops. One engagement leads to the next. One door opens the next. And all of it is taking me away from Love First more than I can stand anymore. Just a few more cities and these pop-up conferences will be done.

I'm lying across the bed, fully dressed, when my phone buzzes. I need to get undressed and put on my pajamas, but I'm just too tired.

"Hello," I say.

"We got the grant for the youth center, babe."

It's Greg. Maybe I'm sleepy or just incoherent, but I have no clue what he's talking about.

"What grant? What youth center?" I ask.

Greg sighs. "I've been telling you about the new grant writer at our church, and how we did a grant proposal to build a new youth center."

"Oh. Right, right."

"You have no clue what I'm talking about, do you?"

"I'm sorry, Greg. I'm sure I do, I'm just so tired right now that the details aren't coming to mind. Please tell me about it."

"You know what? Never mind. It's good. You don't need to worry yourself with the mundane day-to-day operations of our church. You're out there impacting the globe, right?"

"Greg . . ."

"No. It's good. No need to apologize. I know where your focus lies. You're doing what you do."

"You know that I care about what happens in our church. Please don't charge me up over one missed detail. I'm tired. Cut me some slack."

"All the slack you need, babe. You won't

be at church on Sunday, right? Not gonna be home yet."

"No, but I remembered to leave a video greeting for the congregation."

"A video greeting. Are you going to show up for our anniversary celebration or are you sending in a hologram for that one?"

I give a sigh. "Greg, I told you this was my last engagement for a while. Now who's not listening to whom?"

"Yeah, okay, Nya. I'll see you when you get home."

"I can't wait to see you."

"Are you gonna be ready for me?" Greg asks.

"Ready for you?"

Greg sighs. I know what he means, but I'm just playing coy. He's been hounding me lately about a lack of sex because I'm away so much, but I don't know how to resolve that issue except by having him travel with me — something he refuses to do.

"You know what I mean, Nya. It's been too long. The last time you were home you were on your cycle."

"I'm sorry, hun. You're right. I will be ready for you when I get home. That's a need the pastor's aid committee can't help with."

Greg chuckles. "Well . . ."

"I'm not playing with you, man!"

We both laugh, and as always I'm glad to hear the sound come from Greg. Genuine laughs from him are few and far between these days.

"I love you, babe, and congratulations on your grant money."

"Thanks, Nya."

Greg disconnects the call without saying that he loves me too. I've got a mind to call him back, but I don't. I can't make him feel better anyway, and I sure am not in the mood to hear his continued fussing.

There's a knock on my hotel room door. I don't want to get up, but I know it's Tina bringing me the bottled water and fruit that I asked for. I probably won't eat the fruit now, because I'm just that exhausted, but I need the water.

I trudge over to the door and open it. Tina walks in and puts the grocery bag down on the dresser.

"Girl, what's wrong with you?" she asks.

"Nothing. I'm just tired, and Greg is acting like a jerk."

Tina laughs. "What's my brother doing now?"

"Girl, get this. He asked me if I was gonna

be *ready* for him when I get home. I mean, really?"

Tina pauses for a second to grab her midsection. Then she lets out a belly laugh. "Greg is nasty," she says between giggles.

"That isn't funny. He gets on my nerves. He knows I have to preach on Sunday evening and he just talking about getting some. I need to focus on studying."

"Why don't you go and take some nude bathroom selfies and send them to Greg?"

My jaw drops. "I will not."

"I don't see why not. Y'all been married fifteen years. Why don't you spice it up a bit?"

"We have plenty of spice, thank you very much."

Tina shrugs. "I'm just saying. Greg is still a man, and I know men love getting sexy pictures of their women. So if I was you, I'd do it."

"Well, thank God you're not me. You'd have your naked behind all over the cloud."

Tina winks at me. "No, I'd have it all over my husband, if I had one. You don't know how good you have it."

"Good night, Tina."

"All right, girl. You want me to wake you up in the morning?"

"Please do."

Tina leaves my hotel room and I hold my phone in the air and take a selfie of my face. Then I look at it in my gallery. It's a cute picture. I look rather sexy.

On impulse, I send it to Greg and wait for his response.

He texts back. Nice. But you're wearing too many clothes.

I howl with laughter. I guess, for once, Tina was right. Greg is a man first and a pastor second. I suppose I could take one picture . . . and leave my face out of it.

CHAPTER 41
FELICIA

Pastor Greg is alone again in the pulpit on Sunday morning. I checked Nya's itinerary. She's doing a speaking engagement in Philadelphia this evening, so she probably already left. Service opens with a video from her, thanking everyone for their support of the Suddenly Blessed movement. I guess the video is supposed to be a little bit humorous, because at the end Penelope Bowens rushes into the room and tells Nya to shut down the camera because they're about to miss a plane.

The entire congregation laughs as Nya blows everyone a kiss before the screen goes dark. Then there's a huge round of applause, which dies down as Greg takes to the podium. One would think that the cheering would be louder for the actual pastor who preaches every Sunday.

"Yes, it's all right," Pastor Greg says. "You can go ahead and give my rib a round of applause, but let's give God an even bigger hand for being sovereign in our lives!"

At least the congregation responds to this. I was about to get angry, because they seemed mesmerized with Nya's video, and some of them even looked sad when it stopped playing. I wish I could just tell everybody how fake she is, and how Greg is the real deal. He is truly a man of honor. I have been in his presence multiple times and he hasn't said or done anything ungodly.

He is the one who should be out doing speaking engagements. He should be on the preaching tours. He hasn't forgotten that it's all about Jesus.

I watch Pastor Greg carefully as the choir sings. He looks a little pale, and there's a bit of sweat on his brow. He just doesn't look like himself. I wish I was one of the church nurses, because then I'd have an excuse to go and tend to him.

When it's time for him to preach, Greg gets back up to the podium and looks like he's gained a little bit of strength. He opens up with a song. A worship song that everyone joins in and sings with him.

Pastor Greg starts to preach, and I can feel his words reach deep down into my soul. The sound of his voice moves me, and even though he's talking about my Lord and Savior, I believe I'd get salvation from just about anything Greg says.

As he reaches the high point of his sermon, his voice goes up an octave with his excitement. Many in the congregation are standing on their feet right along with me. Pastor Greg seems to feed off our enthusiasm for the Word of God.

I love how he doesn't pretend to operate in the prophetic. He just goes in the Bible and makes it plain. He could teach his wife something with her fake, jackleg preacher self.

I reach down into my purse and look for the envelope I've been holding until just now. An envelope filled with hundred-dollar bills. I know that Pastor Greg doesn't need my money, but I want to bless him.

I step away from my pew and walk down the center aisle of the church. I hold my envelope high in the air so that everyone can see what I'm doing. Pastor Greg smiles at me as I approach and I smile back.

I yell out, "Preach, man of God!" before I lay the money at his feet.

After I do this, several other people follow suit, until there is a long line of people walking down to the altar and laying money at Pastor Greg's feet.

Then Pastor Greg stops preaching. He gets very quiet as the envelopes pile up at his feet.

"You know, this is a new church tradition that I never liked. It is meant to show appreciation for the Word going forth. To bless the man of God. I am humbled by your expressions. But I want y'all to open your Bibles to Acts chapter four, and we're going to start reading in verse thirty-three."

Pastor Greg makes eye contact with me as he flips the pages in his Bible, and I think I can see a faint smile on his face. I would walk up and lay another envelope down if I could.

"All who have it read along," Pastor Greg says. " 'And with great power gave the apostles witness of the resurrection of the Lord Jesus: and great grace was upon them all. Neither was there any among them that lacked: for as many as were possessors of lands or houses sold them, and brought the prices of the things that were sold, And laid them down at the apostles' feet: and distribution was made unto every man according as he had need.' "

I bite my bottom lip, feeling a little bit embarrassed that I'm the one who started the money line, because I feel a rebuke coming on.

"Ushers, come and please collect all of the offerings," Pastor Greg says. "I want to pray over them."

The ushers do as they're told. It takes a few minutes to gather up all of the envelopes and loose bills, but Pastor Greg is patient while they do it. Then they hold the baskets up and he prays with outstretched hands.

"Now that we've read the Word and prayed, I want to do with this money what the apostles would have done. We have several families who have expressed needs. You don't have to know the details of their struggles, but I'm going to ask Geneva Monday and her family to come down to the front. And George Perkins. Bring your entire family, if they're here today."

Both families make their way down to the altar. Geneva Monday has a few kids and they all look dingy, not dirty. Their clothes are faded from having been washed probably hundreds of times. George Perkins's family is just as ragged, but his children are older and don't look like they appreciate their neediness being put on display for the entire church.

"I want to bless you all this morning. Each of you will receive one half of this benevolence offering," Pastor Greg says. "I pray that it blesses you."

Then Pastor Greg looks at the congregation. "If any of y'all put a bad check up in here, you should probably come get it now."

Everybody starts laughing.

"Listen, y'all. I want us to have a different kind of worship experience here," Pastor Greg says. "And I know that my wife concurs with me on this. Love First is about the love of Christ before all. If you want to bless me as your pastor, bless one another. Let's get our church to mirror one of the first-century churches. Let's have an environment where no one is in need."

"I'm gonna pick on Sister Felicia for a moment," Pastor Greg says, now openly smiling at me.

It takes me a moment to grasp what is happening. But Pastor Greg is singling me out in the congregation.

"Stand up, Sister Felicia."

I hurry to my feet. He doesn't have to tell me twice.

"Sister Felicia ran down to this altar with an offering, but she has made a much bigger contribution at this church. She's helped us get a grant for our youth facility."

"We can give of our time, ability, skills, and finances to ensure that no one in our congregation lacks anything. You can go ahead and sit, Sister Felicia. Thank you. I appreciate you."

Greg continues his preaching, but it goes by in a blur. I can only think about how he called me out specially. In front of the entire church. He said my name, thanked me in front of everyone. He smiled down at me and said my name.

I am still on a cloud when service ends. My feet barely touch the ground as I float over to where Pastor Greg says hello to the congregation after service. He smiled at me, so now I want to give him a hug and let him know I appreciate him too.

I'm so focused in on Pastor Greg, I almost crash into Mother Olivia as she blocks my path.

"Oh, hello, Mother Olivia," I say in a friendly tone.

She is frowning. "Good morning."

"What's wrong, Mother Olivia?"

Her frown goes deeper. "What God has for you is for you."

"I receive that, Mother! Why the frown?"

"Another woman's husband ain't for you."

Before I can reply, Mother Olivia struts away and gives me her back. The nerve of her. I didn't do anything. Greg called out to me. I brush off her words, because she obviously doesn't know what she's talking about.

Greg grins as I walk up to him and give

him the approved, church-sister hug.

"I hope you weren't offended. I wasn't trying to call you out specifically. You didn't start that tradition."

"I wasn't offended at all. That was a teaching moment for me. I don't think I ever knew that was what happened when the people threw money at the apostles' feet. I learned something new."

"Well, I just want you to know that I meant it when I said how much I appreciate the service you're doing at this church. We need more like you."

"You're welcome."

Greg shakes my hand firmly, and starts to make eye contact with the next person in the line. That was it? Thank you for your service, Felicia. And walk away? After the moment we shared?

Okay, I see that he is going to be harder to crack than I thought he would be. It's time for me to pull out the big guns. I'm all his, and he needs to recognize what that means, what we could have, once we move Nya out of the way.

Our connection is for the advancement of the kingdom, and sometimes the kingdom has to be taken by force.

Chapter 42
Nya

Something doesn't feel right in my spirit. I have no idea what it is, because I haven't had a vision or anything like that, but I just feel extremely unsettled. I'm getting ready to go and preach this evening, at this church in Philadelphia, so maybe someone in the congregation really needs something from me. A word from God.

Morning service was good. The pastor preached on the sanctity of marriage and the marriage bed being undefiled. It's as if he'd spied into my hotel room the night before. Because the pictures I ended up sending Greg looked like something an Instagram groupie might send to an athlete or a rapper. He was happy though, so that's all that matters. Maybe he'll forget that he was mad at me for not remembering his grant proposal.

Back in my hotel room, I'm having a chicken Caesar salad, although I want something heavier. I never eat a large meal before I preach though. There's nothing like trying to minister with indigestion.

My phone buzzes with a number that I don't recognize, but since it's a Dallas number I answer it.

"Hello?"

"Uh, hello? Hello? My word. Hold on, baby."

I let out a giggle. I can tell it's Mother Olivia, and clearly she doesn't know what she's doing with her cell phone.

"Hello? Can you hear me?" Mother Olivia asks.

"Yes, Mother, I can hear you. How are you?"

"Is this Nya?" Mother Olivia asks. "I need to speak to Evangelist Nya Hampstead."

"It's me, Mother. It's Nya."

"Oh, well. Hello. You need to come home right away."

"What's wrong, Mother? Is everything all right?"

"It will be when you brang yo' behind on home. You been gallivanting around the country speaking at everybody churches, and there's a woman here. I think she's trying to run up behind my pastor."

I take the phone away from my ear and

look at it. Did she just say what I think she said?

"Come again, Mother Olivia? What do you mean a woman trying to run up behind Greg?"

"What you think I mean? Some floozy going up to the altar and throwing money at Pastor Greg's feet, dressed like the whore of Babylon."

I know Mother Olivia can exaggerate sometimes, so I'm gonna take "whore of Babylon" with a grain of salt.

"Mother, are you sure she wasn't just leaving an offering?"

"Whatever she was doing, my pastor put her in check. But you need to get home anyway. Greg is sick as a dog too."

Now why didn't she start the conversation with this? I don't care about a woman trying to go after Greg, but I definitely want to take care of him if he's sick.

"What's wrong with him, Mother?"

"He's got a high fever. I gave him some medicine, but you know how he is. He wouldn't come home with me to let me and Deacon take care of him. Where are you, anyway? Can you get home tonight?"

"I may be able to get on the first flight out in the morning. I don't know if there are any more leaving out tonight."

"Well, you do whatever you need to do."

"Okay, Mother. I will be there. Thank you for letting me know."

The sense of urgency in Mother Olivia's voice makes me worry. As many times as I've traveled over these last five years, no one has ever called me and asked me to rush home.

Immediately, I dial Lady Sandy to let her know I have a change of plans.

"Hello, Nya. Do you need something? Do I need to send someone over to your room with anything?"

"No, thank you, Lady Sandy. I'm just calling to let you know I have to fly out first thing in the morning."

"But we have that brunch for my sorority. They are giving us a pretty high honor, especially since you're not a member."

"I know, but my husband is sick. I need to go home and tend to him. One of the church mothers just called me."

Lady Sandy bursts into laughter. "Is Greg an infant? I don't see why you would need to miss receiving an award and networking with these women just because Greg is feeling under the weather."

I start to explain to Lady Sandy that Mother Olivia wouldn't have called me unless it was truly serious, and that Greg is incredibly self-sufficient. But then I realize that I'm good and grown. I don't answer to this woman or her sorority. Lady Sandy has been overstepping her bounds lately anyway. This is as good a time as any to tell her to stand down.

"Lady Sandy, I am just informing you of my plans to go home. I'm not asking your permission."

There is a long silence. For a moment, I think Lady Sandy has hung up on me.

"Do you have any idea the amount of pull it took for me to get my sorority to honor you?" she asks in a nasty tone that I most often hear from women right before they deliver a spanking to a child.

She has definitely got me confused with Penelope. I'm not the one. Not today. Not when my husband is sick.

"Send them my apologies, Lady Sandy. I will see you back in Dallas. Have a wonderful evening."

I don't wait for her to say good-bye before I disconnect the call. I'm sure this is going to cause strife between us and may have damaged the relationship beyond repair. If it did, maybe the season for this relationship is over. My weariness is now spilling over to everything — the way I deal with my husband, and the way I communicate in general.

I dial Greg's number and wait for him to answer. After three rings he picks up.

"Nya?"

"Yes. How are you feeling?"

"I'm good. Wait . . ."

I hear a good amount of gagging and retching in the background. Enough to make me feel worried and one hundred percent sold on my decision to defy Lady Sandy.

"I just have a little bug, babe. I'm gonna lie down for a little while. I will see you when you get home."

"Wait . . . Greg . . ."

He's already disconnected the call. I toss my phone on the bed and start to pack my bags. I don't want to miss that early flight.

Lady Sandy is just going to have to be mad. If she wants, she can go exert her will over her daughter. As for me and my luggage, we're getting on a plane at the crack of dawn.

CHAPTER 43
NYA

The first thing I notice when I open the door to our home is that it's stifling hot. It's summer in Dallas, and it doesn't feel like the air conditioning is running. I go straight to the thermostat and turn on the air. Like I thought, the temperature in this house is ninety degrees.

"Babe!" I call. "Where are you?"

"Nya?" I hear Greg call out in a weak voice.

He's in the downstairs guest bedroom for some reason. The door is cracked, but as I push it open I can immediately tell that Greg is very ill. The room smells faintly of vomit. Greg is in the bed with the blanket pulled up to his chin.

"You're home?" Greg asks in a soft voice.

"Yes, I'm home. Or do you think you're hallucinating?"

Greg laughs, and it sounds weak. "I might be seeing things. It's cold in here. Did you turn on the air?"

I walk over to the bed and touch Greg's neck. "You're burning up. Have you taken something for this fever?"

"Mother Olivia gave me one of her prescription ibuprofen at church yesterday, but I haven't taken anything since then."

"Lord have mercy. Let me go get you some medicine."

I go into the kitchen and put together a tray with water, orange juice, ibuprofen, and a few crackers. I don't know if Greg can keep anything down. From the smell in the room, I'm thinking he can't, but he'll need to eat something with these pills.

When I walk back into the room with the tray, Greg has fallen asleep. I gently wake him. "Here, take this before you go off to dreamland."

Greg takes the medicine and a glass of water from me. When I try to give him the crackers he frowns.

"No food. My stomach . . ."

"Try to eat one. You need something on your stomach for the medicine."

Greg closes his eyes and takes a bite that he chews slowly. He swallows and washes it down with a little more water.

"I'm glad you're here, Nya. I thought I was going to have to call an ambulance."

"Silly! You don't need an ambulance. All you needed to do was tell me you were sick and I would've been here. Why did Mother Olivia have to be the one to call me?"

"I didn't think you'd come."

I shake my head and wipe Greg's brow with a cool, damp towel. "Well, I'm here. Get some rest."

I finally take a deep breath when I'm outside the room. Trying to exhale out any germs and inhale some crud-free oxygen. I don't think I've ever seen Greg this sick.

Back in the kitchen, I check to see if I have everything to make my chicken noodle soup. It's just what Greg needs to eat until his stomach is solid again.

I take a whole chicken out of the freezer and set it in a pan of water to defrost while I cut up the vegetables. Just now, I wonder what Lady Sandy and her sorority sisters are doing at their award banquet. I might be missed, but I think they'll make it.

I'm surprised when the doorbell rings because it's two o'clock in the afternoon. I don't want to wake Greg to ask him if he's expecting anyone, so I wipe my hands with a kitchen towel and go check to see for myself.

I look out the peephole and there is a woman standing on the other side. She's holding what looks like a Crock-Pot, and is wearing a snug T-shirt and yoga pants.

I swing the door open, half ready to start swinging something else. "Can I help you?" I ask.

"Oh, Pastor Nya. You're home!"

So she's a member of our church. That's the thing about having a church with thousands of members. You can't possibly know everyone, although I think I'd make it a point to know this chick. I wonder if she's the floozy Mother Olivia was talking about. She must be.

"I am. Were you here for my husband?"

She looks uncomfortable. "I'm Sister Felicia. I saw that Pastor Greg was under the weather at church yesterday, and I just wanted to make him some soup."

I lift an eyebrow, then give her a fake smile. Greg ain't eating that soup. Making the pastor soup when he's sick is something the church mothers would do. Maybe even the pastor's aid committee. Not a single (she's not wearing a ring) sister in skintight clothing.

I reach my hands out for the pot. "I would invite you in, but I don't want you to get sick too. I think this house is full of germs."

"Oh, it's no problem. I think I'm the one who infected Pastor Greg. I just got over this same bug last week."

I swallow hard. "You infected him, you say?"

"Yes, we had to have a meeting with a huge corporation that's giving us a faith-based grant for the youth center. I pressed my way even though I was feeling sick that morning."

"Mm-hmm . . ."

"Anyway, we got the grant, so that's a plus, right?"

I cock my head to one side and look at her. She's young. Maybe still in her twenties, but definitely younger than we are. Her body looks toned, like she works out all the time.

"That is a plus. Downside is, my husband is sick as a dog. Thank you for the soup. I'll have someone bring your pot to church on Sunday."

"I can come pick it up."

"No need for you to come back out here. I hope you didn't have to drive far."

She shakes her head. "I live in Southlake too. Not a big mansion like this, but I've got a condo about two minutes from here. It was no trouble at all."

"A single woman with a condo in Southlake. That's an accomplishment."

She gives me a huge smile. "I'm extremely

blessed, Pastor Nya."

"Indeed."

"I will see about getting the pot from Lena on Sunday."

I start to close the door. "All right then. Good-bye. Be blessed."

I walk straight to the kitchen with the pot and empty the soup down the garbage disposal while it runs. It smells good, but something in my gut says this girl is on some mess.

Why can't God give me a prophetic vision right now, to let me know Felicia's plans, if she has any? It never works that way, though.

I go back to chopping vegetables, but I can't take my mind off that chick who showed up at my door. I take out my phone and go peek to see if Greg is asleep. Then I step outside our front door, sit on the steps, and dial Tina.

"Everything okay?" Tina says when she answers the phone.

"Greg is okay. I think he just has the flu."

"Good. Do you think Lady Sandy will be mad that you left?"

"I don't care if she is. I'll probably just meet y'all back in Atlanta next week to tape the next few episodes of the show."

"Okay. What's wrong, girl?"

"How do you know something is wrong?"

"I can hear it in your voice. What's up?"

In a flurry of words I tell my best friend everything about Felicia and her pot of chicken soup that no one is eating.

"So you say she's been working with Greg?"

"Apparently, on some grants for the youth center. But you know what's crazy? Greg has never mentioned this woman to me. He told me about the grant. He even went as far as to say that the church was approved for the grant money, but he didn't say anything about a chick with perfect hair and a perfect body working with him on it. Why would he keep her a secret?"

"Wait. You should get his explanation first. Don't just assume he was keeping secrets. Maybe he doesn't think that you care about the day-to-day operations of the church while you're out traveling."

"I can tell you one thing. We need to figure out how to consolidate the taping of these shows, because I need to be at home more."

"Maybe you should just quit doing the conference dates altogether for a while. Lady Sandy and company can find someone else to preach in your place."

I carefully consider this. I wonder what Lady Sandy would say if I said I didn't want to do the conference dates anymore. They have become a big source of income for her Women's Empowerment foundation, but it's not like she can't bring on one of her big-name friends to preach for me.

"I think you're right. I'm going to talk to Lady Sandy."

"And I wouldn't worry about the chicken-soup-making bird. You and Greg are about to celebrate your fifteenth anniversary. Your marriage is stronger than that."

"Thank you for saying that, girl. I know it's true, but I guess I just needed to hear someone else say it."

"Anytime."

I disconnect the call and place my phone on the ground next to me. I pull my knees up to my chest and try to believe what Tina said to me. Greg and I are solid. We may have a few chinks in our marriage armor, but for the most part, we got this, and I know it.

So tell me why I've got a horrible feeling in the pit of my stomach about this one. I want to call the church mothers and ask them to put us on the prayer list. I think we could use just a few prayers of the righteous.

CHAPTER 44
FELICIA

This is not how this was supposed to happen. Nya wasn't supposed to be home when I brought Greg that soup. I wonder what made her show up all of a sudden. I bet it was Mother Olivia and her meddling old self. She just added herself to my list of people that I need to move out of my way to get my blessing.

It's Thursday, and finally Greg's car is back at the church. It's been several days since he's been here. I guess that flu bug really did lay him out. I hate that he got sick, especially because it's brought everything to a head now.

I didn't want to have to expedite my plan. I wanted Greg to desire me enough to put his marriage in jeopardy. And he was getting there too. Him spinning me around and nearly kissing me is proof of that.

I scan the parking lot to make sure Nya isn't anywhere on campus. For the past couple of days she's been a fixture at the church offices, going in and out, carrying folders and envelopes and everything else. I don't know what she's up to, but she's busy.

I have to watch out for Mother Olivia too. She's been making her presence known every day. She's planning this anniversary banquet for Greg and Nya. It's an event that I hoped to prevent from even taking place, but since it's happening in a month, I probably don't have time to stop it. But I can show up, looking fabulous, and stealing everyone's shine — including Nya's.

Finally, when I think the coast is clear, I rush into the administrative building that houses Greg's office. I'm about to knock on the door when Lena walks up. Darn. I didn't need any interruptions.

"Hey Lena, what's going on, girl?" I ask.

She narrows her eyes at me. "I don't have an appointment with you on Pastor Greg's calendar. How can I help you?"

"Oh well, I didn't have an appointment, but I just found another grant program that he might want me to show to Pastor Nya. He says she has some initiatives that she wants to work on."

The mention of Nya's name seems to throw Lena off. Obviously someone — Mother Olivia, probably — has her thinking that I have bad intentions toward Greg. Why would a woman who wanted to be the pastor's mistress be planning to work with the pastor's wife?

"I still don't have an appointment for you," Lena says. "Especially since you somehow told me the wrong time for that grant meeting."

Oh. That's what she's mad about. It has nothing to do with Mother Olivia at all. She's angry that she got left out of that meeting.

"Girl, you know that was not on purpose. I'm so sorry."

"Mm-hmm. You had Pastor Greg thanking you on Sunday during his sermon like you were the only one who worked on that grant proposal. I did a lot too."

This delay is actually starting to irritate me, but let me go ahead and humor this heffa so I can get her out of my way. "I promise that it won't happen again. As a matter of fact, I was going to start teaching you how to actually write sections of the grant proposals. We're going to have more work than we can handle pretty soon, and I will need someone like you to back me up."

"Really? I definitely want to learn how to write grants. That's a skill I can use outside the church too. Look what it got you. You living like a baller out there in Southlake and everything. You need to hook your girl up."

"And I will. I just need to talk to Pastor Greg really quickly about this research I've done."

"Okay, girl. I was just messing with you. Go ahead and knock. He doesn't have anyone in there right now."

"Good. Could you do me a favor, Lena?"

"Sure."

"Can you make sure no one interrupts us for at least the next forty-five minutes? I need Pastor Greg's undivided attention. There is a lot of money on the line here, and I want Love First to get a nice big chunk of it."

Lena nods emphatically. "Absolutely. I will let the saints know that Pastor Greg is busy and can't be disturbed."

"Thank you."

I tap on Greg's door and his booming voice comes through the wood. "Come in."

He smiles at me as I step inside his office. I'm dressed casually, but sexy enough to where Greg can admire my curves without necessarily lusting over them.

"Sister Felicia. How are you? Did we have a meeting today? If we did, and I had an action item, please forgive me. I'm just getting back into the groove of things after being sick."

"I'm sorry about that, Pastor Greg. I think I'm the one who got you sick."

"I agree. You came in my office breathing germs all over the place. But since we got that grant money, I'm going to forgive you. I'm better now."

"Did my chicken soup help?"

Greg looks confused. "Nya made me some of her chicken soup. You brought me some too?"

"I did. Pastor Nya didn't mention it, did she?"

He shakes his head. "No, but I bet it's in the freezer for another time we're feeling sick. Thank you so much for thinking of us. I appreciate it."

I walk over to sit in the chair in front of Greg's desk. When I sit, I watch his eyes rest on my cleavage, which is very visible in my low-cut blouse. At a distance, he probably didn't notice, but with my boobs at eye level right now, he can't help but gaze. He wouldn't be a man if he didn't.

"So, Sister Felicia, is there something that we're supposed to be meeting about today?"

I breathe deeply before I begin. I take myself back to Atlanta five years ago. Transport my mind to the table where my perfectly healthy child was murdered by Lance and Dr. Tomlinson. I've not thought about these things in a few years. Every time it tries to press to the forefront of my memory, I push it back. But now I just let the memories bubble up and overflow.

The tears flow easily, and Greg quickly hands me a tissue.

"What's wrong, Sister Felicia? Please tell me."

"Pastor Greg, I've been wanting to tell you this for so long, but I didn't know how."

"It's fine. You can tell me anything. Don't be afraid."

I look up at him with tears streaming from my eyes. The concern on his face makes my heart swell with love for him.

"I-I came to this church because of Pastor Nya."

"Oh? Well, why does that upset you so much?"

"I'm the one who received that 'suddenly blessing' prophecy."

Greg nods slowly. "Really?"

"Yes. And my life has been nothing but a nightmare ever since."

I tell Greg about everything that happened to me after his wife muscled her way into my life with her false prophecy. I don't spare him any details.

When I'm finished, Greg sits back in his chair and strokes his goatee. I don't know how to read his demeanor, but I believe he's processing my words.

"You lost your baby."

"My baby was stolen from me."

Greg shakes his head and frowns. "You believe she gave you a false prophecy?"

"I don't know if she gives some people a good word, but I can promise you that nothing in my life happened that even remotely qualified as a blessing. And the things that happened suddenly were the most hurtful things that ever happened in my life."

"There's something I don't understand, though. If you think she gave you a false prophecy, and I'm not saying if she did or didn't, why are you here? Why would you join our church? Sit under our ministry? It doesn't make sense."

"I've been getting up the nerve, for the past five years, to ask her why she would do that to me. Why she would choose me to give that lie to, because for the life of me, I don't understand."

"Would you like for me to set up a meeting?"

"No, Pastor Greg. I don't think . . . when I brought you that soup, she was so mean to me. It was like . . . she thought I was trying to go after you or something."

Now Greg's face crinkles into an angry frown. "Are you kidding me?"

"Honestly, I thought she was going to throw the soup in my face. I was just so concerned about you, especially because I thought I gave you the flu in the first place . . ."

"I can't believe she treated you unkindly. That's not like her."

"Pastor Greg. There's more. She recognized me. I thought she wouldn't because I've lost weight since the conference and my hair is different."

"How do you know she recognized you?"

"She threatened me. She told me that if I tell anyone about her false prophecy that she would make sure I'd regret it."

"What? I'm calling her right now. That's crazy."

"No, no, please don't, Pastor Greg. Please keep this between us. I don't want her to think I'm a threat. I mean, Pastor Nya has built her entire career on the lie she told me."

"All of that 'suddenly' stuff is made up. It's a lie."

Greg says these words, but it's as if he's not even talking to me anymore. He's left the room. Like he's pondering the type of woman he's married to. He should be pondering, wondering, and doubting. She's a demon, if you ask me.

"Maybe I shouldn't have told you this, but it's killing me. I've been holding it inside for so long, and you've been so good to me. I-I just didn't want you to find out some other way."

"No, thank you for coming to me. I'm your pastor. You don't have to worry about me saying anything to Pastor Nya."

"Will you . . . will you pray for me?"

Greg gets up and walks around his desk. He pulls me to my feet and puts a dab of anointed oil on my forehead from a little bottle on his desk.

"Close your eyes. Bow your head," he says.

He takes my hands and squeezes. He says a prayer over me that had to move something in the heavens, because it definitely moved me.

When he finishes, I look into his face with tears in my eyes. Real tears. Retelling that story brought up some genuine emotions.

"Thank you, Pastor."

"You're welcome. If my wife lied to you, she's going to apologize. I don't know if she's to blame for the things that happened to you, but she definitely had you thinking you had a blessing on the way."

"I know it seems crazy that I'm here, but I . . . I guess I'm just looking for answers, that's all."

"And I'm going to make sure you get them. And that you're healed and whole."

"Thank you, Pastor."

Greg gives me a chaste hug and walks me to the door. I wondered how things would unfold if I told him about his lying wife. Part of me expected him to throw me out of his office. To tell me to get out and never come back.

But he didn't. Because Greg is man after God's heart, and a lover of God loves God's people. Me. I am a daughter of the King.

I hope Greg realizes that his wife, the liar, isn't anything like him. She isn't a kingdom builder like we are. She's working for the other side.

CHAPTER 45
NYA

I have worn myself out doing a deep cleaning on my home. I actually am grateful for the break when I hear the doorbell ring. I was scrubbing soap scum out of my Jacuzzi tub, and my knees had just started to burn.

When I open the front door and see Penelope standing there with tears in her eyes, I immediately invite her in.

"I'm sorry to just show up like this," she says. "Obviously you're busy."

"Not too busy. I need to finish up anyway. We have Bible study tonight. Come on in the kitchen. I'll fix us a cup of tea."

Penelope follows me into the kitchen and sits at the bar while I start with the tea.

"What's wrong, girl?" I ask.

"My mother is tripping out," she says. "She went crazy on me. She said you told her I faked a prophecy."

I close my eyes. I should've known that Lady Sandy was going to light into Penelope about that. She's all about appearances. What people think means more to Lady Sandy than the truth.

"I mean, you did fake it."

"That's what I keep trying to tell you, Nya. I didn't fake it. Everything I told you, I felt. It scared me when you said your vision was the opposite of what I saw. I wondered what it was that I experienced, if it wasn't real."

I place a cup of tea in front of her and a few packages of sugar.

"I think that you just want it so badly that you convinced yourself you got a prophetic word."

"It felt so real, though."

"Just like sometimes people feel so good in a church service and proclaim that they're healed, but they're really not. It's almost like a form of self-hypnosis."

Penelope shakes her head and sighs. "You're so right. About how badly I want this, I mean. I think it will finally make my parents proud of me. Imagine it! Me being able to command a room full of believers like you do. People flocking to a conference to hear a word from me. My mother will finally get off my back."

"You know, there was one time that you did something in defiance of Lady Sandy, that I thought was the beginning of a transformational ministry for you."

Penelope gives me a confused look and places her teacup on the counter. "When did I ever defy my mother?"

"You don't remember? You wrote your testimony down in our book. You were going to share your altar-call experience. Remember?"

"Oh yes. And my mother shut that down real quick."

"I think we should've fought back. I think that was the first move you made in actually discovering your purpose."

"Maybe. But that moment is gone now. I missed that opportunity."

"Perhaps not. I have an idea that can help both of us get free of your mother's clutches."

"You're not in her clutches, Nya. You can walk away from her anytime you want. You've got your church and your husband. At this point, you can start making deals without her if you want to do the other stuff too. She's made herself the middleman, but she doesn't own you like she owns me. I am hers. Literally."

Of course Penelope doesn't know why I feel bound. She doesn't know that one lie so many years ago has tethered me to this

333

journey. Made me have to stick around to make sure it doesn't spiral out of control. Yes, I have enjoyed the perks and the celebrity status and the money, but at the end of the day, I didn't want that blessing prophecy to become even more twisted than the initial perversion. I've been doing five plus years of damage control.

I'm ready for it to be over. And I know exactly how to end it with a bang.

CHAPTER 46
FELICIA

I have to dress carefully for Bible study tonight. Very carefully. I choose a long, loose skirt that will billow out around me when I fall to the floor. I've pinned my long wig into a low bun at the nape of my neck. This is perfection, and exactly what I need.

But the item I really need is wrapped carefully in tissue paper. When I saw it at a craft fair last weekend, I knew it was perfect.

I unwrap the ornately decorated, expertly crafted ceramic box. It's small, and can hold maybe three or four ounces of liquid. But that's all I need for my demonstration.

And after tonight, Greg will know beyond a shadow of a doubt that I should be his partner. Tonight is going to change everything.

CHAPTER 47
NYA

Tonight, Greg and I decide to ride together to Bible study. Usually we go separately. Most of the time he's already at the church and I'm either traveling or coming from home. But tonight we were both at home.

"Did you see Melody and her little girl at church on Sunday?" I ask Greg as he drives.

He nods. "I did. Her daughter is getting so big. She told me she was taking classes at the community college."

"I am so proud of her. I'm glad we were able to get her out of that situation."

"Me too. You had a vision about her, didn't you? That first day you saw her in church."

"I sure did. I saw her at the abortion clinic. And she had been thinking of doing that. God wanted to step in and save that baby."

"It definitely was God's will for her to be in the sanctuary that day. *That* day, God truly moved."

Greg's tone is so dry and direct. I don't know what's wrong with him, but he's been acting very strange. I've stayed home ever since I flew back to take care of him when he was sick, so he can't be feeling neglected.

"Greg, is there something bothering you? You feeling okay?"

"Yes. Why do you ask?"

"Just wondering."

Greg cocks his head to one side and gives me a strange look. "Are you having a vision about me? Am I about to be blessed? Suddenly?"

"Okay, now I definitely know you're acting weird."

"Nah, I've just got a lot on my plate. A ministry to run. I'm glad you're home. How long are you gonna be in town?"

"I don't know. I was thinking of quitting the talk show. Let someone else step into that role."

"Why would you do that? You've sacrificed so much for that show. For Lady Sandy and her vision. Why would you walk away before it's finished?"

Greg has always wanted me to quit and cut ties with Lady Sandy. He never wanted me to connect with her in the first place. Now he's giving me grief for considering cutting ties. Something isn't right. All I can think about is that heffa bringing that pot of soup to my house like Greg was her man or something. She was way too bold and familiar.

"I thought you wanted me to quit. Has something changed? You like me being out of town now?"

"Of course not. I want you home for good."

"Okay. I'm working on it."

"Did you prepare something for Bible study tonight?" Greg asks. "Or am I going solo?"

I shake my head. I actually did start studying something, but I'm not feeling it tonight. I think it's stress, or maybe just pure fatigue, but I just don't feel in the mood for bringing the word.

"You're solo, babe. Do you mind?"

"Nope."

Greg is tripping, but I don't have the energy to address it. "I just want to be a congregation member tonight, and receive a good word."

"Do you want to come up to the altar for prayer? Rededicate your life to Christ? You know you can be rebaptized too."

I think these are jokes, but the deadpan way he's delivering them makes me wonder if he's trying to tell me something.

"What are you trying to say, Greg? You think I need prayer?"

"I think we all do."

"Do you think I need it more urgently than others?"

"Do *you*?"

I shake my head and give his dry jokes a dry chuckle in response. I don't need a vision to tell me Greg is on something tonight.

We get to the church, and for some reason it's jam-packed for a Bible study. Although on Sundays we have a big crowd, we typically only see a couple hundred for Bible study.

"Wow. Is Mother Olivia and her crew cooking dinner? There are so many people here."

"No. I've been doing a study series. This is week three. Everyone loves it."

"Really? What's it about?"

Greg laughs. "You haven't even been watching the Bible studies online when you travel? You totally disconnect from your church when you get out there, don't you? I guess Prophetess Nya doesn't have a church home."

Admittedly, I haven't been watching the Bible studies on our website. I've been meaning to get caught up since I've been home, but I've been doing a flurry of other things. Now that I think of it, those other things were pretty unimportant.

"I do need to catch up, but I'm excited. What's the topic?"

"Jesus's one-on-one encounters with people in the Bible."

Wow. He took the topic we were supposed to do together and developed a Bible study series from it. Even though I am irritated, I'm not quite sure if I should be.

We walk into the church together and as soon as we hit the door, Greg and I are separated. So many people want to hug me because they haven't seen me in weeks. I let Greg go ahead and get prepared to minister while I give my friends in the congregation some much missed attention and affection. Besides having Greg by my side, this is the part that I crave when I'm out in unfamiliar places. I miss the safety and security of home.

Tina links arms with me as I walk into the sanctuary.

"You sitting in the pulpit or in the pews with me?" she asks.

"Greg is preaching tonight, so I will sit with you."

I wave at a few more people as I sit next to Tina on the second pew. The praise team is already up and has started to sing.

After a few selections, the church is in an uproar of praise and worship. People are in tears, hands raised to the ceiling. The spirit is so high, God's presence almost feels tangible. I have missed this too. Never experience this on the road. We've had a few moments, but mostly it felt manufactured and orchestrated. This is the real thing.

The people are primed for a word, it seems, and Greg seems prepared with one.

"Tonight we're going to talk about intimacy. I lost some of y'all already," Greg says with a laugh. "Some of y'all went straight carnal as soon as I said intimacy. And some other night we'll talk about that intimacy y'all thinking about. Between a man and a woman. But not tonight. This evening, we're going to talk about intimacy with God."

A round of applause goes up from the congregation. Some stand to their feet.

"You know that's what He wants from you, right? He wants to be face-to-face with you. He wants to rub noses with you in the spirit, like an Eskimo kiss. Who wants to kiss the Savior tonight?"

After another round of applause, Greg smiles. "Okay, y'all, open your Bibles to the Gospel of John, chapter —"

Before Greg can finish his sentence a loud wail comes from the back of the sanctuary. Greg makes eye contact with me and looks down at his notes.

"That's John, chapter four —"

This time the wail is so loud and clear that the majority of the congregation turns to look. I can't help myself, so I look around too. I want to hear who has that kind of despair in the sanctuary tonight.

I narrow my eyes at the pitiful figure stumbling down the aisle of the church. She is wearing a long skirt and it looks as if . . . is she barefoot?

As she gets closer to me, I narrow my eyes and look at her face. Although it's contorted from her screaming and hollering, I recognize her immediately. It's the chicken-soup maker.

I stand to my feet and step out into the aisle. I'm going to intercept whatever it is she's trying to do.

When she gets to our pew, I reach out and grab her arm. She snatches it away like I shocked her. Then she looks me dead in my face, and snarls.

"Liar," she whispers. "You are a liar."

Then she reaches toward Greg with an outstretched arm. She's holding something in her other hand, but I can't see what it is.

"Pastor!" she cries. "Pastor Greg!"

I am about to have security escort this crazy wench out of the building, when I notice that Greg's hand is outstretched too. What in the world?

Greg nods to one of the ministers on the front row. "Bring her up here," he says.

Two ministers jump up from their seats and flank her on either side.

"While she's coming up here, I don't want any of you to sit in your seats judging her. I have knowledge of this woman's situation, and I promise that most of you wouldn't even have the strength to walk down this aisle if you'd gone through what she's gone through."

That heffa wails louder, giving Greg's words extra effect. I wonder if they planned this.

"She's lost everything."

Humph. Not everything. The heffa lives in Southlake, where even a townhouse would cost over four hundred thousand dollars. I wouldn't say she's lost everything.

"I see some of you are unconvinced, but that's okay. God knows what she's gone through. God's collecting her tears right now."

When on the platform, the heffa whispers to one of the ministers, who then whispers to Greg. Greg pauses for a moment and then nods. He steps out of his shoes and removes his socks.

Wait, what? Oh, I don't even believe this. Tina grabs my arm like she doesn't believe it either. Mother Olivia makes a sound like she just sniffed a sour carton of milk.

This *heffa* has kneeled on the floor in front of my husband. She's pouring something on his feet and crying at the same time.

"This is someone who wants a God experience," Greg says. "Pray for her."

"She wants a *Greg* experience," Tina whispers.

I was almost able to stay in my seat, but when the heffa unpins her hair and lets that wig fall over Greg's feet, I have had quite enough.

When I get in the aisle, Mother Olivia stops me. "I got this, baby," she says.

Mother Olivia, in all her plus-size sanctuary-nurse glory, waddles up onto the stage with a huge white sheet in her hand. First, she looks at Greg like he ain't got good sense. She takes one hand and pushes him in the middle of his chest, separating him from the Brazilian hair tangled up over his feet. Then, when she's backed Greg away, she takes the sheet and whips it through the air like the sail of a ship. It billows through the air and lands on the heffa. Perfectly covering her from head to toe.

I guess she's finished. And that's that.

Thrown off his message some, Greg slips back into his shoes, without the socks. He walks down from the podium to speak, leaving the heffa lying on the floor with the sheet over her.

Greg motions with a head nod for the rest of the ministers to go and lay hands on her. When he's sure she's being taken care of, he continues to speak.

I don't hear another word coming out of his mouth. I'm watching the heffa like a hawk, because if she rises from the floor and goes anywhere near Greg, I'm going to turn into one of those women on those ridiculous videos that get posted on social media. The ones where the women are fighting and hair weave is flying all over the place.

This chick is utterly disrespectful. And Greg? Well, he's got more than a few questions to answer.

CHAPTER 48
NYA

We're in the car, on the way home from church. I held it in until we were pulled away and driving down Interstate 35, but now that we're out of earshot of our members, I'm about to cut all the way up.

"Greg."

He glances over at me and pretends that he doesn't hear me. Then he grips the steering wheel and stares at the road. What in the heck is he mad about? There's only one person in this car who has the right to be furious, and that's me.

"Really, Greg? You're not talking to me? I don't understand the nature of your attitude. I just watched a woman, who clearly wants you, pour oil on your feet, cry tears, and wipe them with her hair."

"I think she identifies with the woman with the alabaster box."

"She better be glad her face didn't identify with getting slapped by the open side of my palm. Are you kidding me?"

"Get out of here, woman. All of the theatrics y'all do on your little 'suddenly' outings, and you're going to say something about this?"

"So, who are you? You Jesus or somebody?" I want to throw something at him. "You know good and well that was inappropriate."

"I wouldn't have sanctioned it if I'd known what she was going to do, but I think it was an authentic moment. I believe the Holy Spirit moved her from her seat."

"You cannot be serious, Greg. That was not the Holy Spirit. That was planned and calculated. You can't tell me she didn't wear that getup on purpose, looking like a damn gypsy prostitute."

"You cussing now?"

"Then she just happened to have her hair in a style that she could unpin and let flow all over your feet? Oh . . . and she just coincidentally . . . in her purse had a ceramic box with oil in it. Miss me with that. You 'bout to make me think you were in on it."

"Really?"

"Yeah, really, player. Is it also just mere chance that the same chick crying on your feet brought you a pot of chicken noodle soup? And she's confiding in you? Telling you all her trials? What'd you do, Pastor Greg? Where'd you lay hands to make it feel better?"

I know I've gone too far. To the point of no return, but there's no taking it back now. I've never had a more visceral reaction to any other woman with reference to Greg.

"You can't stand me having a ministry moment, can you? You so used to people fawning over your anointing that you couldn't let that woman get her break-through."

"That was not a ministry moment. The woman came and laid her body across your feet, Greg. How do you think that looked?"

"How did it look when the woman with the oil washed Jesus's feet with her tears?"

"You. Are. Not. Jesus."

As Greg gets off the highway, he hits a curve too fast and nearly puts the car up on two wheels. He's gonna kill us, taking up for this woman.

"Neither are you, but you think you are. You think you're the only one in our church with a yoke-breaking ministry. Felicia was crying out to God. You and Mother Olivia stood in the way of that. Like, what type of pastor does that? Where is your compassion?"

"Why is it that you know all of her struggles, Greg? Protocol is to send wailing women to our female ministry staff."

"We'd gained a rapport working on the grant proposals. There was nothing ungodly about her sharing her pain with one of her pastors."

"I have a problem with it. So, let's find her someone else to link up with."

"You worried about Felicia? You shouldn't be. All she's doing is writing grants for our church. She's already gotten us a quarter of a million dollars in grant money for the youth center."

"I didn't know you were that hands-on when it came to grants."

"You aren't hands-on at all when it comes to our church, so how would you know?"

"So, your message moved her so much that she got out of her seat and lay out on the floor."

"Apparently."

"If it was such an awesome move of God, why was she the only one to come up to the altar?"

I know as soon as the words come out of my mouth that this is foul, but it's too late. The words are out already. The truth is, Greg's message wasn't all that. It was pretty perfunctory if you ask me. Nothing extra-anointed about that message.

"I guess there's only room for one celebrity pastor in our church, huh? All hail, Queen Nya, the most anointed in the land."

I roll my eyes. "Come on Greg! You can't see what that woman was trying to do? Are you so desperately starved for attention that some crazy woman can walk down to the altar and make you feel like the man?"

"You know what that feels like. Feeling like *the man*? You strut around on stage growling. Sounding just like you're possessed. Maybe you think you're truly a man, 'cause I ain't seen a woman doing woman things in my house in a long time."

"I don't feel like the man, Greg. Mostly . . . mostly I feel like a fraud."

Greg shakes his head. "You should. Because you are."

"What do you mean by that?"

Greg presses his lips together and flares his nose. "Nothing. I don't mean anything by it."

Then, at the most inopportune time, I feel the tingle in my spirit that means a vision is coming.

The woman sits at my feet with clothing that is way too tight. Her hair is a mess and so is her makeup, but the most memorable thing about her is the wailing. She wails at the top of her lungs, and her wailing makes me want to give her something. The people are waiting for something.

"Oh my God," I say, snapping out of my vision. "It's her."

"Who?"

I slam my hand on the dashboard. "It's her. Your alabaster woman. She's the one I gave the 'suddenly blessing' prophecy to at that conference. She looks different. Slimmer, with better clothes and a better wig. But it's her."

"And why wouldn't it be? You gave her a prophecy that changed her life. Or, should I say, destroyed her life."

"Destroyed her life? Wh-what happened to her?"

We're not home yet, but Greg pulls the car to a stop at a gas station. I guess he doesn't want to keep driving as he tells me this.

Greg turns to me and gives me a sneer. "While you were off prancing around in half the pulpits in America, she got involved with a married man, thinking he was her blessing," he says.

"That wasn't smart."

"And she got pregnant by him. The man

plotted and schemed with a doctor and they convinced her the baby had such a devastating birth defect that she had an abortion."

"Oh my goodness," I say, not wanting to hear anymore.

"Wait, it gets worse. So then, she gets an infection after the abortion that caused her to have a hysterectomy."

"Father God in heaven."

"Does she sound suddenly blessed to you?"

I don't reply. I can't reply. This is too much. I literally feel like I'm breaking inside, but I don't feel as if I have the right to break. I've not suffered at all from my lie. And even though this woman was off her rocker to think that someone's husband was a blessing, I disrespected the gift. I brought sorrow.

"Why would you do that, Nya? Why would you stand up there and lie?"

"Greg . . ."

Greg takes both my arms and squeezes. "Why would you need to make up a prophetic word? God speaks through you . . . right? Or have you made it up this entire time?"

I shake my head. "Just that one time. I've never lied about it before. You know it runs in my family."

"I don't know what I know. What I thought I knew, I didn't know."

"Can't you see she's trying to get revenge on me, Greg? Through you. She wants me to pay, so she's throwing herself at your feet."

Greg shakes his head and chuckles. "I'm her pastor, Nya. Or have you been gone so long that you forget what pastors do? We have a whole congregation here. They need our prayers, and they're standing in the gap for us when we need prayer. But I guess you haven't been thinking about that because you're a celebrity based on a fraudulent word."

I stare at Greg. Blink a few times and wonder how much time he's actually spent with his alabaster-box woman. How many times has he stood in the gap for her?

I was wrong for lying on God to her. Dead wrong. But she's obviously insane if she thought God would bless her with someone else's husband. And since she's insane, she's capable of anything. It's time to stop her in her tracks, before she does even more damage to my home, to my ministry, and to my marriage.

CHAPTER 49
NYA

I've invited Felicia to meet me under the guise of completing another grant proposal for the church. She quickly accepted my request. Almost too quickly. Maybe because the request looked like it came from Greg.

I'm sitting in Greg's office at the church, waiting for her. I notice a vase of nearly dead flowers on his desk and remember my vision where he enjoyed the scent of roses. I guess I assumed that the flowers in my vision had come from me, but I didn't send these.

I walk over to the vase and remove the card from the bouquet. It says, "Congratulations, Greg! We make a great team. Kingdom business ☺Felicia."

She wrote "Greg" on her card. Not Pastor Hampstead, Pastor Greg, or simply Pastor. This note is too familiar and intimate. This heffa is beyond out of order, and so is

Greg's needy self for allowing it to go this far.

There's a knock on Greg's office door.

"Come in," I say.

The door swings open and Lena shows Felicia inside. Felicia wears a shocked expression on her face to go along with her shockingly tight white dress. She looks like she's on her way to an after-five event. Not a meeting with her pastor.

"I'm sorry," Felicia says. "I was supposed to be meeting with Pastor Greg."

I give Lena a hand wave to dismiss her. "Actually, I called the meeting, Felicia. Have a seat."

"*You* called a meeting with me? Why?"

I haven't decided yet what I'm going to say to her. I guess I just hoped she'd get here and God would give me a vision or show me what to do.

"You don't really think I would allow you to meet privately with my husband after last night, do you?"

She stares at me. Narrows her eyes, like she's sizing me up. I lean forward in my chair and square my shoulders up. Assertive moves. She needs to dial back a bit with her aggression.

"You wanted to meet about a grant proposal?" Felicia asks. Her facial expression indicates irritation, as if she has the right to an answer. She's the one sending my husband flowers. If anyone should look irritated, it's me.

"No. I want to know what your plans are for my husband."

Her mouth opens slightly as if she's going to respond, and then her lips curve into a smile. Not the reaction I was looking for.

"Pastor Greg is an incredible man of God who has poured so much into my life. I feel grateful for him. When I joined this church I was at the lowest point of my life. His ministry helped turn me around."

His ministry? Interesting.

"Are you from Dallas, Sister Felicia? What made you join our church out of all the churches in Dallas? What brought you to Love First?"

Her smile gets wider, almost maniacal. This girl either has mental problems or is possessed of a demon. I can't determine which.

"God brought me here," she says. "He ordered my steps."

I was hoping that she'd tell the truth. That she'd admit to being at Lady Sandy's Women's Empowerment session.

"Where did you serve before you came here?"

"I lived in Georgia, actually. I wasn't at any one church. I'm ashamed to say I did a bit of church hopping. Luckily, I got rooted and grounded when I arrived in Dallas."

"Why do you think God sent you here?"

She looks surprised by the question. Like she didn't expect me to ask it.

"I think God sent me here because my talents were needed by this church. He sent me here for kingdom business."

I point at the dying flowers. "That's what you said on the card. On the roses you sent to my husband."

Now Felicia's shocked expression seems full of worry. Her forehead creases as her eyebrows rise.

"Those were to congratulate him on getting the grant, Evangelist Hampstead. We worked really hard on that, and Pastor Greg impressed the grant makers. It wouldn't have happened if not for his charisma."

"Indeed."

"What? Do you not like the flowers?" Felicia asks.

"I love flowers. Some might find a single woman sending a married man roses inappropriate. But then I'm assuming that you're single. Are you?"

"I am, but I'm waiting for God to suddenly bless me with a covenant partner."

So she knows that I know, or at least hopes that I know. I'm not going to give her the pleasure.

"That's what God does sometimes. You could just be living your life and He'll just pop up out of nowhere with a blessing. Just like he sent you out of nowhere to bless our church with your talent."

"He did. Isn't God awesome?"

"Yes, and my husband speaks highly of you."

"He does?"

The excitement in her tone when she says this makes me want to jump up and choke her. Girlfriend better recognize. I may be an evangelist, but I can and will set it off if necessary.

"Yes. I'm going to be working on some grants for homeless teenagers in Dallas, and would like your help."

"Is this a Suddenly Nya initiative? Is this a part of your television show?"

"No. It's a Love First International initiative. Something Greg and I have been passionate about for years."

"Oh. He didn't mention it to me," Felicia says as she lifts one hand and glances at her manicured nails.

"And he probably wouldn't. He's not in the habit of talking about his hopes and dreams with our members. I'm sure you understand that. It wouldn't be —"

"Appropriate," Felicia says, finishing my sentence for me.

Felicia looks at her watch as if she's suddenly bored with the conversation. Then she reaches in her purse and hands me a card.

"E-mail me when you're ready to work on your grant proposal, Evangelist Nya. I want to respect your time, and let you go. Is there anything else you'd like to discuss today?"

There's a lot I would like to discuss, but maybe not today. As much as I want to go in on this heffa like she's any normal home-wrecking husband stealer, I don't. Somehow I wounded her with that prophecy. She wouldn't be here if I hadn't.

I need God's help on this one. I don't know how, but I have to right this wrong.

Chapter 50
Felicia

I look at the rectangular piece of paper in my hand. I ball it up and then I immediately change my mind. I smooth out the paper and place it on my bed. I stare at the words. FIFTEENTH WEDDING ANNIVERSARY GALA FOR PASTORS GREG AND NYA HAMPSTEAD.

I bought the ticket before Nya came home. Before she stepped back up into the church, ruining my plans and interrupting my seduction of Greg. I'm kicking myself for not moving faster, for thinking that I had all the time in the world, for acting like Nya would never come home.

Greg was touched when I brought my box of oil to the church. Of course the oil was symbolic. I was pouring all my gratitude out at his feet. He's the one who has made me feel loved. He's been the one to show compassion to me. Not his lying wife.

And that Mother Olivia. I ball my fists up

and pound against my chest, thinking of her. She embarrassed me by covering me with that sheet. She even covered my head, like she was a magician trying to make me disappear. I owe her. I don't care if she is older than dirt, I am getting her back for that.

After church a few women came up to me and asked to pray for me. I didn't want nor do I need their prayers, but I let them do it anyway.

What I really wanted to do was to go find Greg and fall into his arms. I knew I'd feel better if I could have him pray for me.

Their anniversary gala is tonight, and I am ready. Although, I was hoping that after Bible study, they'd be on such poor terms that they'd cancel the whole thing.

But then Nya summoned me. Called me to Greg's office like she's the one with the upper hand. Sitting there asking me about my life, when she knows that she's the one who lied to me and destroyed it.

Or maybe Nya doesn't know who I am. I don't put it past Greg to keep my secrets, and she's too narcissistic to even remember the people she's lied to. These days she probably just flies through the sanctuary knocking people out in the spirit. This is more confirmation that she is straight-up fraudulent. A real prophetess would know who I am, and what I came to do.

I hold up my dress. Some people might look at it and think it's a wedding dress, but to me it's just a gorgeous, white lace gown. It's symbolic of the pure relationship that Greg and I have. The covenant bond.

He told the ministers to bring me to him. I will never forget that. Nya tried to stop me, and I called her a liar right to her face. Then Greg made them bring me forward. Like they were giving away the bride.

The next day, I went and got this dress to wear to the anniversary party.

I'm sure the church members are preparing right now to celebrate their pastors on fifteen years of marriage. They will also be able to bear witness to the new order, 'cause I'm gonna usher it in right before everyone's eyes.

I have bathed for three days with ginger, frankincense, and myrrh. I want to be ready for Greg. This is our coming-out party.

I apply my makeup meticulously. Primer, then foundation, little dabs of concealer to hide the tiny blemishes, and more foundation to cover it all. Carefully pencil in my eyebrows, add a thin layer of golden eyeshadow. I want to glimmer and glisten like a bronze statue. My nude lip gloss completes my understated and classy look. I look perfect.

I pull on my dress. It fits perfectly, hugging where it should, and flowing where appropriate. My white, jewel-encrusted pumps are fairy tale–like. Definitely appropriate for me to stake a claim on my blessing.

My look is complete. Wait. It's almost complete.

My bed is covered with copies of my child's first ultrasound. The one I had before Dr. Tomlinson and Lance became accessories to his murder. Actually, I don't know if my baby was a boy or a girl, but since Lance kept calling him his son, I'll go with that.

I fold one of the ultrasound photos and slide it inside my bra. Then I take several more and pin them right underneath the hem of my dress. I roll yet another copy into a tiny scroll and slide it into the corsage on my wrist.

My baby was sacrificed for this. It's only fitting that he be present when it all comes together.

My cell phone chimes with a text message. I smile as I read it. My limo has arrived to take me to the party, and to my blessing.

CHAPTER 51
NYA

All day today, I've been in high stress mode. I can't concentrate on anything. Dropped coffee in my lap at breakfast and broke a nail. My entire spirit is on high alert. I am vexed and nervous and can't stop fidgeting.

I sit on the edge of my bed and look at the dresses Tina has selected for me to wear to our anniversary party tonight. Honestly, I'm having a hard time getting into a party mood, so I can't decide.

"Greg, can you come in here?" I call into the bathroom.

I hear Greg's electric razor stop and he walks into the center of our bedroom wearing only a towel. Seeing him there, glistening and with muscles bulging, makes me want to forget being Pastor Nya today. I'd rather skip this party and go off to the beach somewhere to enjoy my husband.

Things have been strained since he found out about my fake prophecy. I feel like he's lost some respect for me. For the gift. Maybe he believed in it more than I did.

"Can you help me choose one of these dresses?" I ask. "I can go with the turquoise because that was our wedding color. Or I can do the white one. It's kind of symbolic, I think. Like a renewal."

Greg strokes his goatee and presses his lips together. I wonder if he's only pondering the dress or if there's something else going through his mind.

"Go with the white," he says finally. "And it is symbolic. Of what happens after we get washed by the blood of Jesus."

"Funny."

"I'm not joking. I hope you repented for your lie."

I close my eyes, hating the way his voice sounds. Hating what his words mean. "I did. That same night. I have begged God for forgiveness."

"Well, He's already done with that matter, I suppose. I guess it's just taking me a little bit longer."

"Why, Greg? Why is it taking you so long to forgive me for this?"

"Nya. I love you with all my heart. But this is *crazy*. You know how I feel about the people of God. I am questioning how I can even serve in ministry with you anymore.

You do realize we built all of this from your lie. How am I supposed to thank and praise God for this when I know how it came about?"

I blink back tears. "I know, Greg. You don't think this has haunted me over the years? I've always wondered when the other shoe would drop. When someone would find out. What would Lady Sandy do if she knew? How would I be received? It's been torture."

"Torture." Greg says the word, then chuckles. "Getting television shows, touring the country and writing books has been torture? You would've made a horrible apostle."

"Please, Greg, don't pile it on. I feel an incredible amount of guilt behind what happened to Felicia."

"I'm sure your guilt doesn't equal her pain."

It bothers me hearing Greg defend Felicia. I definitely did her wrong — I would never argue that, but there is something not right about that woman.

"Thanks, Greg. I'll wear the white dress."

We get dressed for the party in silence. Several times I want to call Mother Olivia and give everyone our regrets for not attending. I want to stay home. Crawl in a

366

corner somewhere and have a long, ugly cry.

When we're downstairs in our living room, waiting for the driver to arrive, Greg walks up to me and touches my face. It feels like a tender gesture, which I need right now.

"Babe, this is our wedding anniversary party," he says. "We're celebrating our marriage tonight. Not Suddenly Blessed, not our ministry, not our church. We're gonna do some line dances with our friends, just like we did at our wedding."

He kisses my forehead and I feel relieved. I know he loves me, but today I needed a reminder.

"I am furious and disappointed about what you did, but you're still my wife. I love you. You're my boo."

This makes me laugh. "You're my boo too."

"Good. So stop looking all sad. There's a limo waiting for us outside. Let's go enjoy our night."

The smile on my face is genuine, and fifteen years of marriage is a lot to celebrate. I take Greg's extended arm and allow him to lead me into our awaiting chariot. Tonight, I will not think about "suddenly" anything. Tonight, I will have fun and enjoy my husband.

CHAPTER 52
FELICIA

Accomplishing my plan tonight will not be easy. After my alabaster box presentation, Mother Olivia has had her one good eye on me every time I walk into the church. I need an ally. Someone who loves Pastor Greg but isn't one hundred percent sold on Nya.

I tap Lena on the shoulder when I see her in the foyer of the hotel ballroom. She turns to face me, but she doesn't smile.

"I can't believe you're here," she says.

"I bought a ticket, didn't I? Why wouldn't I come and celebrate my pastors?"

Lena glances to her left and right and over her shoulder. I guess the coast is clear because she pulls me into one of the hotel's small conference rooms.

"What was that you did at Bible study, girl? The whole church thinks you're trying to sleep with Pastor Greg."

"I would *never* try that. I was honoring the man of God."

"Wait, why are you wearing a wedding dress?"

I look down at my dress and shake my head. "This isn't a wedding dress. It's a white formal gown."

"It looks like a wedding dress to me," Lena says. Then she twists her lips to one side and lifts her eyebrow.

Shoot. I have to get her on my side.

"Pastor Greg is the only one who knows my story. He has ministered to my very spirit, Lena. I honor that man on everything."

"What story?"

Telling Lena can't hurt at this point. Soon everyone is going to know how much of a liar Nya is, and it will all make sense.

"Remember the Women's Empowerment conference that made Pastor Nya famous?"

"Yes. We talked about this before. I was there."

"I am the woman who was supposed to be suddenly blessed."

Lena's jaw slackens as she tilts her head to one side. "That was *you*? Well, God surely did bless you, 'cause you looked a hot mess."

"He's blessing me now, but not because of Nya's prophecy. After she told me that lie, I lost everything, including my ability to have children. She is a liar."

"I mean . . . I was there, Felicia. She didn't really say anything specific in that message. What did you do afterwards?"

I tell her about Lance, about the baby, about the murder, and about my infection that destroyed my reproductive organs.

"Damn." Lena says this one word in response to it all. And what else could someone say?

"When I told Pastor Greg about this, he was so compassionate with me. He told me that Nya would be held responsible for destroying my life."

"Okay, but you chose to sleep with that married man. You can't have thought that was a God move."

"David and Bathsheba gave birth to Solomon," I reply.

Lena gives me a frustrated head shake. "I understand why you might be blaming Pastor Nya. I'm just saying you should take a little responsibility too."

"I do. And that's why I want to thank Pastor Greg tonight."

"What you mean?"

"I know Mother Olivia won't let me on the program, but I know you're the mistress of ceremonies. If you can just slide me in. I have this proclamation that I want to read to both our pastors."

Lena gives me a skeptical look.

I pull the plaque I had made for this occasion out of the bag. The inscription reads: FOR MINISTRY EXCELLENCE — PASTORS GREG AND NYA HAMPSTEAD.

"Is this even appropriate for tonight?" Lena asks. "They're celebrating their wedding anniversary."

"I know. It's just a token of appreciation."

Lena shakes her head. "No. I don't think you should be on the program. You can bring this to church and present it there. Mother Olivia wouldn't forgive me for allowing you to speak. Sorry."

"Sorry? That's it? After I told you what's happened to me?"

Lena touches my arm. "All of that is sad, and I'm praying for you. I even think if Pastor Nya lied to you then she should apologize, and she should pay for that. But I won't have anything to do with it. And it won't be tonight."

Lena reaches for a few tissues out of a box on the table. She hands them to me.

"I will leave so you can compose yourself. Your makeup is smudging."

Oh no. I can't let her leave. Not like this. She will ruin everything.

I take the tissues from her. "Thank you."

Then, as she reaches for the doorknob to leave the room, I do what I have to do. I take the pastor appreciation plaque and bring it down on the back of her head. She lets out a yelp as she slides to the floor. There's just a small trickle of blood. She'll be all right, and out of my way.

CHAPTER 53
NYA

Greg and I arrive at the hotel and are shown to the honeymoon suite. Tina will be here soon to refresh my makeup and fix my broken nail so that I can look perfect for our entrance.

"Did you see this spread?" Greg asks from the bedroom. "Mother Olivia sure knows how to spoil us."

I step inside the bedroom and my stomach rumbles at the sight of all our favorite snacks. Chocolate-covered strawberries, shrimp dip with pita crackers, grapes and watermelon chunks.

"I love Mother Olivia. Did I ever tell you she's my favorite?" I say with a laugh.

"She is definitely my favorite," Greg replies.

My phone buzzes in my hand. It's a text from Tina. On my way up.

"Tina's about to come up here to finish my makeup and stuff. I'm gonna close this door so she doesn't get our snacks."

"Please save the snacks from that greedy woman." Greg laughs as he chomps a huge strawberry.

I laugh as I go back into the living area of the suite. I am so happy about this, because Greg and I couldn't afford a honeymoon suite or a honeymoon when we got married in college. Our reception had mismatched potluck foods and we got a hotel room at the Marriott down the street from our campus.

There's a knock on the door. Finally, Tina is here to fix this broken acrylic nail. That sting is worse than a toothache.

I swing the door open. "Hey . . ."

It's not Tina. It's Felicia. Her face is tear-streaked, she's wearing a wedding dress, and she's holding a gun in her hand.

"Hello, Nya."

I open my mouth to scream, but she rams the gun into my midsection. The pain is horrific and it knocks the wind out of me. When I double over, she pushes me through the doorway and forces herself into the room.

Still holding the gun on me, she knocks me onto the couch.

"If you scream," she says, "I swear I will shoot you right now, before you get a chance to repent for your sins."

Now I'm wishing that the room wasn't so big. Greg is in the other room, and probably can't hear anything happening out here. I need to stall this crazy chick until Greg finds a reason to come out of that bedroom.

"Felicia, Greg told me what happened to you."

"He told you how you destroyed my life?"

I nod slowly. "He told me that you were the one who got the 'suddenly blessed' prophetic word."

She points the gun in my direction and I flinch.

"It wasn't a prophecy. It was a lie," she hisses.

"With everything that has happened to you, I agree. That word wasn't true for your life."

"It wasn't true for anyone's life! You are a fraud."

I nod again. "Maybe I am. I'm so sorry for what happened to you."

She looks surprised by this. Maybe she didn't expect an apology. I sure didn't expect to give one while she's got a gun in my face, but I'm going on autopilot right now. Survival instincts have kicked in.

"Can sorry bring my son back? Can sorry

bring my uterus back? I can never have another child now. Because of you."

"I wish I could change what happened in the past," I say. "But I can't."

She presses the gun to my temple, and I tremble. *Lord, please don't let me die like this.*

"You can't change anything. But you can get out of my way. Greg and I are connected in the spirit realm. He is meant for me. All of this has worked together for *my* good. But first, I have to get rid of you."

She presses the gun harder. Lord, Jesus, please let Greg come out of that room.

"Do you have any final words before you go tell Jesus everything you've done?" she says.

I hear the bedroom door open.

"Nya, this dip is off the chain!" Then he sees what's happening. "Felicia, what are you doing?"

She waves the gun in his direction. "Stay back, love," she says. "You may not understand why this has to happen right now, and I don't want any of this blood on your hands anyway. This is my mission. I have to do this in order for us to be together."

"Felicia," Greg says, "you don't have to kill her for us to be together."

"I do. The only way we can be covenant partners is if she dies and you are widowed.

You can't just divorce her."

Greg swallows and glances down at me. "But, Felicia. She's a liar, right? You don't think that God will understand me walking away from her? It will be like an annulment in God's eyes."

"And then . . ."

"Then we can walk in what God is calling *us* to do. I knew from the moment you brought that alabaster box to the altar that you and I have the same heart for the people."

It's working. Her attention is completely on Greg now, and she's dropped her arm to her side. The gun is no longer at my temple.

"Come . . . lay your burden down, Felicia. God wants to give you rest."

She walks over to Greg as if in a trance, still gripping the gun in her hand. She sobs loudly and holds her arms out for Greg.

He holds out his arms too, and I look for something to use as a weapon. Quickly, as if the Holy Spirit has taken hold of my limbs, I snatch the fruit bowl from the table. I take three steps and then lunge at her, swinging the bowl with all my might. It hits her in the side of her head, but it only stuns her. She drops the gun and stumbles to the floor. Greg swiftly retrieves the gun and points it at Felicia.

"Nya, call the police," Greg says.

I dial 9-1-1 while Greg picks up the hotel room's phone. I listen to him talk to hotel security while I tell the police what is happening here.

Felicia sits on the floor kicking her feet like a temper-tantrum-having toddler. Then I notice something sticking out from the bottom of her dress.

"What are you looking at?" Felicia screams at me. "Don't look at me."

She looks at where my eyes are trained, and then wails. "That is my baby. You killed him with your lies. You did this."

My heart sinks when I realize that the blurred image on the paper is an ultrasound photo. She really has experienced the worst kind of pain. Now, instead of anger and hostility toward the woman who just held a gun to my head, I feel a deep kind of pity.

"Felicia," I say, "I am so sorry for your pain. We're going to get you some help."

She hisses and spits in my direction, and even as the hotel security bursts through the doors and takes her into custody, she glares at me with nothing but hatred in her eyes.

"Take care of her," Greg says as he hands the gun to one of the security guards. "We're praying for you, Felicia."

When they are gone and the door to our hotel room is closed, Greg lets out a huge sigh. "Jesus," he says. The one word being more than enough.

"I can't believe this just happened," I say.

Greg crosses the room, closing the space between us. He wraps me in an embrace and kisses my face, lips, neck, and forehead.

"But it's over now," he says.

I shake my head. This isn't over. It's far from over. In order for me to leave this all behind, there's one more thing I have to do, and it's not going to be pretty. In fact, I'm terrified that after I do this one final step, things will never be the same. Not for me, for Greg, or for our ministry.

Chapter 54
Nya

Rumors of what happened at our anniversary party have spread all over the Dallas church community like wildfire. The stories range from Felicia being Greg's secret lover to her being *my* secret lover. I even heard that she gave Greg a lap dance in front of the entire church. Folk know they can spin a tall tale.

Right now Felicia is in a jail cell, although I assume she will undergo some psychiatric evaluations. She isn't well. I pray for her healing.

Because of the scandal, I don't have any invitations to speak anywhere. Lady Sandy informed me that we have several cancellations of speaking engagements that were already on the calendar. So be it. But the plan that I have for me to retire from Suddenly Blessed requires a pulpit and an audience. I suppose the one at Love First International is going to have to do. Our church is about to get a Sunday-morning big reveal.

I invited Penelope to sing right before I speak, and although her mother told her not to be seen in public or private with me after the scandal, she ignored it and showed up anyway.

"Are we still on for the plan?" Penelope asks me in the minister's room at my church.

"Yes, if you want. Are you ready?"

"No, but I have no idea how to get ready."

"Don't think about it. Let God have His way."

We hear the praise team start service, which lets us know that soon it'll be showtime.

"You still have time to back out if you want," I say to Penelope. "I won't think anything bad about you if you do."

"I'm good," she says.

We go out onto the pulpit and the congregation receives us with much clapping and cheering. It's almost like they want me to know that they don't blame me for what happened with Felicia. But, of course, they don't know the entire story.

"Praise the Lord, everybody!" I say into my microphone. "Can y'all give a warm welcome to my little sister in Christ, Penelope Bowens?"

The church roars with applause.

"You guys are used to seeing us together on TV. No, we're not going to do a dating game this morning, and nobody is getting a glam squad."

"I wanted the glam squad," Penelope says into her microphone. And her comment draws laughter from the congregation.

"We're here for a different reason this morning," I say. "We're going to call it 'see-through Sunday.' "

Penelope nods. "Exactly. Because we're going to let you see through us the way God sees through us."

"Transparent, like a window your mother just cleaned on a Saturday morning. With vinegar and newspaper."

"She's so country, isn't she?" Penelope asks.

When everyone laughs again, I realize that we need to pull this service in. They're used to seeing us banter and entertain them. What we're about to say isn't going to entertain anyone.

"So, can we get real with y'all this morning, saints? Can we tell you the truth without judgment?" I ask. "It's what we all want God to do — hear our flaws, our mistakes, our mess-ups, and unconditionally forgive. But we rarely extend the same forgiveness to one another or to ourselves."

The laughter slowly dies and silence falls over the congregation. Now they want to know what I'm talking about. The truth sounds juicy. And in this case it certainly is.

"I want to go first," Penelope says. "If you don't mind."

I give her a head nod, indicating that she has the floor.

"How many of you-all read the book we wrote about the altar-call experiences of women?" Penelope asks.

Many of the women clap and some hold their copies of the book in the air, as if they brought them to the church to be signed.

"I have a chapter in that book, but my real altar-call experience isn't anywhere in there. I tried to write it. The first draft of this book had my true testimony in it, but I let the devil steal my testimony."

"I have a secret," she continues. "And when my parents found out about it, they told me to bury it. They wanted me to hide it from you, from the church community, and from the world. In their defense they thought they were saving me from your criticism. But they couldn't save me from being disappointed in myself. And guess what? My secret wasn't buried. It was planted. Today it blossoms forth."

Penelope closes her eyes and takes a deep breath. "When I was sixteen, I got pregnant. Please don't blame my parents for having a church. It wasn't their fault. I got pregnant, and because I wanted to handle it on my own, I didn't ask for their help. I got an abortion and thought that I'd handled it."

"No one prepared me for how broken I'd be after that. No one told me how many nights I would cry myself to sleep at the loss of my baby. But I did. If there's any woman here who is grieving a baby they aborted, I want you to either pray at your seat or come to the altar, so we can lay hands on you and let you put your shame behind. And if you're thinking of having an abortion, come down to the altar too. It's not too late to let God come into your heart."

I am shocked at the number of women who come to the altar with tears streaming down their faces. They connect with Penelope's story. I am not sure if they'll connect so closely with mine.

But it's time for both me and Penelope to get free.

"Praise God for this altar call. Praise God for the women coming and for the women in their seats who couldn't find the courage to come. God can touch you right at your seat," I say.

I gaze out over all the women standing in front of the altar. "Y'all stay right here. We're going to pray in a minute. But first, I need to share my burden as well."

"How many of y'all in the congregation heard my Suddenly Blessed message?"

There are claps, amens, and hallelujahs from all over the sanctuary. I'm pretty sure that almost everyone in this church has heard of the Suddenly Blessed movement.

"And how many of y'all believed that word, made changes based on it, and pursued a new business or venture, because you thought that message was prophetic for you?"

There is more chiming in; not as much as the first question, but still many, many people respond.

"What if I told you that it wasn't a prophetic word at all? What if I said I felt pressured that day, so I said that God told me something that He didn't? What if I said the prophecy wasn't a prophecy? Would you feel differently about me if you knew I thought up those words in that moment and said they came from God? I'm sorry, church, but that one time, I misrepresented God and disrespected my gift. Not a day goes by that I don't regret it."

From the heaviness of the silence, no one would guess that there are thousands of people here. This is deeper than a teenager getting an abortion because she made a mistake; my sin was deliberate. The woman of God will be held more accountable than the poor teenage Penelope.

For a moment, I regret saying anything. Maybe I should've taken what's left of my secret to the grave.

I look over at Greg, and he can't hide his shock. I know he never thought I'd tell. Never thought I'd give it up. But I don't care if I never preach in another pulpit or never utter another prophetic word. I want my joy back.

Then Greg jumps up out of his seat and rushes over to me. He grabs the microphone from my hand.

"Y'all not gonna encourage my wife?"

After a very pregnant pause, the applause starts. It's spotty and from different parts of the sanctuary.

"Some of you are confused right now. Or maybe you're even mad. You're upset 'cause you think my wife lied to you. And she did lie. God didn't give her a *prophetic* word that night, but He did create her to be an encourager. She has the innate ability to look inside someone's situation and give them a word of encouragement that can change their lives around."

"We love you, Pastor Nya!" someone screams from the audience.

I feel a tear form in the corner of my eye. I didn't know how hard this would be.

"Does anyone know why my wife decided to reveal this now? In an open forum like this? The Bible tells us to confess our sins to one another. She gave that word in front of you all. In front of the nation. In front of the Bowens' Internet audience. The day she lied on her gift was the lowest moment of her life. She told you this way, because she preached the word this way. Those of you who might be sitting in judgment of her, I want you to ask yourselves one question. Would you like to be judged on your lowest moment?"

Something about this question floors me. I grab hold of Greg's arm as I feel my legs buckle. He holds me up, though; he doesn't let me fall.

Still holding on to the microphone, Greg kisses my forehead and squeezes me.

"This woman is a prophetess. But more than that, she's my wife and I love her. She's apologized to us. Laid her sins at our feet. If we're striving for Christ, there's only one option. Forgiveness. Who forgives her with me? Come to the altar and surround her with love. She needs it."

Some people move from their seats to the front of the church, but many do not. Part of me just wants to stare at the ground, but another part of me wants to see who doesn't forgive me. I scan the church and notice many harsh stares from founding members who always sit in the front row. They've been with me and Greg from the very beginning.

Perhaps my assumption was that I would confess, get the weight of my lie off me, and that it would all go away. Greg and I could be happy and our church would just move on.

I always teach that forgiveness is a process. And it is. But I never thought about that process applying to me. Some of these faces look like they'll never trust me again.

So I will focus on the ones who *do* come. They close in tightly around me. There are hugs, whispered prayers, and hand squeezes letting me know that I have their support.

It fills me with hope. And with this fractured and wounded congregation, Greg and I will start over. We'll stay strong. We'll build again.

We have to. God gave me a vision, and He

is the same yesterday, today, and forever. His Word is true and His prophecies always come to pass.

EPILOGUE

Felicia sits in the quiet room at the Red Oak Psychiatric Facility. The staff always lets her have the quiet room at this time every day. She's very difficult to handle if they don't allow her to watch her favorite ministry channel every day at four-thirty p.m. For an entire year that has been her daily routine.

When she first arrived at Red Oak, Felicia would watch Nya's talk show and get furious every time she saw the woman's face on the screen. Felicia wanted Nya to lose everything, including that talk show. But she hasn't. Nya and Greg are still preaching. Their church is still open, and from what Lena wrote Felicia in a letter, everything is back to normal except that a few members have left the church.

Now, it's against doctor's orders to allow Felicia to watch anything featuring Greg and Nya Hampstead, but she can, however, watch other ministers if she wishes. Her favorite one comes on at four-thirty.

To Felicia, Blaine Wilson is the epitome of preachers. He uses a cane to walk, but that doesn't hide his charisma and it doesn't take away from his handsome and dazzling smile. When he takes the microphone and sings, it always brings a smile to Felicia's face.

Felicia waits patiently for the broadcast to begin and for Blaine's handsome face to flash on the television screen. She has done her research on him. He was almost killed in a tornado right here in Dallas. It changed his life.

Felicia understands adversity and trauma. She and Blaine Wilson are kindred spirits, connected in the heavenly realm.

And the most important part is that Blaine's wife abandoned him at his lowest point. He had to crawl back from losing everything, and now his ministry is exploding with popularity. He is anointed. He is blessed.

And he is a bachelor.

Felicia knows better than to trust any prophetic words, but she *does* trust the feeling in her body when she sees Blaine's face on the television. It's like he is speaking directly to her. Trying to reach her over the airwaves. Wanting to make a connection with her.

"Come unto me, and I will give you rest," he says.

A smile forms on Felicia's lips. She'd lay her burdens down for this man. All she has to do is complete her treatment plan, and she'll be released.

Felicia feels no anxiety about the delay, though. She can feel in her spirit that this is ordained of God. And when she's healed enough and prepared enough, she will step through the doors of Blaine Wilson's church and claim her blessing.

This time, Felicia will be ready for the attacks of the enemy. She'll take her time. It's not like anything that happens suddenly can be trusted anyway.

It's the end of the thing that matters anyhow. Not the beginning.

"The Word says that you will find comfort in Him," Blaine says. "Eternal rest."

The words resonate with Felicia. Eternal rest is what she needs. Blaine Wilson feels like an angel. God said He would send a comforter. Felicia always thought that scripture was about the Holy Spirit. But then again . . . the comforter *could* be a man, couldn't he?

Felicia's grin widens as she lifts one hand

in the direction of the television screen.

"Yeah, God!" she whispers.

■ ■ ■ ■

A READING GROUP GUIDE: THE PASTOR'S HUSBAND

TIFFANY L. WARREN

■ ■ ■ ■

ABOUT THIS GUIDE

The following questions are intended to
enhance your group's reading of
THE PASTOR'S HUSBAND.

DISCUSSION QUESTIONS

1. Nya and Gregory are in ministry together as co-pastors. What do you think of that dynamic when it comes to married couples? Is a wife better suited as a first lady (in a supporting role) or as a co-pastor?

2. What do you think of Nya's prophecy? What about Felicia's subsequent actions? Were they reasonable?

3. Do you believe in the gift of prophecy? What about Penelope's desire to learn how to prophesy? Do you think it's possible to learn?

4. What do you think of Nya's revelation at the end? Would you have admitted the lie or taken it to your grave?

5. What do you think is in the future for Nya and Gregory? What about Felicia?

The employees of Thorndike Press hope you have enjoyed this Large Print book. All our Thorndike, Wheeler, and Kennebec Large Print titles are designed for easy reading, and all our books are made to last. Other Thorndike Press Large Print books are available at your library, through selected bookstores, or directly from us.

For information about titles, please call:
  (800) 223-1244

or visit our Web site at:
  http://gale.cengage.com/thorndike

To share your comments, please write:
  Publisher
  Thorndike Press
  10 Water St., Suite 310
  Waterville, ME 04901